Praise for *Partitions*

"Amit Majmudar's exceptional debut brilliantly captures India at its most turbulent . . . dazzling narrative."

Daily Mail

"Heart-wrenching."

New York Post

"A greatly human dramatization of the persecution each religious group experienced at the hands of the others . . . Poignant but never maudlin."

Booklist, starred review

"Magnificent . . . Written with piercing beauty, alive with moral passion and sorrowful insight – a rueful masterpiece."

Kirkus, starred review

"Vivid."

Metro

"Ambitious and impressive . . . an accomplished and praise-worthy novel."

New Internationalist

"Superb . . . This novel will make you angry and sad, as it should; it will also leave you with a heightened sense of sympathy and hope for the people on both sides of an arbi-trary border."

Wall Street Journal

"Unforgettable."

Boston Globe

"Shimmering prose . . . and a poignant surprise ending."

Seattle Times

ALSO BY AMIT MAJMUDAR

Partitions

The Abundance

Amit Majmudar

ONEWORLD

A Oneworld Book

First published in Great Britain by
Oneworld Publications in 2013

First published in the United States by Metropolitan Books,
an imprint of Henry Holt and Company LLC, New York

ISBN 978-1-78074-268-7
Ebook ISBN 978-1-78074-269-4

Printed and bound by CPI Group (UK) Ltd, Croydon, CR0 4YY

Oneworld Publications
10 Bloomsbury Street
London WC1B 3SR
UK

The Abundance

CONTENTS

PART ONE

ABUNDANCE

They arrive after midnight on the twenty-third. Mala had called from Indianapolis at around 10 PM and said they were having dinner at a Denny's. I told her I would put everything in the refrigerator, it wasn't a problem. She said she was sorry, but they had left home later than they wanted, it hadn't been in her control, the snow had been heavy since they crossed into Indiana. The weather was clear where we were, I told her. She said yes, but it was snowing where *they* were, and she really had tried to get home in time.

I could tell she was frustrated. The children were still awake, and the food hadn't arrived yet. I could hear Vivek's demands in the background and her own pleading, cajoling, halfhearted threats. Sachin had taken Shivani and was pacing back and forth in the waiting area, hoping to calm her. The tone of Mala's apology was reproachful. She assumed that I was reproaching her, even though I wasn't, even though I don't think like that. I know she is harried, overstretched, a mother and a career woman. I cut the call short so she could focus on Shivani and Vivek.

I am still awake when she calls my phone again.

"Were you asleep?" she whispers. Her mood seems improved, I can tell from her tone. "We're here."

"Did you take the exit already?"

"We're outside, in the driveway."

I smile into the darkness. "Okay, I'm opening the door." I tap Abhi's arm, and he sits up and pinches the bridge of his nose, squeezing out the sleep. I get out of bed too quickly. The pain pills make me sway. Abhi throws off the covers and guides me to a sitting position. He lays his pillow at the foot of the bed, then stacks mine on top of it.

"Lie back and put your feet up."

"They're in the driveway."

"I'll open the door."

"No. I'm coming."

"Lie back."

"They'll know something's wrong."

"Something *is* wrong."

"Don't say that. Don't even think that. Not for these next few days. You promised."

We sit for several long seconds. Stalemate.

"They're in the driveway," I repeat.

He scoots to my side and, arm around my shoulder, helps me stand. As we get to the top of the stairs, my fingers press all the light switches, upstairs chandelier, downstairs chandelier, the fixture over the stairs. They will be watching from the van. They will see the light through the windows, the face of the house brightening in welcome. My daughter home, and my grandchildren: Will they see us on the stairs through the high oval window, Abhi with his arm around me, helping me down? I ease his arm off me and hold on to the railing; he hurries down a few steps and looks back, below me in case I fall.

"I am not dizzy anymore."

"Slowly, okay?"

"I sat up too quickly. That's all."

The winter silence has a presence like sound. The bright snow draws its glow from the track lights and the cat's cradle of Christmas lights in our front yard maple tree. The light inside the van comes on, and I can see, between Mala and Sachin, the children in their car seats, symmetrical, brother and sister sleeping with their heads fallen aside to face each other. They look warm, serene.

Sachin tugs down his hat. His skin, still used to Indian weather, is more sensitive to the cold. Mala is already outside, no hat, no gloves, sliding Shivani's arms through the car seat straps. Mala covers her with a coat and a scarf and hurries her to the porch steps, footsteps crunching softly.

I have been standing with the door open, feeling through my nightgown the same cold they feel. I want my focus of sensation to shift from inside, where the pain is, to my body's surface.

The moment Mala comes inside, I worry about being seen in so much light. I worry she will notice at once a change too gradual for me or Abhi to detect.

"Is everything ready upstairs?" Mala asks, pushing off her snowy sneakers, sole to heel.

"It's ready," I whisper.

The house, sensing the cold, starts up the heating system. *White noise*, I think. *Good, this will help them sleep.* I follow mother and daughter up the stairs, keeping my face close to Shivani's lying on her mother's shoulder, cheek pushed up until the eye is just lashes. Abhi, who has gotten into his boots and coat to help with the luggage, pauses at the door. He waits until I make it to the top. Sachin arrives behind him, holding Vivek. Sachin greets Abhi in Gujarati. His voice is much too loud. He sits down on the stairs with Vivek still on his shoulder. He bites each glove's fingertip to pull his hand free, then begins unlacing a boot. When he drops it next to Mala's sneakers, the snow scatters over the floor and doormat.

Vivek shifts and mewls. He squints into the light, and my hand leaps to the switches, hoping to salvage his sleep. Sachin gets to work on the second boot. I hurry down the stairs, thinking I should maybe take Vivek myself. Abhi arrives at the door, a bag in each hand held off the ground, his frail shoulders sloping. He is just in time to see me fall.

I am not out long. Mala rushes down when she hears the noise. Abhi props me against his coat's cold sleeve. He smells of the outdoors and of the snow.

"Where are you hurt?"

"It was just a few stairs." I look into Abhi's eyes, and he understands he must not tell.

Mala turns the lights back on and kneels beside me on the stairs. "Is she okay? Dad?"

"I'm fine," I say, moving away from Abhi so I don't appear dependent or weak. I glance upstairs, toward the guest room door where I have set up the mattresses. "Did I wake her?"

"How many stairs did you fall, Mom?"

"Just a few. Two steps, right here. Go close the door, Mala, she'll wake up."

Sachin speaks to me in Gujarati. "There's a bump. I'll go get some ice."

I touch my forehead, embarrassed. "I shouldn't have turned off the light. I slipped."

"You go in the room with the kids," Mala orders Sachin. "I can get the ice."

Sachin nods. I turn to find Vivek's face close to mine. He is still a little disoriented. He blinks at me.

I kiss his forehead.

Sachin picks him up, and he puts his head on his father's shoulder right away. I bring my knees close to give them passage. Mala, at the foot of the stairs, pauses. "Are you hurt anywhere else?"

"I'm fine."

She comes up to touch my arm and my knee, as if to see if either gives. "Your legs? Are your legs okay?"

I know what she is thinking—that I have fallen and fractured my hip like an old woman. "I haven't broken a hip," I say with a little impatience.

"Just have to check," Mala says, and kisses me, unexpectedly, on my widow's peak.

She goes to the kitchen. Abhi holds me. I can hear the refrigerator's ice dispenser. "Did you tell her?" I whisper to Abhi. In Gujarati, the question is only two quick words.

"When could I have told her?"

I nod.

"Let's get you to the bed."

"No. The couch. Downstairs."

"Everyone's going to sleep."

"The couch."

He takes me to the couch, tracking snow on the hardwood. Mala's ice pack against my forehead, I watch the bits of white boot-print soften and clear. Sachin is still upstairs with the children, so Abhi brings in the rest of the luggage. Mala helps take it up the stairs. I lean forward to listen. Are they exchanging whispers? Mala turned on the kitchen lights to get me ice. Did she see me here on the couch and guess? She is a doctor, after all. She has called a patient's name, swished the penlight over each glassy eye, knuckled the sternum. She has seen illness before, and she will see mine. Haven't I seen it myself lately? Every night, I feel a stranger staring at me while I sleep, nose to nose. His shadow remains on my face.

Mala comes down with two bottles and starts washing them in hot water. I would have done it for her, but she has a specific ritual, and I have learned not to interfere. Abhi opens the closet. I hear a click and slide of hangers as his hand parts and pushes aside our coats, making room.

Sachin joins me. In his white socks he walks through Abhi's melted boot-prints and doesn't seem to notice. When he sits on the couch, his thighs tilt upward because he is so tall. He grew up in India, where everyone is shorter, and learned to slope his spine to hide his height. Resting on the carpet, his feet point slightly inward, just as they do when he walks.

Sachin asks me in Gujarati about my fall. He is relaxed, almost garrulous, anticipating Abhi's arrival. When Abhi, smiling, comes into the still-dark family room, Sachin rises to hug him. They begin chatting immediately in Gujarati.

Abhi turns on the light, and I fear Sachin and Mala will see everything. I move the ice pack to hide my face. I am ashamed of this stupid bump that has brought me so much attention. Abhi, sitting close to me, murmurs a question about the drive. I know how happy Abhi usually is to see Sachin; I want to tell him he doesn't have to distract himself with sympathy, he can sit next to Sachin.

Sachin eyes my forehead periodically. He is also a doctor, but maybe he doesn't see the change in me, either. I wonder whether my slip on the stairs might be a windfall, this tender swelling distracting from the harder lump inside me.

Sachin turns the conversation, predictably, to OSU football. It's what Abhi and he would usually talk about at this point. Mala, over by the sink, looks up in annoyance from the running faucet.

"Sachin?"

"Yes?" He is already on his feet.

"Sippy cups. I'm missing two."

"Where do you think they are?"

"The back row. Or else check the floor between the car seats. I know I gave her apple juice."

Sachin heads to the door and begins the process of lacing and zipping. Abhi says it is too cold to go out for two cups, but Sachin, in English, says it isn't a problem. Abhi acquiesces. This is between husband and wife. Mala turns the faucet off, grabs a hand towel, and looks down the hallway at her husband. "What are you doing?"

"Putting on my glows," he says, the *v* becoming a *w*. Most of the time he sounds American. Suddenly, under Mala's glare, his accent comes out strong. Abhi and I keep our eyes on the carpet.

"Take your time, all right?"

"Okay."

The sarcasm has not registered. She keeps drying her hands while he pulls on his hat and gets his hood over it. She looks at us.

"Mom, Dad, you can go back to sleep. You don't have to wait."

Abhi smiles. "We'll go up with you."

Sachin closes the front door behind him, at last.

"How's that bump, Mom?"

"It's fine."

"Let's see."

She comes close and draws a gentle fingertip across my cold skin. "It's fine now," I say. The bump is at my hairline. I haven't colored my hair in some time. Neither has Abhi. Although we are stocked with L'Oréal boxes in the bathroom closet, one shelf below the towels, Soft Black, we've lost the desire to do it. From this close, Mala must be noticing my gray hair.

Though I, too, see some disturbing signs up close: the sink-hole above my daughter's collarbone, the brittle lines from elbow to wrist, the too-sharp outline of her jaw. She needs to eat. She does not eat.

Have I gone completely gray under the dye? Would what is happening inside me seem less of a shock if I didn't fool myself with young hair? I have my mother's hair, loose at the roots, every morning a matted tangle over the shower drain, and wisps wound around two fingers and tugged free of the comb.

Sachin returns with the sippy cups. He takes off his gloves and boots but stands with the winter coat still on, shoulders dusted in fine snow. His hands look small at the ends of his puffy sleeves, the plastic Mickey Mouse cups even smaller. Mala takes them without saying thank you. As Sachin removes the rest of his gear, the talk turns to weather, how many inches of snowfall in St. Louis versus here, how bad it was last year—and I think how merciful it is that all people have the weather in common, the one subject everybody can talk about. We three speak in Gujarati, Sachin at ease again, his pleasantness undiminished by his humbling. Steam rises from the sink as Mala turns the fixture all the way left and holds the cups under the water, her face set, as though proving to herself she can withstand the heat.

Upstairs, in the dark, Abhi sits on the bed. I tug at his pajama sleeve.

"Do you really think we can do this?" he says. "Pretend this way? Let them know."

"It's late. The little ones will be up early."

"Tomorrow morning. Take Mala aside."

"This is their last visit before things change, Abhi. I told you."

"You will have her as she is, then."

"That's what I want. You saw, she was sweet to me when she came in."

"Tonight she snapped at Sachin, tomorrow morning she may snap at you."

"I don't mind."

He shakes his head. "How can we walk about as if there's nothing crushing us?"

"This is their last visit before they find out and things change."

He covers his face a moment, palms side by side, then slides the heels of his hands up to his eyes and presses in frustration. "Things have already changed. You are in pain. I know it. I see it every time I look in your eyes."

"It's nothing."

"It's not nothing."

"You should sleep, Abhi. Mala says the kids have been getting up lately at six thirty."

"It's not nothing."

"Come here. Come here and sleep."

Abhi shakes his head again and joins me under the covers. He lies apart from me for a few moments, then he turns and sets his thigh over mine, brings his arm under my breasts, nuzzles my neck. Once, this used to be a signal that he wished to make love; now it is the burrowing of a scared creature. The thigh and arm that rest on me make sure that I do not vanish without warning. I cannot remember when we last made love. I do not want to remember, either. If we let it happen now, I will keep thinking, *This may be the last time.* Maybe I will think it just once, then concentrate harder, focus, shake the thought from my head—but the pleasure, if there can be any pleasure, would rise between my legs like a lump in the throat. I would be conscious of every moment. And later I would remember this one night, our last, more intensely than all the others we have spent together, back when we were time's millionaires, rolling in nights.

I lie on my back for a while, unable to sleep. I trace Abhi's arm across my chest, the soft hairs of his hand, his rough knuckles, his fingers limp now that he has fallen asleep. I find the white gold of his wedding band and turn it around and around, as though winding a clock.

I made everything in advance the morning we went for the second opinion. I poured the dahl still steaming into a casserole dish. Condensation jeweled the glass lid. The fan over the stove kept me safe. I thought of its roar as a leaf blower's, scattering my apprehensions. Anything not to concentrate on the appointment.

Two events were crowded into that day after weeks of waiting: my appointment at the Cleveland Clinic with Dr. D'Onofrio, and the arrival, from Buffalo, of Abhi's nephew and his wife. Life is like that, a long lull, then all the phones ring at once. We had to leave at 10 AM to make it to our 12:45 meeting, then, after two hours, come back here to pick up the guests from the airport.

Of course we hadn't planned things this way. Abhi called Dr. D'Onofrio's office and got me the first available opening. His nephew Shailesh's itinerary arrived by e-mail three days afterward. We hadn't been able to attend his wedding in Ahmedabad, so showing this hospitality, during the couple's visit to America, was crucial.

Abhi asked me whether he should request that they fly into Cleveland. We could pick them up on the drive back. I didn't want that. His nephew would never tell us whether the airline had penalized them for changing flights, or if it cost more to go through Cleveland. I didn't want to lie, either— though we did end up lying that evening, not with our words but with our bodies and faces. Eyebrows high, lips stretched, we hugged our young guests outside baggage claim after they bent to touch our slush-caked shoes.

Did they sense that something was off? Did Abhi's eyes look sunken? He had been sleeping even less than usual. My weight loss, at least, was hidden by the winter coat. We quizzed them about their parents and their honeymoon during the car ride home. Abhi did well. How was Niagara? Where else were they going? I made sure not to leave all the work to him. How was Kaka's health? And Kaki's health? Always the inquiry about health. In Gujarati, you say it without thinking. You are asking about general well-being, not the heart medications or last year's stroke.

Shailesh noticed a change when we got home. I was putting their heavy coats on hangers. They were well-worn coats, brought out for them, I suspected, from the basement of his aunt in Buffalo.

"Kaki," he said with surprise, "you have reduced!"

Reduced was the English word he used, though the sentence itself was Gujarati. *Healthy*, in Gujarati, means chubby, ruddy, a second chin; *reduced*, having noticeably lost weight, is not the compliment it is in English. It is asked with concern. If it's the husband who looks thinner, the next joke is usually, "Isn't she feeding you anymore?"

Abhi played off the joke and patted his stomach. "You're right, she *has* reduced. She cooks so beautifully, I leave nothing for her!" Polite laughter gave me cover to get into the kitchen.

Henna, Shailesh's wife, followed me, offering to set the

table. I wanted to be alone, like a wounded deer, I wanted my kitchen's familiar niche. But with Henna there, I wouldn't have the chance. Maybe this was for the best. No opportunity for despair. Having guests would keep me heating and ladling and stirring for a few days. I would have some continuity between my life before and my life from now on.

Henna filled the pitcher tentatively, with skinny, delicate fingers, her wedding mehndi's paisleys a faded red-orange, only the pads of the fingers still dark. The jostle of ice cubes put an absurd lump in my throat. The sound, for me, meant time to call everyone to dinner. I always brought the water out last. I liked to set it cold and dripping under the chandelier. I always told the children to drink water with their meals. Enough so they could taste the food, but not so much that it would fool their hunger.

Most of the meal I had set out on the counter to cool. I had made masoor dahl—the amenable lentil, a cop-out. But in the deepest casserole dish I had something to impress them: stuffed breaded baby eggplants with yams, potatoes, onions, and even segments of banana cooked in the sleeve, the peels blackened and edibly soft. This was a dish our mothers used to cook in open-field fire pits when I was girl. That and the bhartha spiced with its own burning. You could hold an eggplant to a ring of natural gas, and the shiny skin would crinkle. But nothing flavors eggplant quite like red fire and wood.

I observed myself emerging from my mood as I set everything to heat. *You are getting everything ready, you are still functioning.* Then I saw the stray pot on the dormant back burner, and I remembered immediately the dahi. I curdle mine the old way, seeding it from the last pot. I had left it out overnight to take on body and the right hint of sour. It had been perfect this morning. I had tasted it and made sure. Why, why hadn't I moved it to the refrigerator? Distraction. I had skipped forward, in my mind, to the appointment. And now, hours later, there it was.

I checked on Henna at the dining table, then hurriedly tested a spoonful. Too sour: first the pucker inside the cheeks, then the smart of it down the throat. Ruined. I slammed the lid on it as if it had a stench and hid it in the refrigerator.

The meal needed something else for coolness. What else, what else? I remembered the mango pulp. I'd gotten three dented orange cans from Bharat Grocers last week. I hurried out to the garage where we kept them to chill. The door swung shut behind me but the garage light was still on. The can felt icy under my hand, its flat top coarsely dusty. I lifted it, and the garage light timed out. I was in utter darkness and silence but for the dripping minivan. *Will it happen to me like that?* I brought the cold can of summer sweetness against my stomach: sweet and orange and preserved forever. I shuddered. *You will come to wish it happened like that.*

In the kitchen, I slid a drawer open and found the can opener. My hand shook as I clipped and pushed two triangles into the top. I realized I had forgotten to rinse the can. I went to the faucet and paused; Henna would see I had made the punctures before running water over the lid.

"Which bowls should we use? These small glass ones?" she asked. I reached past her and picked up four bowls myself. I must have seemed annoyed. Henna backed away, eyes on the ground, pulled into herself like a touch-me-not. I handed her the bowls and wiped the punctured lid with my sleeve. The dust came off visibly on my cuff. The can had been out a long time. It had come from the grocer's shelf dusty, too—who knew how long it had sat there, across from wet coriander in the glass cooler?

Henna took the bowls with a small nod and hurried out of the kitchen. I had offended her. I had made her feel uncomfortable. I was in my kitchen, nowhere so powerful as here. Yet I did not feel in control.

I told myself I had done this thousands of times by now. *This is my empire.* I turned the gas up a little, took out two large spoons, and stirred the pot on the front burner and the one on the back. A familiar crackle. These scents comforted me. Only grandchildren in my lap could have calmed me more. I eased back into my mastery. I opened the drawer where I kept my hot plates and my salt-and-pepper-shaker mitt. The hand I slid into it did not tremble.

I press the lump on my forehead, exploring the pain. A hard knot of blood, nothing sinister. The sinister lumps are the ones you cannot feel, the ones that hide.

We had sat on the bed until two in the morning the night of Henna and Shailesh's visit, roughly the time it is now. My face hidden in Abhi's neck, I had cried, wringing out the heart's old rag. I was careful not to be too loud. The guest room shared a wall with ours.

Abhi asked when and how we should tell Ronak and Mala. I shook my head. I didn't want to tell them. They had their rhythms: morning alarm clocks, blue toothpaste for the children, granola in this bowl, Lucky Charms in the others, changing the children out of their pajamas, the commutes, the jobs, the microwave beeps at dinnertime, bedtime routines, that last hour padding around a quiet house, picking up toys, checking e-mail, paying bills, thumbing appointment reminders into the corkboard beside the fridge.

And then, suddenly, this? It would throw off the finely balanced movement of their lives. Over every meal: *I talked to Mom today. How's Mom holding up? What did the oncologist say? How is she feeling? Is she in pain? . . .* I did not want the spotlight of their concern. I imagined the phone calls between Mala and Ronak, the news dominating every conversation. The idea embarrassed me. I wanted them to talk about their week or the upcoming ski trip or Shivani's new word or Nikhil's report card. Not me. Not this.

"But we have to tell them," Abhi whispered. "This isn't something we can keep a secret. We should tell India, too. Your brother may want to visit. We will cover his ticket."

I wiped my cheeks. I could breathe and speak again. "I want everyone to stay as they are."

Abhi shook his head.

"Things will change for me. But things shouldn't have to change for them. I want them to stay as they are."

"Things are going to change for all of us."

"I want them to stay happy."

"Of course you do."

"As long as they can."

"Yes. We both want that." He gazed at the carpet, imagining, maybe, the act I was asking us to stage: three weeks' pleasantries over the phone, and finally Mala's Christmas visit, five days face to cheerful face. "You can't not tell them. You can't."

"I will. But later. Not while I am still strong. You saw. I cooked today. A full meal. Dahl, rice, rotli, shaak."

"Things change. There's nothing wrong with that."

"I am still strong, aren't I?"

"You are. But it's okay to feel tired. It's okay to rest."

"I don't need to rest. You'll see tomorrow. It will be like always, for now."

Abhi put his elbows on his knees, his face in his hands. He looked up. "We have to tell the kids. I can't hide this from them. Not even on the phone. It's hard enough with guests."

"No. Please. Not yet. Mala is coming during Christmas week."

"You'll tell her then? Face-to-face?"

I thought ahead to her arrival. It felt good to do that. Only three weeks from now, attainable happiness. "I want to have one last time together, Abhi. Without this coloring everything."

"You want to hide it from her the whole stay?"

"And I want Ronak here, too."

"You know he's spending Christmas with Amber's family."

"In Pittsburgh. It's not far. They can spend Christmas there, but the next day they can come here. He has until the second off. He told me so."

"They celebrate Christmas in a way we don't. It's—it's religious for them."

"They go to church on Christmas day. The day after, there aren't any services. They can drive here."

Abhi shook his head. "The only way to convince Ronak," he said, "is to tell him why."

"We'll both call him."

"When has he listened to me? He doesn't pick up his phone when he sees it's me."

"You call him and invite him. I will, too."

"You're going to exhaust yourself getting ready for it. I know. This is no time for that kind of hard work."

I shook my head. "I have to get a few things."

"Give me a list."

"There are things only I'll know how to get."

"I'll ask."

I stood up. "You're acting like I can't walk. You're acting like I'm already bedridden."

"All right. All right."

I could tell from his eyes he was afraid he had offended me. The last thing I wanted was for him to watch himself around me, or to swallow his benign Gujarati puns and jokes, to give up his weekend swims and his nightly retreats to the study. I didn't want him to alter our routine as a couple, in however minor a detail. But he would, wouldn't he? The change had already found its way between us.

I stood and held his head and shoulders to my stomach, the way I had once, long ago, when I felt our first child kick.

The second pregnancy is supposed to be easier to carry and easier to drop, but that wasn't the case for me. Ronak was easy. Mala kicked me awake in the last trimester. She took an eternity parting from me. In the end they had to cut me open and cut her from me.

Mala, the second born, had been strangely fearless, unlike our expectations of a daughter. Pictures show her wild-eyed, shirtless, barefoot. Wild-haired, too—she pulled out her hair bands, unraveled the careful braids I gave her. You would think I was a neglectful mother. In pictures she looks almost feral, crouched atop our old coffee table or the hood of our car. Me in a saree, Abhi with his black hair, Ronak close to my hip, a shy five. And Mala, two years younger, always apart, always in some spring-loaded pose. The most memorable snapshot (Where is it now? Where have I saved it?) is the one where Abhi caught her jumping off a fence. The pink clip sits askew in her messy black hair, her mouth is open, her arms wide, her eyebrows high; the maroon velvet birthday-party frock has fluttered up to show her skinny calves as she braces for the landing. Had we tamed that tomboy? And if we had, why?

I could not reconcile that Mala with the woman who, at twenty-nine, undernourished from a resident's life, said she was scared she would never find someone to love. A girl like Mala—beautiful, successful. The men her age had done their playing, she sobbed, the men had dated around, and now they

were marrying twenty-three- and twenty-four-year-olds. She
would soon be thirty and the pool kept getting smaller. Who
was left?

Mala had waited until Abhi left for work, and then she
broke. She had said nothing of her despair before. He must
have broken it off with her. I have no name, just *he*. Who, she
never told me. Maybe an American boy. Virile, athletic, hair-
less on the back and chest. Had she worked to impress him?
Had she studied his favorite movies so she could talk about
them? Had she made him agree never to call her at home?
Had he introduced her to his parents—"my girlfriend," nothing momentous, the father waving hello from behind his
computer—and never understood why she wouldn't do the
same? Or had they pretended for as long as they could, growing closer, wearing each other's T-shirts sometimes, sleeping
in each other's dorm rooms when a roommate went home for
the weekend—everything shared except this fenced-off part
of her?

"You can make your phone calls now," she had said, giving
us the go-ahead to send inquiries about marriageable boys.
(Twenty-nine was her cutoff, but still we called them "boys."
A "boy" for our "girl.") Had there been resentment in her
voice? *Go, have your fun, do the thing you've always wanted to
do.* Even so, how wrong of me to treasure her resignation. To
rejoice as I hugged her and stroked her arm.

My fingers could touch in a ring around her arm, above the
elbow no less. I thought she was "picky," I called her "picky"—
until the ninth grade, when she collapsed during track practice. (Ronak ran track, so Mala had to run track.) I drove to
school to find her looking sheepish, a scrape on her forehead
of shallow parallel red lines, an ice pack to her cheek and ear.

Apparently she had been crouching at the starting line when she blacked out. A few tall, broad-shouldered blond girls and a compact, exquisitely formed black girl were sitting beside her on the bleachers. I had seen Mala go running with these girls, their ponytails bouncing in synchrony. Two sets of two on the sidewalk, Mala just behind them and alone. The black girl was named Shaunte, which came, I assumed, from Shanti. Her legs and arms were so taut the flesh on them wouldn't pinch, her calves were two sleek vases, her arms faintly muscled, but she still looked healthy. Part of it was her eyes, which were not set deep in her face, but rather on a plane with her forehead. Mala looked at me, and her eyes were sunk in dark holes. She had a layer of softness on her thighs, girl fat, normal Indian girl flesh, but her skin had no luster. I saw, for the first time, that she had been starving herself. Yet the starving had shrunk only her torso, which was wasting away atop a woman's hips, the hips she inherited from me. Her friends had gotten her to suck on a straw without interest. "She got hypoglycemic," they said confidently. I drew the ice pack away to check Mala's ear and cheek, then guided it back. Mala handed me the juice box to let me inspect her scraped palm. I didn't know how long she had been sipping, but the juice box was still heavy.

When Mala told me to start looking into a marriage partner, I was too thrilled to speculate why she had reached this point. I had been given the go-ahead. She wanted my help. During her early twenties, I had sometimes suggested this or that friend's son, and she would snap at me or, if she was in a good mood, roll her eyes. "You and Dad had an arranged marriage that worked out, but you're lucky. That's not the rule," she would say. My answer was that arranged marriages had a lower

divorce rate than love marriages. She countered that couples
who could be forced by their parents to marry were also the
sort to force themselves to stay together. I would say no one
was forcing her, just as no one forced me; we only wanted her
to meet this boy, whose family we knew very well. I probably
was forced back then, she would say, I just didn't know I was
being forced. "Then forcing me to marry your father was the
greatest gift my mother ever gave me," I would tell her. We
would go back and forth like children after that. "That wasn't
what I meant." "That *was* what you meant." No it wasn't, yes
it was—she would clench her fists in frustration, close her eyes,
and, in a quiet voice, declare she couldn't have a conversation
with me. That would begin a silence we both maintained for
altogether too long.

But at last, I thought, she was willing. She had come around
late, which made my job harder, but it was welcome work
and something new to do. I called India, I called California, I
called New Jersey and Chicago. Grandmothers were my best
resource—even if their grandchildren were married, they
always had a nephew's son in Baroda or Jamnagar. I tracked
every youngish man at the weddings of other people's children, checking for a ring, checking whether he placed his
hand in the small of a woman's back or brought someone a
drink. A receding hairline and a thick watch suggested a
professional—such boys drew my attention. I made unsubtle
inquiries. I traded e-mails, I sent and received biodata, the
standard JPEG and Word file with which we advertised our
aging children (some mothers, I suspect, without their sons'
knowledge). Age, caste, job and education, hobbies: year,
make, model, maintenance history.

My picture showed Mala at twenty-four, but the fudging
was customary. It was the same photo she had posted when
she tried an online Indian dating site. About that experience

she had told me with a mixture of horror, self-pity, and mirth. Because she had failed to click on a box of some sort, her profile had been made public. That night, within hours, her cell phone came alive. Men in India and the United Kingdom called to woo her without understanding the time difference. Men across the world desperately wished to meet her—she, being a doctor, could provide airfare, yes? Men in the States with student visas, men who attended obscure community colleges in Indiana, Minnesota, Connecticut, four bachelors to an apartment. She turned her phone off in horror and collected seven messages by the time her alarm clock went off. Later, she got callers who sounded like they had been born in America. They were the nervous ones. "The fobs were never nervous," she said. They were blissfully free of insight.

I worried about her meeting them in person. No knowledge of the family meant no safeguard. A lot of the profiles, Mala told me, were posted by the parents themselves. She could tell from the grammatical mistakes and the British spelling for *colour*—as well as the list of Indian dishes the boy enjoyed.

One caller had something in his voice that she responded to—the faintest trace of an Indian accent, the way his *v* softened into a *w*—he had come to America at eleven. They talked twice more, asking questions about their lives and plans, but it went nowhere "We had nothing to talk about," Mala said, shrugging, "but who we were."

I laughed when she made fun of fobs and their accents. She imitated her callers vivaciously, viciously. Yet hadn't Abhi and I been like that only three decades ago? Had we appeared to Americans as that inept, that silly?

I knew I had best avoid showing her boys too recently arrived from India, or worse, still in India. We would have gotten along with such a boy, I imagine. He would have made a good son-in-law. But Mala would not have respected him as a man, I could tell. I was heartened that she had been open to a boy who had come over young and, during his teens at least, had grown up here. Soon after our conversation, I invited Sachin to meet her.

While Abhi took Shailesh and Henna back to the airport, I went to the supermarket and stocked up for Mala's visit. I kept moving. I set chickpeas to soak and Osterized the mint leaves for chutney until they tasted as bright as their green color. I rinsed the blades and ground some walnuts for dessert that evening—a roar as loud as a construction site. I felt better making that noise to fill the house. It scattered the black-birds off my nerves a while.

It was not yet time for Mala's dutiful daily call, and for that I was glad. I couldn't be sure I wouldn't let the shock slip, or reveal it in my pauses or my tone. I made my first call to Ronak's cell. *Hey, this is Ron, leave me a message, thanks.* Brusque, unwelcoming. I left no message. He would see the missed call—maybe he had already seen it and silenced the ringer. Left to himself, he would return it later in the week. I planned to try him more than once. *Hey, this is Ron.* We hadn't named him Ronak with a mind to its American abbreviation. We had kept to easy, two-syllable names for both children precisely to prevent that. "Ron" made things easier, of course, in his line of work. Amber mingled the two versions: she called him *Roan.* A horse whose dark hair is interspersed with white.

I had shortened Abhi's name from Abhishek, but not to something American. (At least "Ron" had some logic: we knew a Vrijesh once who did business as Mike.) I liked Abhi's shortened name more. *Abhishek* means the bathing of an idol. *Abhi* means *now*—in both English senses, *the present moment* and *immediately*. I valued, more than ever, the urgency and the short-term focus of that name. Naming the one I loved, I said how long I would have him.

When Abhi got home that day, the rice cooker's light had blinked off, and the rotli dough held the smooth divots where my fingertips had tested it. I loved working little rips of dough into balls. The palms were held parallel, circling each other, a few ounces of softness between them. The rolling got easier until there was no friction at all. Then the dough was worked smooth and flat by the pin. The dough seems heavy compared to the rotli itself, bright with brown pocks, steam-swelled. I had the stovetop fan going and didn't hear Abhi come in. He still had his coat on.

"How are you feeling?"

"Fine."

"How is the pain? I didn't ask you this morning. Did you take those pills they gave you?"

"I'm not in any pain. I'll take the pills if I am."

"I'm worried you won't."

I looked down into the black round of the tawa. "Are you ready to eat?"

"I talked to Ronak."

"I called him earlier today. I got a message."

"I was persistent."

"How many times did you call him?"

"He picked up on the fourth call."

"Four calls? He will suspect something is wrong."

"He didn't sound like he did."

"What did he say?"

"He said they're going to his in-laws for Christmas, as they do every year."

"You told him we wanted the twenty-sixth, right? After

Christmas? Even the twenty-seventh would do. Mala will still be here."

Abhi unzipped his coat and turned from me, sliding it off his shoulders. "I wouldn't count on him."

"What did he say, exactly?"

"He said he would check with Amber."

"Maybe I should talk to Amber."

"She picks up her phone, at least."

He left to hang his coat. I was used to this bitter abdication in matters pertaining to Ronak. Abhi felt he had no control. In earlier years, he used to raise his voice because he still believed shouting might accomplish something. He would shout, always in English, at Ronak's closed door or closed stare. The reproach would start with phrases like *how dare you* or *by what right*. Sometimes he would repeat the words *I am your father*, as if that settled things. He was appealing to bygone rules of hierarchy and submission. How late Ronak came home on weeknights, his social drinking, the never-acknowledged but never-denied girlfriends or (Ronak's phrase) friends-who-happened-to-be-girls—in America, this was normal teenage behavior, as natural as any physiological change. In Ronak's case, it was harmless: he was too keenly self-interested to do anything that would give him a record. No matter how late he stayed out, we never got a call from the police, unlike some parents we knew. And he used this as a counterargument: *Have you ever gotten a phone call? Ever?* As if we ought to praise his moderation. In those years, the voice deepened, the height increased, the tongue grew cutting. All to be expected. Yet in India, we never saw such things. *Who are you to tell me, Dad?* We had never spoken that way. No stranger had to remind us, *I am your father.*

I cooked a lot those first weeks after the diagnosis. Usually I did not like making food and freezing it. It troubled me to see the furry crystals, the way tilting the container didn't tilt the sauce, the potatoes embedded as if in a rock. I felt an unease, irrational I know, about living flavor hardened to tasteless ice. It could not come back the same once it had known such cold. And after that, the microwave, and the unnatural way microwaves heated the periphery first. The heart could still be icy though the container hurt the fingers. I preferred reheating dishes on the stove the few times I did freeze them. I would use a spoon to break a Tupperware-shaped square into floes that would soften, flatten, merge, and settle into a comfortable simmer. I distrusted my own food after its artificial wintering. I would bring a spoon to my lips critically, half expecting the spices to have blunted or the vegetables to have gone to slime.

But the food never really altered. The resurrection matched the life. So, those first weeks after we knew, I stocked and stored as industriously as a wintering squirrel. Who knew for how long I could keep these little crowns of blue gas going, four at a time, like plates spinning on sticks? Who knew when my own dials would click, click, click, click, and nothing would flare? Better do this while I could.

Abhi brought home a small refrigerator. I noticed that he had come home late and stayed in the garage long after he pulled in. It had gotten very cold that week. After waiting for him to come inside, I investigated. He had unpacked the gift and was plugging it in. The refrigerator was a white cube, knee high, and he had tucked it between the unused bikes and two sacks of black soil I had never gotten around to using.

"For overflow," he said, opening and shutting the door.

My hands covered my smile and I clapped them gently. "Perfect!"

"You're happy?"

"Of course, Abhi. This is perfect. I was running out of room."

"You're happy." He tapped the refrigerator distractedly. "You know . . . this is only for now. They will deliver a bigger one tomorrow. Full size."

He had only just had the idea, I could tell; he had probably gone to the appliance store, debated between the two sizes, and chosen the smaller, cheaper one. Now, seeing how happy it made me, he regretted his choice. "What will I do with two full-size refrigerators?" I said. "I can't possibly fill two."

I thought about the huge refrigerator a year from now, silent, its triple-pronged plug resting on top. Its freezer the same temperature as the garage. Nothing in it except an open box of Arm & Hammer.

"Are you all right?"

"Of course."

"Your face changed."

"I just remembered. I have the gas on." I looked beyond him to the parallel tire tracks in the driveway snow and the salt stains speckling the lower half of the Camry. A blue sedan passed the house. It must have been parked outdoors, because its speed blew the snow off its roof. It rode ahead of a halo.

I was right about Abhi's decision to buy the bigger refrigerator after he saw my pleasure. He hurried into his study, called the store, and gave his credit card number over the phone before he came to have his after-work snack. An apple or a few pretzel sticks were all I allowed him. Come dinner I wanted his appetite. It's the same in all things. Satiety is an honest judge, but hunger is a favorable jury.

Mala checked in by phone every day, out of love, out of habit, out of obligation. I kept to the planning for their trip and asked what Vivek preferred to eat now.

"Mostly mac and cheese," she said.

"That I can make from a packet. I want to make something."

"I don't know what to tell you, Mom. It's what he wants. That and those veggie dogs. Did you pick those up?"

"There must be something I can make."

"Mom, we're dealing with little kids here. They're picky. It's how they are at this age."

"I will make a variety. We can see if they like any of it. Good food."

I shouldn't have said that; it was very easy for Mala to assume I meant she wasn't feeding her children good food. Sure enough, her voice went hard, defensive.

"Sorry to disappoint you," she said, "but things haven't changed since last time. He's just not showing interest yet, Mom."

"He won't show interest on his own. You have to offer options."

"I *do* offer him options."

"Let him be hungry one meal. That way, next time, his stomach won't let his tongue refuse."

"I'm not having him go hungry, Mom."

"It is your duty to teach him what to want." I used the wrong word. "Duty" sounds like a reproach. Maybe I should have said her *right*? But even *right* she could have taken wrong: she'd think I implied *I* had rights, too, over *her*, and indirectly over Vivek.

"My first duty," she said, her voice rising, "is to treat my son as a human being."

"I know, Mala. I am trying to help."

"That means he has likes and dislikes."

"I *know*—"

"And if one of his likes is a soy dog with no mustard, no

ketchup, and no bun, I'm fine with that for now. I'm not going to force-feed him at every meal. If he's thirty-eight years old and that's all he eats, then yes, I've failed as a mother. But he's five now, and you know what? I'm not worrying. Can we just not worry about it for now?"

I sat back, phone to my ear, and wondered how the conversation had spoiled so rapidly. This was not the first time we had had this quarrel; we'd had this same conversation, with different words, the month prior. Mala and I had five or six regular quarrels. Our daily chats, usually affectionate, might dead-end in one of these quarrels by an infinite number of routes.

In the silence after this one, though, I was grateful. I wondered whether part of me sought it out: bringing up Vivek's diet, baiting her, watching her fume. Our quarrel was more than just a distraction. It was a routine from the old life. After Mala found out, she would behave differently. She would be careful. That occasional harshness of hers—I would miss it. Because harshness, paradoxically, is intimate. You have to be very close; you have to be family. My nearness to death will estrange me. My family will become as well-spoken as they are around strangers and acquaintances. Already Abhi is careful not to be short with me; already he is lingering in the kitchen after his early-evening snack. When had he ever idled in a chair while I cooked? Abhi *never* idled. Before, he would spend that hour in his study. Things are different since the diagnosis. *I* am different. He gives me company as if I am a guest.

Of course, I feel like a stranger in my own body, so naturally I expect others perceive me as a stranger, too. If I were to ask Abhi why he lingers, his answer would be simpler, sweeter: that he wants to spend all the time with me that he can. Scarcity has made every minute precious. This is true for me, too.

I love watching them sleep, daughter and granddaughter spooning, Shivani resting in the curve of Mala. I used to sleep with Mala that way. It is uncanny how some of the behaviors of love recur on their own, without being taught, as if particular configurations of embrace are encoded in the genes. Did my own mother hold me to her chest that way, too, and crook her arm beneath my temple, giving me the smooth pale swell of her inner arm as my pillow? I imagine slipping behind Mala so the three of us might layer like skins of a bud.

Even better than watching Shivani sleep is being woken up by her. I am on my side, near the edge of the bed. Shivani comes over so she is face-to-face. Girls usually talk early, but Shivani is taking her time. She has only a few words. So I am awakened by her small hands patting my pillow. Perfect: first thing, my eyes open and see her face. Auspicious. Mala, too, is in a good mood, smiling from the doorway, her eyes half closed and her head resting against the door frame.

Savor this, I think, looking at Shivani and her tiny brown fingers on the white pillowcase. *Remember everything.* The thought distracts me, detaches me, but only briefly. I lift my granddaughter and sit her on top of me. It feels like having

Mala here again. There is no wakefulness like a well-rested
child's, no weight on her eyelids, thoughts whole and simple.
Shivani doesn't sit on me for long before she ventures into the
valley between Abhi and me. Abhi rolls to look at us and
closes his eyes again. I get up on my elbow and tell Mala I can
change Shivani so that she can get more sleep if she wants,
but Mala says she's got it and claps her hands softly. Shivani
raises her arms. Before Mala carries Shivani out, she tips her
so she can give each of her grandparents a small, wet kiss;
then coaxes her to use her words and say a froggy *Good morning*. I ease myself back down to the pillow and wait while the
kiss cools and dries.

My spirits are high. Between bed and toothbrush, I don't
think of it at all. Then my brushing slows. When I soap and
splash my face, the protective sleep has gone. I have full knowledge again. I look in my mirrored eyes above the towel, and
she and I both know.

Downstairs, after opening the blinds, I peel and twist a
cylinder of croissant dough. The soft, white-yellow dough
pops through the cardboard. I don't get these croissants usually, I don't like the perfection of the triangles and the almost
voluntary way they curl into their shapes. But Mala and the
children like them. So I set them to bake. I hear the buzz of
Vivek's toothbrush from the top of the stairs and rush from
the kitchen to catch him. He jumps up and down and starts
talking—so happy to see his grandmother! Sachin, his brush
still in his mouth, says, "Ho, buddy, wait till we're done brushing," and wipes a drip of toothpaste foam from Vivek's pajama
shirt. Vivek follows his father back up into the bathroom. I
return to the kitchen and get out the two boxes of cereal I
have gotten for their visit, Lucky Charms and Cheerios, not
knowing which is in favor recently. I get two skillets going on
low and tilt them to slide the butter squares. Everyone comes

down, one after another, chatty. They are all here: Abhi doing his stretches in the light through the east-facing bay window, Sachin with his collar wet from splashing his face awake, Mala with her hair up in a bun, holding Shivani, who is pointing at the cereal boxes, Vivek jumping on the couch and being ordered off it. Booster chair and high chair, and the chairs where the parents wait with spoonfuls dripping, open up, big bite, come on. Bowls and plates and silverware clash on the table. I bask in the joyous hubbub of a family morning.

I made sure to shower quickly and dress before everyone came down. I even put on a touch of foundation and a brush of rouge. I rarely wear makeup and certainly not at home. But this morning I knew my face would give me away if I didn't cover it somehow. So I closed the bathroom door and painted my shadows bright.

They say flesh is grass, and flesh does grow and wither the way grass grows and withers, but not so that the eyes notice. You need an old photograph to realize how much you have changed, or the exclamation of a friend you haven't seen in years. Or word of your mortality from a pale bespectacled man in a long white coat, practiced in giving sympathy and news—a chart of the circulation system on the wall behind him, a swath of crinkly paper on the examination table, the back of your gown open to the air.

After the examination in Dr. D'Onofrio's office, I had gotten dressed again, and we had waited for twenty minutes, saying nothing. Abhi had brought a travel magazine from the waiting room—he turned its pages but stared past the impossibly blue seas at the floor. The nurse practitioner came and said they needed the examining room, could we wait in the discussion room, where the doctor would meet us shortly? Abhi got to his feet and followed her out. This left me to gather my purse and both our heavy winter coats.

I walked down the hall, my arms full, raging silently. *I am carrying his coat*. The discussion room was smaller and contained a round table and a rack of patient information brochures. Abhi had found new reading material. I stopped at his downturned head, waiting for I don't know what, waiting for him to sense me glaring. *You had me carry our coats. You had me carry our coats even though I am the one dying!* Through the whole discussion with Dr. D'Onofrio, my slender manila chart laid open before him, his voice slow and dry, I kept thinking how I had to walk down the hallway with my arms full. My mind gnawed at the dry leather of anger. It was a better chew toy than fear.

Later, I told myself Abhi had been distracted, but I knew that wasn't it. Over years I had let him get into the habit of ignoring the small chivalries. I was uncomplaining. I always made things out to be more trivial than they were—the opposite of some wives I knew (the opposite, too, of Mala). I waited out my anger in silence. And the anger went away eventually, like an itch fizzing away to nothing. On the drive home, I thought of my anger with detachment and said nothing of it to Abhi. What was the use? You couldn't change a relationship this late. You could not force small kind gestures. They didn't occur to Indian men, at least not to Indian men of Abhi's generation. (I wonder if we need expectations to perceive ingratitude. Was that why I could think of Ronak or Mala as ungrateful, but never Abhi?) Still, the larger love was there. The larger love I never had cause to doubt. Just as on every other occasion, I was happy I hadn't spoken my anger. Abhi was a good husband. Plenty of philanderers came home with brooches and tennis bracelets for their wives, making up ostentatiously for hidden transgressions. Abhi was a good husband, a good man. So what if he didn't open doors for me? So what if he didn't pull out chairs for me the way Ronak did for Amber?

Abhi likes three whites with one yolk marbled through it. Sachin likes his eggs with all the yolks mixed in. Men first: the traditional reflex. Besides, Mala is focused on feeding the children. She shakes one cereal box, then the other, giving them a choice. I do not break the eggs as cleanly as I usually do. My fingertip chases a fleck of eggshell through the jellied egg white until I draw it up the bowl's slope and beach it on the lip. I spill the eggs onto the heat and I let them whiten.

Abhi is sitting straight, lotus position, lengthening his spine. He never did these asanas when he lived in India. Neither had our parents. Yoga was for sadhus, not for engineers and students. Only after seeing white women on the Fitness Channel do it, five of them on mats, blue bay and white boats behind them, he had become fascinated with this sublime science from India's past. I set two slices of rye bread to toast for him, just in case he doesn't want the croissants. Soon he will be restless while everyone lingers over breakfast. How wonderful these indoors winter days are! Brownies on a plate, child laughter and child tantrums to disrupt my brooding, plastic trains and picture books and stray stuffed animals on the carpet. Yet these days drive Mala *stir-crazy*—that is her word—come the afternoon, when dinner is as far away as the children's sleep time is from dinner.

Abhi loves these days, too. But he is subject to the inward pull of his mind, which revolves beyond the reach of our ruckus. After Vivek takes Mala's requisite two more bites, Abhi will play with him for a few minutes. He will roar, he will chase and capture and release and chase again, but then he will get distracted. The chasing will grow listless, the tickling less furious, and once Sachin finishes eating (Sachin is very slow), Abhi will slip into the study, body following mind.

Half an hour alone with his numbers refreshes him. He can't accomplish much in that time. I told him once that he returned to his mathematical work the way some obsessive-compulsives wash their hands. He said that was right—except it wasn't work, it was play.

Vivek asks for croissants, just as they are due out. Mala gets up to fetch something from the refrigerator and stops, the door wide, her profile bathed in pale, cool light.

"What's all this?" she asks. "Mom? Is this just for the next couple days?"

Tupperware stacks are each topped by a plastic-wrapped basin of a different dahl. On every dish, I sprinkled the shredded coriander in a circle, as in a cookbook. I even have ready dough, covered in a stainless steel bowl. "I made it all yesterday. It's fresh. There's more in the freezer."

"Isn't this a little much for the four of us?"

"The kids will eat, too."

"Good luck with that." Her hand goes for something, then drifts back, thwarted.

"What do you want?"

"The skim milk, but . . ."

"Here." I slide things out, slide things aside. "I'm sorry, I should have kept the milk more accessible."

"No, you know what? I don't need it. Just leave it."

"It's fine."

"No, Mom, it's all right."

"This will only take a second!"

She crosses her arms and waits. Vivek has his mouth full of steaming croissant. He opens his mouth and breathes out the heat, then gets up on his knees on the chair as if to show everyone the food.

"Don't stuff your mouth like that," Mala says. "Sit down in your chair. You'll fall."

Vivek doesn't respond until Sachin looks his way, makes a sound like *shhhp*, and points down with two fingers. He turns back to feeding Shivani. Mala sighs while I get her the skim milk. Sachin, his curiosity piqued, sets down the spoon in Shivani's bowl and comes over to where I have put out some of my dishes. Mala passes him without a glance.

"What do we have?" he asks in Gujarati.

"Surprise, surprise, you have to wait until lunch." I put my hand halfheartedly over one of the bowls.

"This *is* a lot."

Abhi, his exercises done, approaches the table and the plate I set for him. "You didn't see the refrigerator in the garage, did you?"

"What's this now?" Mala asks. "You bought another refrigerator?"

"Full-size. And she filled it, too. You should have seen the cooking she was doing yesterday. She sprouted two extra arms, like Durga."

Mala shakes her head. "These two aren't going to eat Indian food lunch and dinner."

"Can we have lasagna?" asks Vivek through a full mouth.

"Chew your food, V."

"Can we?"

"Ask Naani. But chew your food first. This is the last time I'm going to tell you or you lose those croissants."

"I know," I say. "It is too much food."

"Not if I am set to work on it," says Sachin pleasantly, returning to his seat in front of Shivani's high chair. Shivani is playing with two spoons, one in each small hand. "Home cooking! After a long time."

Mala has just poured herself half a glass of skim and is raising it to her lips. "A long time?"

"Naani, can we have lasagna for lunch?"

"I meant we hadn't had your mother's cooking in a long time."

"If I had free time, I'd spend all day in the kitchen, too."

"Not for lunch, Vivek. I've made a lot of nice things for you. You like raita, right?"

"Sorry, husband, but I have a *job*."

"Mala," Abhi interjects sharply. I close the refrigerator door. Abhi would have let the comment pass if circumstances had been different. Things are about to escalate. Vivek is not going to forget the lasagna, either.

That is when the doorbell rings.

The day before Christmas Eve? At nine in the morning?

"I'll get it." Mala leaves the table.

Sachin and Abhi glance at each other. Shivani, quiet, amenable Shivani, opens her mouth for another bite, and her father obliges. I listen. The door opens. Mala gives a sound of delight, a laugh crossed with a yelp. "What are you doing here? You know I saw that Spurs jacket of yours through the window and I thought, *Naw, it can't be him*. God! You didn't even tell me. And I thought I was going to be alone this whole weekend! Don't you smirk at me!"

Abhi is looking at me with his mouth open. I rush to the door, shouting, "Ronak?"

He is standing in the doorway, looking a little abashed. I throw my arms around him and feel the chill of his jacket against my cheek. He smells of coffee. I step away and look up. He is unshaven.

"So, uh, Merry Christmas," he says, not at ease, his eyebrows twitching, the way they do when he is nervous.

Vivek comes running full speed down the hall and jumps into Ronak's arms. Abhi and Sachin with Shivani on his hip approach in puzzled delight. Sachin puts his hand out. "Brother, welcome, quite the surprise!" Ronak shifts Vivek to one side and shakes the hand, then draws Sachin close. The shake becomes a sideways hug. Ronak kisses Shivani on the forehead.

Abhi waits. He pats Ronak's shoulder, studying the scruff on his cheek. "So let's get my grandkids in here," Abhi says, his voice just short of elation. "And Amber, too—where are they all hiding?"

Mala glances out at the driveway. "You brought the Beamer?" Meaning the sedan; meaning not Amber's minivan, not the car seats, not the kids. "They didn't come?"

"Right," says Ronak, and swallows. "They're in Pitt right now. With her parents."

I flush. "You . . . you came for me?"

Ronak hesitates.

I look at Abhi and breathe deeply. "You told—"

"I said nothing." I take one look at Abhi's eyes and believe him. "Ronak?"

Ronak, seeing me and Abhi tense, grows calmer, offhand. "They're in Pitt, like every year. But I came, you know, to be here. Here with my boy V."

"Where's my cousins?" asks Vivek.

Ronak purses his lips. "They're in Pittsburgh with their mom," he says. "But they did send along a whole bunch of presents."

"So you dropped them off and came here?" Mala asks. "You took two cars?"

"Right."

"So you left their house at what, six thirty in the morning?"

"Yeah."

Mala smirks playfully. "Kind of early for you, isn't it, High Finance?"

"Once in a while's okay. You know, so I can see how the other half lives. Doctors and surgeons and that kind of riff-raff."

It pleases me to see Mala and Ronak teasing each other. Abhi is tense. "They must be up by now, right? We can do a video chat so the cousins can see each other."

Vivek smiles. "Yeah, I want to see my cousins on the computer."

"Okay, V, they're probably still eating breakfast, and then they are going to see some relatives this morning . . ."

Vivek sticks out his lower lip, his disappointment not lost on Ronak or Abhi, who says, "Let me get my phone. I'll see if we can catch them."

Ronak sets Vivek down and tips his suitcase over. It is a large bag with wheels, the kind you would take for a longer stay, or a trip to a place that wouldn't provide everything the way our house would. Presents, probably. He unzips a front pocket and brings out a Buzz Lightyear figure. "There's an early Christmas present for you, V." Vivek is successfully distracted, clawing at the packaging to get it open. Abhi returns with the phone on speaker ringing in his hand, over and over, until Amber's voice-mail comes on. Her voice slows Ronak's hand as he zips the bag.

Now that Ronak is here, the house takes on an air of celebration, mostly thanks to his effect on Mala. Abhi relaxes more as the morning goes on, like a moving body warming to water. Vivek plays on the couch, climbs on his mother, basks in her good mood.

It is unusual for Ronak to spend this much time with family at a stretch. His laptop is usually out by now, or he is sliding a fingertip across his phone, the screen's reflection turning his glasses white, impenetrable. Generally he leaves the chit-chat to Amber. His children, too, would divert us, freeing him from the obligation of interacting. This morning, he seems curiously free of his itch to retreat. Maybe, without Amber and the children, he has consigned these hours to us. Yet he seems happy to be here. Does he know? I wonder. If he doesn't, I don't want to tell him. I don't want to ruin this unexpected warmth.

For a while, the grandchildren and I do some fingerpainting with a set I bought at the dollar store. Vivek keeps showing his work to Ronak, and Ronak scratches his chin, sticks out his lower lip, and says, in a British accent, "A work of astonishing grandeur!" or something like that, which pleases Vivek greatly. Shivani paints the paper and her face alternately; when she runs out of cheeks, I offer her my own. In the bathroom mirror, we look like we have been celebrating Holi. Ronak goes upstairs to shower and shave when Mala teases him about his "terrorist-mug-shot shadow," which I think means his two-day beard. When Sachin comes down from his own shower, I slip into Abhi's study.

He is at his desk, an architect's table by the window, and has three separate books open, his graph-paper notepad at the center. He registers the door opening with the surface of his mind and commands his right hand to rise. His left hand keeps writing. It is his "stop where you are and don't talk" gesture. I walk up behind him and pluck the pencil out of his moving hand, which moves for a few seconds before he startles, as if shaken from a dream. He looks over his shoulder at me, closes his eyes, and rests his elbow on the table, his forehead on the heel of his hand.

"It's like walking a tightrope," he says. "And you cut the tightrope."

I clack his pencil firmly on the desk. "I never interrupt you."

"What is it?" He picks up the pencil and begins worrying the eraser with the pad of his thumb.

"Did you—"

"I told him nothing."

"Did you hint at it?"

"No."

"Did you say something to Amber?"

"I never talked to Amber. I still haven't got ahold of her. I am worried."

"You think they had a fight?"

Abhi nods. "He will tell Mala first. He may not tell us at all."

I bite my lip. "Do you think they fought because we asked them over?"

"No."

"How can you be sure?"

"They wouldn't fight over coming here."

"Why did they fight then?"

Abhi shrugs. "What do couples fight about? What do *we* fight about? Some trivial thing or another. Enjoy him while he's here. She seems to have given him a sound thrashing for us."

I smile and kiss his head where the light from the window shines on it. I tap his notebook. "You are overthinking things, Abhi. The answer is four. Two and two is four. Now come out and play with your grandchildren before they grow up."

I wonder how much Vivek understands of the moods and shifts and silences above him. Does the chill between adults drop like cold air and discomfort him, an unplaceable draft? For the most part, he seems to soak up Mala's moods. The only time he ever spoke to me defiantly was back in June, right after I had an argument with Mala. I had known he was mimicking his mother and had not taken offense. Still, I had expected Mala to reprimand him. She didn't. (What had his outburst been about? I think it was the color of his Gatorade cup; he had a special Gatorade-only cup I was supposed to know about.) Mala had let him speak to his grandmother in that tone. The sting had come out in our tearful reconciliation later that night, after the kids had gone to sleep, when as usual we traded apologies and self-defense in whispers at the kitchen table.

Eventually we lapsed back into argument: "We shouldn't have to scold him when he does something out of line around you, Mom. You can tell him, you're his grandmother."

"But it's not as effective coming from me as it would be from you, Mala."

"That's not true, he never listens to me."

"He listens to you all the time: he listens to how you speak to me."

"I was speaking my mind to you because you're my mother, but you know, I guess I'll watch myself in the future."

"You don't have to watch yourself around me."

"Well, obviously I do . . ."

Old quarrels: forget them. We are happy right now, aren't we? And I am watching myself. I made no comments on her eating habits or her children's. It is a sensitive topic with her and has been ever since her teenage years, when I began pushing her to eat more than a few spoons of rice and the skim water off the dahl.

Vivek shows Abhi two action figures he brought from home. Mala slides an *India Today* from under the coffee table. Sachin, Shivani in his lap, is pointing at a picture book and counting. Even Ronak, when he comes downstairs, looks lively. With his freshly shaven face, a light seems to have been switched on somewhere inside him. But the eyes are bloodshot. The eyes are not smiling.

"Did you eat anything before you left?" I ask. "You've been on the road for hours."

"I grabbed something for breakfast." He goes for the pantry and starts scanning shelves; he is hungry, he just isn't saying it.

"Let me make you something. Go sit down. What do you want?"

"I'm fine, Mom. I'm not hungry." He finds the cashews and shakes some into his palm.

"How about eggs?"

Mala speaks from the couch. "Might as well save room for lunch, Ronak," she says. "There's quite the feast coming our way."

Ronak glances at me, and I name the dishes I made for lunch as he strolls to the glass doors that open onto the deck. Inches of snowfall balance precariously atop the legs of the upside-down patio chairs. The only color is from the patio umbrella, collapsed late last fall, propped at an angle. Its floral yellows break the snow. I will open that umbrella again. Even if I do not respond to treatment, spring is almost guaranteed me. I will get to shake the April water from that umbrella and screw it to the hub.

Ronak stares out at the backyards. Our swing set with its chairs rusted in place, a neighbor's trampoline fenced in black netting, another neighbor's pool, drained and covered for the winter. I remember the blond children in their blue swimming trunks, front teeth coming in outsize, shouts audible over the lawn mower two yards down. They ran and ran and flung themselves down the Slip 'n Slide. The water dried on their golden backs. Then one morning, a station wagon was loaded full of cardboard boxes, clothes and shoes, posters rolled to go up on the dorm room wall. The children came back as twenty-somethings, their hair a few shades of darker brown. In the backyard they sat and chatted at Fourth of July barbecues, beer bottles in their hands and fat watches on wrists, slightly sunburned, khaki shorts, button-down shirt sleeves. The grown rich children of rich parents, the life cycle continuing, and me at the window unchanged.

I go over to Ronak, who is still pensive, his cashews finished. "Is she upset?"

"You got ahold of her?"

"No, no. I am just wondering, is she upset? And her parents—what did Dottie and Don say?"

Mala looks up from her reading and watches for Ronak's response.

"They were fine with it. They know I've spent every year there for . . . for years now. Even before the marriage."

Sachin stops counting. Mala says, "Did you two have a fight?" Her tone is playful—*come on, out with it already, it's not a big deal*—and I fade out, knowing his sister has a better chance of getting the information than me, assuming there is information to be gotten.

Ronak's face stays blank. "No. She's fine."

Mala had closed her magazine over her finger, but now her finger slips out. "Funny, for a guy who hustles old ladies out of their savings for a living, you're an awfully bad liar."

"I'm not lying, Mala. Everything's fine."

"You're telling me your rifle-and-Bible in-laws are okay with you missing Christmas? That's some real Christian forgiveness, I'd say."

Sachin smiles at me in faint bewilderment, having understood nothing but Mala's suddenly aggressive tone. She has a way of making her voice turn sharp all at once. I am not sure she always intends to be sharp, but this time probably she does. I have been on the receiving end of it before.

Ronak is used to her and smiles serenely. "You know,

they're good people, Mala. Bibles and all. You keep talking like that, and I may just take offense someday."

"All right, all right. But think about what it looks like. You here, them there."

"I know what it looks like. And it's not like that."

Abhi chases Vivek around the coffee table and between brother and sister, shouting, "I've got you, I've got you!" It is intentionally disruptive; he is breaking the tension. Mala, rebuffed, opens her magazine and sets it down forcefully on her knees. Ronak takes out his phone and brushes at its screen, wandering distractedly to the kitchen counter. At first I think he is calling Amber, but the screen has a graph on it, and all I can make out is uptick, uptick, uptick.

Ronak.

Mala is sometimes sweet, sometimes cutting. Her brother is neither. Better love that is quarrelsome than indifference, which is what I fear underlies Ronak's perfectly unruffled composure whenever he comes home. With Mala, homecoming carries a charge. Without fail, at least once, she and I will fight and make up. The fault line is active. Ronak fights with no one.

That may be what happens when the father is not a template. The boys born here could not look to the fathers for a model. To know how to hold himself, what to say, when to laugh, Ronak had to look elsewhere, and elsewhere meant friends. We set out love and waited for him to come home and be a son to us, as if his teens and twenties might be just a fitful phase. As if the man might resemble the small boy, everything in between an aberration.

During those years, as now, there was no way to yell at him. At Mala we could yell. She wanted love, she wanted approval—and that meant we could say no. We could say, *That is not how we do things*, and it had an effect.

I could stand in Ronak's doorway and demand to know

why he hadn't answered me when I called his name. I had lunch warm on the plate for him. Ronak would pause his game and look at me over his shoulder, there in his mess of clothes and game covers. I demanded, rapid-fire, arms crossed: When had he last showered? Was this the third straight day? Yes, this was summer vacation, but had he slept in that T-shirt and shorts? He would eye me, bored, unmoved by my reproaches. "I'll be down in a sec. I'm almost done with this level."

Why had we gotten that game system for him? Even his friendships were time spent in an elbow-to-elbow frenzy over controllers, laughing and shouting at the screen. The system and libraries of games he wanted—"needed"—changed every year or so, each system sleeker. Controllers grew crowded with buttons and cross-shaped pads. The screens were bewilderingly colorful and intricate. How could he keep track of his own tiny character amid so much activity? We shouldn't have bought him those games. What if Mala had demanded something that cost over a hundred dollars, purely for her amusement?

If not the games, though, it would have been something else. There's no sure way to win, raising children. They turn out how they turn out. Sushila, a friend of ours, refused her son Vijay a Nintendo 64 and every system that followed it. Vijay went to books instead and studied writing in the university. He lives in downtown New York now, still single, and his apartment has no room for his parents' luggage, much less for a guest bed or sleeping bags. Sushila hardly knows him; he makes next to nothing teaching books in a dingy city college there— Vijay, the son of a breast surgeon and an anesthesiologist.

All you can do is set out love and hope they come. Ronak would eat the meals I made him, scarcely aware of what I had put on his plate. He took second helpings, but only to fill the hole with something. Not out of pleasure. Nothing was savored.

The only time I saw him taking an interest in food was during sophomore year. His body had grown thin and hard, and a scrap of track shirt hung from his shoulders. I never thought of food as fuel. I always thought food, properly enjoyed, was close to rest and leisure, to a massage and hot bath, something to make you sleep well. Ronak ate for fuel's sake before his track meets, tossing pasta brusquely into boiling water. I was never part of those carbohydrate meals. I offered to make him rotli, insisting it was just flour and a smear of ghee. He said that pasta was "better" before a meet, garnishing his steaming rotini with oregano and Sriracha— apparently some ritual meal he and his teammates had come up with.

Whatever he was, he became by watching other people, frantically recombining himself from the boys around him. He collected comics in seventh grade because his friend Nick collected comics. He tried out for track when his best friend, Philip, tried out for track. The team was a kind of family. I didn't know about Amber, but she was part of his life by then, too. He slept at our house, but that was all.

One day, I could see no higher than Ronak's chest. One day, I picked up the phone, and his voice was deeper than his father's. He ate more, but the fat on him disappeared, it seemed, over a single summer. With that softness went the last of his childhood. I saw him from behind and thought: Who is that? Is that man my son? Yet I never felt older. I thought sometimes, too, of some girl's white hand tracing the sharp loveliness of his shoulder blade—and never felt more fearful for his future.

Abhi, in the days when he had more of a temper, used to call his son lazy—but how ferociously Ronak ran at the gunshot, palms cutting the air, like those sprinters in the Olympics! His back was straight, and I could see how tall he was, even compared to the American boys on either side of him and often behind him. I cheered from the bleachers with the other parents. If we had stayed in India, he never would have grown into such height and grace. He would have hunched over his notebooks the way we did at that age, learning things by rote.

Here a boy grows a foot taller than his father. Here he raises a fist as his legs slow their rhythm and the losers go slack, walk, spit, stop, put their hands on their waists, and bend. Here, even a boy can experience triumph. But the triumph made him proud, and pride made him still more distant. Ronak would glance up at the stands where we were waving at him, nod once, and raise his hand. An acknowledgment. *Yes, we know each other.* And a caution. *Now, don't embarrass me.*

This country gave us clean quiet luxury and charged us nothing but our children.

Abhi had four brothers, I had one. We left them behind. They didn't score as high as we did. We put sixteen hours and thousands of dollars between us and our widowed mothers— and then dared complain to each other, years later, about a son who applied to a college two states away when there was a good one in town.

Still worse: in college, Ronak studied neither mathematics nor science—economics, something Abhi considered inferior. After that, with no postgraduate training, he got a finance job in Manhattan. These two choices bothered Abhi more than any others. Ronak took the talent he had inherited and pursued a worldly, debased form of mathematics. Numbers-work, yes, but in a suit and tie, shuffling and dealing. Meanwhile, the father, in his study at 1 AM, inked square-root signs like a bygone Brahman drawing the bar above Sanskrit.

Numbers were sacred to Abhi. He had no gods. He downplayed his dedication, of course. His code for *"leave me alone"* was *"I'm going to go doodle for a while."* Then he would disappear into his study. Those doodles made him famous. Six years ago, we watched him stride onstage at the University of Berkeley, a star. The professors there thought him miraculous because he had no training. He did his neurologist's work day after day until six, sometimes seven in the evening. Then, after eleven, when we were all asleep, he would stay up writing in the graph-paper notepads his brother sent over in bulk from Ahmedabad. Always the same brand: black cover, weak thready binding, and the smell that reminded us both of school. Abhi said that smell prompted his best insights—as if he had known all of mathematics once, in his childhood or in a past life, and the smell of the notebook triggered his memory. We had learned math and penmanship in those books, each letter in its own square.

Of course he disapproved when Ronak twisted that inborn love of numbers into love of money. Ronak thought his job placement such a triumph, he gave us the news with a small involuntary pump of the fist. He never understood why his father's face fell. Abhi muttered only to me. "You don't know what that kind of banker does. Ronak is a gambler now. Our son will gamble for a living." Abhi divided professions into noble and ignoble ones, and *lucrative* did not necessarily mean *noble*. Abhi would have been more pleased had Ronak become a schoolteacher. Medicine and teaching were noble. Playing the market for a living was not.

For everyone but Abhi, though, *richer* meant *better*. I confess: at dinner parties, I passed on the stories Ronak told me of recruiters and their thousand-dollar wine bottles. I enjoyed the envy. Our circle was all doctors and doctors' wives. Their children were premed. Our son alone had made it to a higher level of wealth. How proudly I claimed Ronak for my own when he was away! When he came home—just once, that first year—I was reminded how he was mine in name only. New clothes, new shoes, a new watch, and his hair no longer parted on the left like his father's.

I asked him whether he made any Indian friends in Manhattan. He grinned a new grin, only one side of his mouth rising. He was thinking, probably, how old-fashioned I was to make these distinctions. "Oh sure," he said. "There's a huge Desi singles scene, too."

Day-c; it took me a while to realize that was our word for other Indians. His offhand comment made me wonder, helplessly, what kind of girl he would bring home. Whoever it was, we would have to acquiesce. When had we squandered the right to say what we thought? To say, *We don't like this girl.* To say, *We want someone who will fit in this family.*

I realized, as I watched him cut open a bag of coffee he had brought from New York (how specific his tastes had become!), that we had no say. Even if he did find someone in that Desi singles scene, it would be some Asha on the neighboring gym equipment in his apartment's workout room, some party-scene Sheena behind colored contact lenses who could talk with him about wines. This Desi singles scene was the only time he mentioned dating. Still, I thought, Indian would be better than white, even if Indian meant Bengal or Uttar Pradesh or the south.

So I came to expect an Asha or a Sheena. My accent—which is slight; I barely have an accent anymore—and my cooking wouldn't be completely foreign, at least. I listened for hints or slips when he spoke of ski trips with friends. What friends? Who else had gone? He didn't tell us until he was ready, and it came as a surprise. Amber accompanied him on his Christmas visit home nine years ago. I opened the door and thought this young couple had the wrong house. His smile—another new smile—made his face unrecognizably joyful. She was standing just behind him, slightly wary of me, her slender gloved hand in his.

In those first seconds, as I understood that this was it, this was *her*, I eyed her cruelly, coldly, as I never would afterward. She was shorter than Ronak and her legs were thick at the thighs. This was not the athletic, high-cheekboned white woman I had always worried about. Amber's cheeks were as round, and her body as plump, as any Gujarati girl's. I thought, *If this is what he wanted, I could have found it for him*. It was twenty degrees outside. Amber's cheeks and ears had turned red. Brownish-blondish hair under her hat, a purple scarf. I did not sense wealth or finance or Manhattan from her clothes and boots. Her skin was the white that burned before it tanned. I thought, *Mixed with that skin, his children will look completely American*. I could not see her figure under her puffy jacket, but she seemed full at the bosom; the scarf gave her the appearance of a small bird puffed against the cold. I wondered: *Does he know what childbearing will do to a figure like hers?* And: *Americans age worse than we do—is she at least a few years younger than him?* Shamefully petty, snobbish thoughts, but I thought them. *She isn't, compared to other white women, what Ronak is compared to other Indian men.*

When he led her inside, I could judge her figure better, though blurred by a snowflake-printed sweater. I said distractedly, as Ronak took her coat, "That is a lovely scarf." I paused and formed the next word. "Amber."

"Why thank you, ma'am," she said, lighting up. Briefly I thought she said *mom*, but it was too early for this; she had said *ma'am*. Her green eyes met mine directly, and I looked away. "My grandmother will just love to hear that. We get one from her every Christmas. In fact she'll probably knit you one for next time we visit."

I looked from her to Ronak and back, and I could not connect them. This girl with a local, almost a country accent, speaking of her grandmother; Ronak, distant, money-minded, this his second time home all year. Out of her coat and hat now (was that my Ronak putting her coat on a hanger?), in the gold glow of our chandelier, animatedly speaking, her hair free over her shoulders, Amber was transformed. Her liveliness changed my perception of her. Everything that seemed plain in isolation or awkward when motionless now appeared as beauty. She exercised a calm command over Ronak that did not seem like domination. Abhi glanced at me incredulously when Ronak pulled out her chair at the dinner table. How had she made him a gentleman? We could not have imagined that Ronak was capable of monitoring another person's comfort.

"I did not know," I apologized, not specifying what it was that I hadn't known—that Ronak was bringing an American guest to dinner. (He had intended to spring the visit as a surprise so that he wouldn't have to deal with us "throwing a fit," he told us later.) "I fear I made only Indian food."

Ronak said, "It's no problem, Mom. She loves Indian food."

"Even more than Roan does. Roan's always wanting Italian or Mexican, and I'm always the one pushing for Tandoor Oven."

"You mean the Tandoor Oven here in town?" I asked.

She nodded. "I like the aloo gobi there. That's what I like, right, Roan? The aloo gobi?"

"That's right. She also likes onion naan."

Abhi and I knew the owners. Mr. Mishra or his wife or both were at the restaurant every night. Sharmila handled the seating. I flushed. She had known. Sharmila Mishra had known about them. Who else had known?

"Roan tells me you're a great cook. I've been looking for-

ward to this. Good Lord, look at all these dishes. This must
have taken you days!"

"You haven't seen Mom cook," said Ronak with what I was
surprised to hear was pride. "She's so fast, she could run a
restaurant. How long did this take you, Mom?"

"Not too long, an hour and a half or so," I murmured. I
pointed at the eggplant bhartha. "This may be a little spicy
for you, Amber."

She threw her head back as she laughed and touched Ronak's
arm. "Don't worry about me, I can handle spicy. Your son's the
one always asking for more water at Thai restaurants."

Ronak nodded. "She's amazing like that. She and Dad
should have a contest."

"We'll see about that," said Abhi, who hadn't said much
until then, watching the three of us. "Help yourself, Amber."

She said she was dieting, but Amber ate with great pleasure, and it was a delight for me, seeing such obvious relish
in my food by someone other than Abhi. Mala usually took
thimble-sized portions; Ronak ate without recognizing what
he put in his mouth; Indian guests gave formulaic praise.
Amber actually inquired about what I had put into each dish.
Had Ronak told her how to ingratiate herself with me, or was
she naturally friendly? She accepted seconds when I pressed
them on her. She ate the bhartha without resorting to her
glass of ice water.

Abhi began putting the questions I wanted to ask but didn't.
How, when, where had they met? How long had they known
each other? The answers saddened me. They had met in biology class. Biology? But wasn't that . . . eighth grade? It was.
Ronak and Amber had been paired for an owl pellet dissec-
tion. They had been going out for that long? Oh no, of course
not. They didn't go out until tenth grade. I had imagined
girlfriends, but he had been faithful to this one girl all along.

He had loved her and never told us. And college in Pennsylvania? And the job in New York? "On and off, you know," murmured Ronak. "But mostly on."

"And you didn't feel you could tell us? All these years?"

Ronak said nothing.

"We made the decision together," said Amber lightly. "We waited till it was the right time. No point rushing things, right?"

Abhi nodded and looked at his plate. I thought I could read guilt in the way he pushed his dahl about in the bowl, using the back of his spoon. I know I felt it. Guilt, but also embarrassment at not knowing this immense fact about our son.

Growing up in India, we hadn't had this kind of love to conceal from our parents. Ronak's or Mala's children, a decade and a half from now, would never have to conceal their boyfriends or girlfriends. But during the in-between years, during the shift from Indian to American, love, for our children, was both treasure and transgression, a joy they could not bring home. Ronak had been caring and dutiful—but in secret.

No wonder he seemed remote to his parents. He had sent an effigy to live with us. His feeling self had escaped to her.

Without being asked, solely because she had noticed, Amber refilled Ronak's water. She did it the way I would have done it, tilting the pitcher slowly so the ice cubes caught at the fluted lip. He held the glass steady while she poured, his whole hand around it. I had poured for him hundreds of times, and he had never held the glass.

I foresaw, in that moment, the mother she would be someday. I saw the dark blue minivan with cheddar cheese Goldfish crushed into the mats. The sinkside rack where she would dry the sippy cups she had handwashed in hot water. The cart at Walmart with her toddler's creased thighs sticking through the upper basket, two cubes of Huggies stowed below. The toddler would be fair-skinned and have light brown hair: no trace of us. And then, beyond that, my teenage grandchildren unplaceably handsome, unplaceably beautiful. Maybe once, for some relative's wedding reception, a granddaughter would be brought to me so I could dress her in Indian clothes. And she—what would they name her? something easy and dual-purpose, Maya, Nina, Sheela—she would look the way attractive white women look wearing Indian clothes, sharp-featured, strangely hard underneath, like those too-tall, too-slender mannequins at saree stores.

Within two years (he had introduced the girlfriend so he could make her his fiancée), Ronak and Amber had their wedding, or more accurately, weddings: the morning at their small church on a downtown street corner, close to boxy houses and a taqueria. I had never been inside one of these churches before, not in America. It looked exactly like the ones Abhi and I had seen on vacation in Switzerland and Austria; the builders had reproduced the darkness, the stained-glass windows, the organ pipes up front. I had thought such artistic churches existed only in Europe, but we had one just down the highway, with old Dodges and Fords in the parking lot behind it. We walked down the aisle to our places in the pew, as we had been instructed. Everyone twisted in their seats to look at us. The whole wedding took place in a funereal hush; no one behind us talked.

That afternoon, we changed our clothes and had the Hindu ceremony in a Hyatt ballroom where a mandap and wooden thrones had been set up. Red silks, marigolds in a stainless steel thali, Christmas lights spiraling up the columns, the pandit's half-mumbled Sanskrit like the droning of an engine; and the audience free to turn and shake hands with an old friend, to follow a bolting two-year-old into the lobby, to chat.

I had made a trip to India with Amber's measurements written on a chit of paper. I chose the darkest red that was not yet maroon and, for the reception, the darkest blue that was not yet purple. In Ahmedabad, I went to fetch my mother-in-law's old jewelry sets from a State Bank of India safe, for which Abhi had vouchsafed me the key. He had kept the key inside a deposit envelope, a length of coarse twine for the key chain. I was very careful with that key and tucked it in with my passport. During the journey, I checked on it every time I checked on my passport. The key, especially with that twine, promised me access to the past, to our deceased mothers. It was time to hand those sets over to my daughter-in-law, just as Abhi's mother had given them to me.

Brittle, faded velvet cases; their hinges resisted at first, and then, recognizing me, gave way all at once. Inside, the sets were as fragrant as old books. The gold was a deep yellow, and the work was in a busy older style, thick loops of chain and tiny dangling bell-beads. I tried to imagine the necklace resting on Amber. It would be only for a moment, the pose, the smile, the press of a button. I would not expect or even want her to wear this weight to the ceremony. After the photograph, this set would be hers to store away. Would she think it was gaudy, overdone? Even if she disliked it, she would never say so. Or maybe she would be indifferent. She would have no way to distinguish it from the bangles on her wrists or the bodice I laced up her back. No, Amber would take her cue from me; if I told her what the jewelry was, if I spoke of its history first, she would say it was "beautiful." She would offer praise without comprehension, praise for my sake.

I returned the jewelry to the safe and buried the key in my purse. Outside the bank, though, I saw a billboard with a giant watch on it, and I changed my mind. I took off my watch, put it in my purse, and went back inside the bank. I told the clerk I had forgotten my watch inside the safe, where I had left it while trying on some old bracelets. Tick, tick: the future is stronger than the past. Would things have been any different if Ronak had married an Indian girl? Raised here, raised there—girls were different now. Abhi and I came from an India that did not exist anymore. We had sold my own father's house in Jamnagar to make room for a multiplex. I put my watch back on, and I brought the sets to America.

The afternoon of the wedding, when Mala and I helped her get ready, I told Amber about the necklace and bracelets. She said they were "beautiful, just beautiful," as I knew she would. Mala had a digital camera, and I looked over her shoulder at each new image of Amber wearing the set. When I went around to take the necklace off, her hand rose protectively to the heavy gold resting on her chest. "What are you doing, Mom?"

"I'm taking it off, of course. You wouldn't want to wear this to the ceremony."

"Why not? Didn't you say it belonged to Roan's grand-mother?"

"I did."

"Am I allowed to wear it?"

I looked at Mala.

"You can wear it, if you want to," said Mala. "It's not really the style anymore, Amber."

"Neither were the earrings I wore in church this morning. Those were my great-grandmother's opals. She wore them at her own wedding back in Germany."

Mala frowned. "It looks uncomfortable."

"It's not uncomfortable."

"You're sure you want to wear that for two hours?"

"If I'm allowed to wear it, I want to wear it," Amber said. She pressed both hands to the necklace, last night's mehndi dark on her skin, a brown that glowed orange. The bracelets slid noisily down her arms. "This can be my something old."

I like to take refuge with Sachin and Shivani. The enclave of the chaise longue feels like a clearing. Father and daughter. Both, I feel, harmless, without darkness or cruelty, even of the domestic kind. If Mala could see this quality in Sachin, as I do, maybe she might love him for that. But harmlessness wasn't something women of her generation could love in a man.

A girl with her saree pulled low over her forehead, though, surrounded by relatives, being shown a potential husband over tea—such a girl might feel attracted to harmlessness. She would see whether her suitor looked capable of cruelty. What to watch for, in an interview that short? A certain thinness of the upper lip. Thick forearms, thick fingers. A rough way of setting the teacup back on the saucer.

My own yes to Abhi had been based, in part, on his slender fingers and receding hairline. Such a man, I had thought, will let me visit my mother and father. A similar conviction—he will be kind—had made me want Sachin for Mala.

I sit at the foot of the chaise, and Sachin moves his feet in their droopy white socks to the side. Shivani isn't saying the animals by name yet, but she does point to orca, dolphin, walrus, and penguin as Sachin names them. He looks at me, raises his eyebrows, and points at the book to ask if I want to take over, but I shake my head and let them continue. I like the sight of them together. A turn of the long, glossy cardboard panel: tiger, gorilla, rhinoceros, elephant.

I begin pretending I am not there. I witness this scene as a ghost, unable to alter it. My presence does not change their awareness. I don't even dimple the chaise cushion. This doesn't sadden me. It is a pleasing fantasy, the kind some people have of fame or heaven.

Abhi and I noticed, from the start, how much closer Mala is to her son. Shivani came second, after Mala's love for Sachin, perhaps, had cooled. Or maybe she felt no sense of discovery with this second child, seeing only the familiar chores. Mala would deny favoritism; she would be devastated, and then enraged, if she found out Abhi and I murmur this to ourselves. But the difference shows. Maybe she allows it unconsciously, but Sachin is always handling Shivani. He does it well. He is quick with diapers. It pleases me to see him clip the tiny ankles, raise the buttocks off the changing pad, slide the diaper under, and spread its crinkled fringe with a deft finger-splay; then fold up, wrap from the sides, and blow a raspberry on her chest for the finale.

Just one generation ago, this simply did not happen. In India, you didn't need the man to help. You had mother, mother-in-law, sisters, cousins, grown nieces to share the shushing and cradling. For keeping the house clean, there was always a mute and serviceable bai who swung a wet gray rag over the floor tiles, fifty rupees a month and the gift of two old sarees on Diwali. Somehow, in India, you could leave a child to itself a little more confidently. In retrospect, this doesn't make sense—the insects were more dangerous, and the outlets were uncovered. Still, collective watchfulness substituted for constant supervision. In America, in a small, resident's apartment, the constellation of females vanished, but the husband did not register the tasks to be done. The aristocratic idleness of the Indian father came over on the same plane as the Indian husband's entitlement to a hot meal. Even with a man like Abhi. I never expected him to crook Ronak over a forearm and rinse—and he never did. To Sachin's generation this came naturally.

I make myself small and dwell in Shivani's presence for a while. My storm shelter. I am happy here. She has no idea of mortality, and so, in a sense, no mortality, there in her father's lap.

Already—*beetle, bumblebee, earthworm, spider*—words are getting attached to things. In a few years, words will proliferate and swarm and carry off the pictures in the books she reads, black ants hauling off the butterfly. Eventually just words will be left. The things themselves will have been devoured. What a loss! All creation. To be stuck reading instead of looking. But for now, Shivani is the first human being all over again.

After the book is finished, I give her my finger, and we walk together, kitchen, dining room, hallway, back to the family room. It is nice to have her to myself for a while. The circuit of the house becomes a scenic trail where I look up at things from her vantage. I stop her by a photo collage on the wall and lift her. Early pictures, more recent ones. Mala is in at least seven of the ten. I ask Shivani, *Where's Mommy?* And she points, without hesitating, at the black-and-white photograph of my wedding ceremony, at me in my nose ring and thin gold side chain, little mehndi dots above my eyebrows, my girl face small behind the garlands.

Was there really just a year between that picture and New York City?

Abhi had just started hating his Internal Medicine residency (he would switch to Neurology that July) when I came over from India, six months pregnant with Ronak. We were still strangers then. The training programs had no work-hours restrictions. Mala, two decades later, would just miss the law limiting the workweek to eighty hours. As a new attending physician, she would see her own residents, including the senior ones just a year below her, get each other out before noon, postcall. Mercy, she realized in outrage, had been possible all along. Abhi, in those days, would go forty-eight hours straight sometimes—fourth floor, down to the Emergency department, sixth floor, fourth floor again, Emergency department again, the pages clustering, beeps interrupting one another, the operator's cigarette-coarse voice mispronouncing his name on the overhead speakers. At each stop, he would lay two fingers in a limp palm and ask the patient to squeeze, or float his pen side to side across a fixed stare. Click, penlight in the left eye, penlight in the right eye, click. Then off to scribble a note, the phone crooked in his ear, ordering insulin in response to bed 327a's blood sugar.

In our apartment, alone, I sang to Ronak. I kept my hands on the dome of us to complete a circuit. I imagined the water inside me shivering with my voice. I thought religious songs would make him a good child, even though I was never very religious. From medical school (still fresh then), I knew when the ears canalized. I imagined the intermediaries. Protozoan, fish, salamander: A half-dozen halflings passed through like past lives until the gills sealed and the vertebrae notched. An outsize skull trailed a torso like the radicle of a sprouted chickpea. At last the eyes glazed with eyelids. At last the fingers lost their webs. Two cells had frothed into a boy. Embry-

ology was probably the closest I have come to feeling a religious
tremor. The problem is, you can't sing it. So I sang the old
bhajans in the old language. I thought such songs would make
him a good boy and a good man. Pious, even. Sound doesn't
travel well through water.

Months later, my bare still-swollen foot rocking Ronak's
cradle, I was studying for the exam that foreign medical grad-
uates had to take. I should have waited a year. But he didn't
sleep the night through until he was three anyway. I would
cup him to my breast, left thigh bobbing him, while on the
other thigh I laid a textbook. He would fight it. He would
crush his eyes and turn away in anguish, then, without warning, open his mouth and grope with his whole face in my
direction. I swear he sensed my distraction and would not
tolerate it. His mouth accepted me only when I curled over
him and whispered. Rise a few degrees, turn to the book, and
he broke the seal and wailed.

I went to the exam the first time with spit-up stains on my
shoulder and no pencils. I kept thinking of the Latino woman
who was babysitting him for those hours: she ran a day care in
her living room, the television always on, six contagious older
boys with cheese puff fingertips and Kool-Aid lips, all six
infected with the same rhinovirus and using their sleeves.
They were all delighted to see the baby. I was late. I had to go.
She wished me luck and settled Ronak against her giant
bosom and sat down in front of the television as the older
boys gathered.

Ronak's cold over the next two weeks prevented me from
dwelling very long on the examination results. The cold got
better, briefly, then worsened again, became a pneumonia,
and got him admitted to the hospital for intravenous antibiot-
ics. I received the letter late on a Tuesday night. Abhi, done
with his shift, came to the Pediatric floor, set his white coat

on the rocking chair, and sent me home to shower and cook (we lived in walking distance from the hospital). How distracted I must have been! I forgot to check the mail until, done cooking and packing dinner for me and Abhi, I passed the boxes. I set down the brown grocery bag full of containers and unlocked ours. The box was stuffed with several days' junk mail, a tattered blue aerogram from India, and the envelope.

We dined beside Ronak's hospital crib. The IV dripped noiselessly in the monitor's green glow. I did not know which catastrophe to focus on, Ronak's pneumonia or my envelope. I sent my thoughts to one as refuge from the other. I felt guilty for feeling shame more keenly than worry.

I could not tell Abhi. I had never failed anything before. How did people phrase such news? How, after saying it out loud, did they bear being gazed upon?

I was to stay the night in Ronak's room. Abhi was covering the adult intensive care unit, which meant a 4:30 AM wake-up. As he gathered his white coat, I rushed to embrace him and slipped the envelope into his already cluttered pocket. He was very sensitive to changes in me, even though we did not know each other very well yet. He put a finger under my chin, lifted my face, examined my eyes. Would he figure it out? Would he tell, from my face, that I was not really the smart person he thought I was?

"Ronak is going to recover," he said. "He's a strong boy."

I nodded and began to cry. I was never sure what I was crying about: The results? Ronak's illness being a direct result of my leaving him to take the exam and pursue my ambition? Or the realization I was thinking about the trivial thing while Abhi gave me credit for thinking about the life-and-death one?

I cried a long time. It held him up. I remembered his shift

the next morning and forced myself to stop. Then, as he was getting up to go a second time, I thought to myself: *What if he finds it at some inopportune time? What if he is in an elevator with his superiors, and the envelope drops as he pulls out his notes on the next patient? What if someone sees the score and thinks it's his?* I stuck my hand in his pocket to take the envelope back. I was clumsy. He looked down in surprise and brought out the envelope. I fell back into my chair. He opened the letter. I could not look up. Ronak awoke and began to cry. I hurried to his crib and rubbed his head and shushed him. Abhi pressed himself to my side and kissed the top of my head. A chain of consolation. He stayed up talking me through things until well past midnight. By then it made sense to stay. We crowded onto the one couch. He smelled of my food, and under that of coffee, evaporated cologne, stale stress. Forced flush, we breathed each other in, and finally we kissed, my mouth for the first time opening to his tongue.

The full shock and shame waited until Ronak's recovery. Abhi would come home and could tell from my eyes that I had been crying. He insisted he wouldn't have been able to do it either if he had had to care for a newborn. He sat for the exam, he said, after two straight months of loneliness, the apartment empty and the country strange. What had he done but study?

I was not so charitable. I blamed myself, not motherhood. Hadn't I always suspected it? In medical school it had been that way—the boys playing cricket, laughing aloud in groups of two or three even on exam mornings—me and my friends the studious, nervous girls, whose notes were far neater and color-coded, but whose scores were never quite as high. It felt like a law of nature back then, in India. As girls, we were doing something against the order of things; naturally we did it with more effort, less well.

Yet Ronak, who inherited all Abhi's intelligence, had been third in his high school class. Both the valedictorian and salutatorian had been girls. I wondered at the conviction we girl students had back then—the conviction that we were lucky to pass. Was it the perception of us that had changed our self-perception? Were my male classmates ever "naturally" smarter? Or had their superiority, like any myth, become true by being universally believed—and shaped our scores accordingly?

I took the exam again the next year. The first time, I fell just below the cutoff. The second time I wasn't even close. I'd had the whole year to go over the material. But the information had a strangely old feel. Not old as in familiar, but old like Scotch Tape that had lost its stickiness. I pressed my mind to those pages but nothing clung. Ronak was no easier to care for, either—twenty-two days before the exam date, he decided to start crawling. But the real factor was lack of confidence. I went in knowing I would do worse than before. My memory's hands were shaking. They dropped everything.

For long afterward, Abhi used to encourage me back into medicine. Ronak was older now. I would have time. Things would turn out better. The old information would come back; the new information he would help me with. I put it off. Mala was born. I couldn't possibly take the exam then—the conditions were even less favorable. More time passed. I wouldn't just be retaking the exam. I would have to do whole years of residency with two children at home, hurry floor to floor with note cards in my pocket—hemoglobin and hematocrit, chest x-ray in AM, grand rounds, afternoons at clinic—impossible, I told myself. Impossible.

I start the preparations for lunch. Mala looks up from her reading. "Mom? Can you wait maybe five minutes? Just while I finish this article?"

"Take your time. I'll set a few things on the stove."

"I want to help. Just wait five minutes before you start."

"It's okay." I keep moving. "There's nothing to do. Finish what you're doing."

She sighs, closes her magazine, and joins me in the kitchen. "You can read."

"It's all right. What do you need me to do?"

"Go. Go, finish."

"Should I set the table?"

This is something clean and quick that she could do. "Sure," I say, "if you want. Two bigger bowls, one smaller one for the raita."

Her face doesn't change. She looks glum. She slides out two stacks of bowls and uses the stacks to knock the cupboard shut. I watch her, apprehensive, as she goes into the next room with them. Annoyance surges in me, and I think, *If she wants to get angry over something as small as this, let her.* I roll some potential words on my tongue, waiting, just waiting to say them to her if she acts sulky. She isn't a teenager anymore, why is she acting like one? Did I tell her to stop reading her little article? My annoyance, oddly enough, makes me feel healthy and normal for a moment. The moment lasts just as long as it takes me to lift the heavy pot of dahi from the refrigerator and set it on the counter. I become an observer again, I grow detached from my own emotion and think, *Coming up with biting things to say to your daughter, are you? And you have how many months?* Sadness comes through, and shame. I cannot taste my dahi when I sample some. I focus, try another spoonful, and stay focused to check for any after-shock of sour.

I make my own dahi because I love the continuity. Each pot curdles thanks to a spoonful of the one before it. With every batch, I set some aside. Every generation tastes differ-ent, of course, depending on how warm the milk is, and how long it sits on the counter before I take it to the refrigerator. But the cultures—the *bacteria*, Abhi likes to say, teasing me because he knows how seriously I take this dynastic succession—the cultures stay the same, like genetics. Probably Mala and Ronak don't recognize it when they come home, not on their tongues, at least. But their bodies sense the past. Their bodies know.

I was very careful about saving that crucial dollop. Origi-nally I smuggled some from India in a sterile stoppered test tube. Customs never searched that zippered pocket in my purse. Abhi, on our first evening together in our first New York City apartment, picked up the emptied test tube and glanced at the standing pot of milk, incredulous. Finally he laughed. "Now this," he murmured, "is preserving Indian culture!"

Its lineage was magical. The consistency might vary, but the flavor never—pot after pot thickened identically in taste. Magic: I might have expected as much, as it came from my mother's kitchen. Guests used to praise my dahi specifically. They were tasting Gujarat. Wherever we moved, I had at least one friend who asked for some in a stainless steel bowl. So the lineage branched.

There were breaks, inevitably, as with trips to India. Sometimes I could get away with simple refrigeration. During my long visits to take care of my mother, I left some at my friend Sujata's house, then came home and took a little back. Sujata understood the crucial nature of such living artifacts from home. During her and Arvind's two-week Europe trip, I cared for a tulsi plant descended from the one in her father's courtyard.

Later, I made sure to colonize my grandchildren with the magical cultures. For those first bottle-and-burp-cloth months after each birth, I always brought some dahi in a red Igloo cooler when we visited, along with other still-warm Tupperware containers. I make sure there is dahi at every one of their stays, too, including this one, even though the grandchildren have grown used to the smooth, store-bought kind, scalloped neatly with a spoon, no murky whitish water at the bottom. Mala and Ronak are used to that kind of yogurt, too, but I offer my homemade anyway, lumps and all—to their tongues as to their bodies, familiar.

Mala and Sachin don't eat in shifts the way they did when the grandchildren were babies. So one heating suffices for all. I ladle straight from the CorningWare. No need to stagger the eaters and microwave the meal plateful by plateful. That always feels so makeshift, so paradoxically impersonal. Sachin carries Shivani's high chair into the dining room. I notice, with a mixture of pride and embarrassment, how my lunch has crowded the table. It has grown by accretion and without my awareness. Karahi potatoes. A dahl in which I substituted New World zucchini for Old World bottle gourd. My dynastic dahi and its close cousin, the raita. More cooling: cucumbers and tomatoes, diced, salted, dusted with cumin. Heat, too: a small bowl of ginger shreds in salt and lemon juice. Kerala peppercorns pickled on the twig. Eggplant bhartha intricately beaded with seeds. Shredded carrots that have leached a crucible-sizzle of asafetida. I wonder if this proliferation looks desperate. In a way my secret lies in the open there, giving off steam and fragrance. But they are used to the table having little room left for plates. I fill the glass pitcher, and the ice cubes skate on the splash, knocking and bobbing in a circle. I call everyone to the meal.

Mala takes quarter ladles and half scoops of everything. I know not to pressure her, though even after all these years it is a reflex.

"I'll take seconds if I need them, Mom, don't worry," she says, preempting me.

"I won't be taking seconds, Mom," declares Sachin. "I'm taking firsts and seconds, at the same time!"

He is looking at Abhi, his eyebrows high and his mouth open. Abhi and I laugh. Ronak and Mala only smile.

"Okay, we've got the cheesy mac, but you need to work with me on *one* thing. What do you want, V?" asks Mala, holding his plate.

Vivek scans the table. "Um . . ."

"Do you want to try a little of everything, Vivek?" I ask. "Take little bites, and try?"

"Um . . . I want . . ."

"Come on, V. You want some bhindi? You like bhindi."

She raises a few okra in the scoop and tilts the scoop by the plate, waiting for the go-ahead.

"No. Wait. Let me see."

"You can try a little of everything, Vivek."

"There's too many choices for him, Mom."

"Just give him a little of everything."

"I'm going to give him what he wants to eat—V, I'm waiting."

"Hold on. I want . . . um . . ."

"Listen, V," interjects Ronak, "you've got to get your bhindi, or you're never going to get strong like your daddy."

Sachin flexes his free arm, his left hand offering a spoonful of dahl to Shivani while his own food grows cold. "Try the bhindi, V," he says.

"Okay."

Mala spoons a small pile onto his plate and sets it before him.

"No dahl?" I ask. "Not even the cucumbers?"

"You want the cucumbers, V?"

"No."

"No thank you. Remember?"

"No thank you."

Vivek picks up a single okra nib and puts it in his mouth. I check Abhi's plate and give him a second rotli from midstack, where they would be moist and lukewarm from their neighbors. Ronak has overlooked the raita and the shredded carrots, so I supply both. He uses the back of his spoon to shove aside the fenugreek-flecked potato slips and make room for the touch of orange on his plate. "Thanks," he says quietly. I am surprised at how amenable he is; he must really be hungry.

My eyes go back to the near blank of Vivek's plate, and I cannot help myself. I scoop some more shredded carrots— such a simple dish, not too spicy, not too strange a taste—and stretch to bring them near his plate.

"Your plate is empty, Vivek beta," I say. "Do you want to try some of this?"

"Here we go," murmurs Abhi at my elbow, then pushes a bite into his mouth.

Mala speaks before Vivek can say yes. "Look at *your* plate, Mom. You're hardly eating anything."

Ronak looks at my plate. He never noticed my plate before. "Jeez, Mala, you're right. Are you on some crash diet, Mom?"

I set the carrots back in the dish, let go of the spoon, and glance at Abhi.

"Your mom and I are watching what we eat. We're not as young as we used to be."

"You've been losing weight," says Mala. "That's not a bad thing, if you do it healthily." Ronak eyes Mala: the cups of shadow behind her collarbones, the eyes dark even without kohl. Mala is oblivious to his scrutiny. "Mom?"

"It's not a crash diet," I say.

We are lying now; Abhi hadn't wanted to lie. This is exactly the kind of exchange he had wanted to avoid.

"What diet is it?" she presses.

"What diet?"

"Like, Atkins, South Beach, Weight Watchers, what?"

"I'm just eating smaller portions."

"Are you getting enough protein?"

"Of course she is getting enough protein," Abhi says irritably. "We are all doctors here, Mala."

"How is she getting her protein?"

"Not me," says Ronak. "I'm not a doctor."

"I'm not a doctor either," says Vivek, looking at Ronak in sympathy. Sachin is tearing a rotli into pieces for Shivani. Vivek pops some cheesy mac in his mouth. "I'm a boy."

Ronak grins.

Mala insists, "Really. Look at her plate. Other than that spoonful of dahi, what source is there?"

"Dairy. Lentils. Spinach. All sorts of things."

Ronak shakes his head. "Mala, lay off about the food, all right? Not everyone's obsessed about this stuff."

"Indian food is full of protein," I assert.

"Naani, if you don't eat protein, you can't get muscles," explains Vivek.

"Vivek," says Sachin. "Eat."

Mala is glaring at Ronak. "I am not obsessed."

"All right. You're not."

"I'm not."

"There was a Christmas carol I heard last week," I say abruptly. "I need to know what it's called. I really liked it."

"Don't try and change the subject, Mom."

"No, Mala. Listen. I asked Abhi, he didn't know."

"I can't tell these carols apart," says Abhi, working with me. "I know 'Silent Night,' that's it."

"There were children singing."

Silence. Mala, in a sulk, rolls her okra with her fork. "You're changing the subject. It's transparent."

Ronak says, "That carol could be anything, Mom. A lot of them have children singing. How does it go?"

"I can't sing it. There was a piano in it, too."

Ronak takes out his phone and begins touching the screen with his free hand's ring finger. "I have this app. Just sing a few bars of it."

I don't like him taking his phone out at the table, but it helps divert everyone's attention from my plate, and mine from my own nausea. (Which is still mild, no worse than going down in an elevator forever.) Sachin looks interested, too. Ronak holds the screen so it faces me.

"Go ahead."

"I can't sing."

"Hum it then."

"Are you recording me?"

"No. This app ID's the song from a few bars."

"Bars?"

"Leetis," explains Abhi. "Lines of the song. Try it."

I shake my head, flushed. Of all the things I could have interrupted their escalation with, why did I choose this? Feeling ridiculous, I lean close to the intelligent little device, and I hum the five notes I remember. The whole table is listening. It doesn't sound right to my ears. The machine doesn't like it, either. Ronak checks the screen, frowns, and taps something. "Let's try it again."

"She's talking," says Mala, "about the Charlie Brown song."

Ronak raises his eyebrows. "Let me look it up." He taps and brushes the screen again.

Mala glances at me. "He'll play it in a second."

"I knew you would know."

Under Ronak's fingers, the screen grows suddenly bright, and the carol begins to play. He lifts the phone to take the speaker off the table, and the sound comes out very crisply. I smile. With family around and food on the table, the song doesn't sadden me as much as it had when I heard it in the supermarket the week before. I liked its festive sadness. Now the song floats in our dining room, too mysterious and lovely to play during a chatty lunch, deserving noiseless snowfall and deep night. "That's the one," I say. "You can turn it off."

Ronak taps something, and the carol stops. "Here you go, Mom." He taps again and smiles. "I just bought the song. I'll have Dad put it on your iPod. Merry Christmas."

"Thank you, Mala." I thanked the wrong person. I see, from the corner of my eye, Ronak glance up. I turn immediately to him. "And Ronak. Both of you."

Ronak asks Mala, "How'd you figure it out so quick?"

"Piano, children." She shrugs. "It's my favorite carol, too. Ever since I was a kid."

Ronak nods and looks down at his screen. "Check that out. Mom likes the Charlie Brown Christmas song," he says softly, shaking his head. I do not know why this strikes him as hard to believe. I am in the world, I have ears. I can be charmed by music other than the old Lata songs I listen to while I cook.

As I watch, he grows increasingly distracted by his e-mail. Soon we are talking of other things. A short struggle with Vivek keeps Mala from bringing up again how little I am eating. The struggle ends with me microwaving him a soy dog until it blisters, and Mala stabbing the straw in a Capri Sun.

We have put up a Christmas tree. Mala instituted the tradition the year Vivek turned two. She had watched clips of her nephews on Christmas morning. Ronak's Sony handheld captured it from the top of the stairs: Dev sprinting downstairs, shrieking with joy; Nikhil, not yet three then, wary of stairs, scooting, taking them one by one, shouting, *Wait up!* (Raj, Ronak's third, had not been born yet.) Amber held up a hand—that was all it took—and the older brother stopped with a Simon-says-stop abruptness to wait for the younger. Then, antsy at the new starting line, the boys ran to their presents, stacked two deep under a ceiling-high Christmas tree.

I could imagine Ronak standing apart, recording it all. The open viewfinder served as a convenient wall. Being the cameraman allowed him the remove that some part of him wished to preserve. It was a curious reluctance that had shown up even in his church ceremony. He had no particular affection for Hindu ways or Hindu rituals. In fact, he liked to mock such things. But try to impose anything else, and he grew possessive, proud. There was a wafer he was supposed to eat at the end of his church ceremony, some Christian prasaad that he scandalously refused to accept in his mouth. After the wedding rehearsal, he had called me and Abhi to forbid us from doing so, too, though we were perfectly willing. ("What do

you mean, why not? 'Cause it's not our religion, Mom.") Even
at the reception, Amber had to wear Indian clothes, our clothes,
though she would never have imagined her wedding this way.
The Sinatra song was the one she picked out for her father-
daughter dance, but she danced to it wearing a *sarara*.

Watching Ronak's Christmas morning videos, Abhi and I,
too, had grown jealous. Mere love could not compete with
such dramatic gift-giving. Birthday counterstrikes did not suf-
fice. The buildup wasn't the same. Only one child got presents
on a birthday, and he never tore the wrapping paper with quite
as much frenzy. The birthday grandson embraced us gratefully
afterward, upon instruction, while the other two looked on.
Not the same! We had seen their Christmas morning gratitude.
We had seen them throw their arms around Dottie and Don.
Sometimes our birthday presents were opened along with others from the party—midsequence, indistinguishable, often
outclassed. (Ronak, because of his work, had very rich friends.)
Does a child even remember the giver when he plays with a
gift? The warmth and gratitude spike for an instant, but you
must have him in your lap as he opens it. Lately I have been
buying gifts for all the boys, and the day before the birthday
party, I make a game of it and have them hunt for clues.

The boys should be spoiled, but Amber is raising them, as
she says, "with values." Ronak has never, in my memory, actually reprimanded the boys. Sometimes he claps his hands
twice, which the boys obey because their mother has trained
them to do so. Ronak is relaxed to the point of indifference.
And why should he worry? Amber isn't working (she had
done some secretarial work before the children, to pass time),
Amber handles all that, Amber takes care of discipline . . . and
meals, and potty training, and the sippy cups and Fruit Roll-
Ups during road trips, and the shoes with little lights in the
soles. Each day each boy gets to request one toy from the base-

ment. One toy comes out for the morning. This toy is returned after lunch. A second toy is then brought upstairs, to be played with until bedtime, which is always at the same time.

We have never felt wholly at home in that gated, hilly scatter of four-car-garage houses. Ronak commutes over an hour each day, each way. You couldn't peek through the door-length strip of window beside the door and glimpse a Ganesha or a Krishna-Lila painting that says yes, you are at the right house. The house never has the smell of an Indian house, either. I mean the turmeric and canola oil that leaches into the carpet, the couches, the guests' winter coats piled on the guest room bed; the smell that breathes out from the coat when you sit in your car, overpowering the outdoor cold. I need that smell, I guess, to feel completely at home. What Ronak's house has is shrink-wrapped ground chuck in the refrigerator. Crimson beads, strangely jellied. And cold cuts folded limp inside a plastic deli Ziploc, stickered with weight and price. A pale fluid, wept by the ham itself, pools along the crease and leaves the plastic murky. I always see a dark dispenser-box of beer cans—on the bottom shelf, no less, in Dev's reach. Only a few years from now, he will have his first taste, given a sip by Ronak himself, or maybe Amber's father, Don—during one of their backyard cookouts, hot dogs and patties striped black and flipped, Ruffles on a Styrofoam plate, ball game on the plasma screen indoors, here, Dev, here, *Dave*, here you go. The sound of beer pouring and foaming in a red plastic cup. An American rite of passage. Manhood is the first beer can, not a thread across the chest for this grandson of Gujarati Brahmins.

Ronak didn't convert for her. Maybe Amber knew he didn't really have anything to convert from; the children would be

hers by forfeit. But he did stop brushing his teeth before
breakfast, the way he had done his entire life, and switched to
after-breakfast brushing. Amber taught the children the same
habit, which I found much more disgusting than cold cuts. At
least he didn't give up scraping his tongue. His was the only
one by the master bedroom sink, though, a stainless steel
arch with little loops at the ends of the handle. I brought him a
rubber-banded half-dozen once when I came back from India.
I asked him, in a whisper, what Amber did. Apparently she
"brushed her tongue." I tried doing that the very next morning, just to see, and my tongue wasn't nearly as clean.

Why Amber chose him, I can understand. If he had been
a doctor, she would have been one of the pretty nurses who
paged him on the pretext of a blood sugar, then coaxed the
call into a conversation, a flirtation, a date . . . The analogy
doesn't entirely fit, though. Ronak had found Amber in high
school. So early! How young he seemed then—his boyish face
nicked after its second shave. Did that face kiss her, open-
mouthed? I shudder to picture it. Had one of them been an
adult, it would have been called corrupting a minor. But
because both were so young, it's puppy love and they are high
school sweethearts. Their minds had an adult part and a child
part. The adult corrupts, and the child is corrupted. It is twice
as horrible.

Put tomatoes in a plastic bag, and they do the same thing:
side by side, soaking in each other's scent, the green ones red-
den, the red ones ripen, the ripe ones rot. That's what happens to boys and girls in high school. They grow each other
up before it's time. *Young* doesn't mean what it meant when I
was young. The parents encourage it, sending their daughters
in low-cut homecoming dresses. The schools themselves
arrange and host such dances; the young don't need secrecy.
And the red flower on the front of the dress, that American

tradition, the corsage, pinned where it will draw attention to the girl's breasts, the literal flowering to mark the figurative. A child's breasts. They are still more girl than woman at that age, no matter how they dress or speak or, in their Victoria's Secret push-up bras, look.

But was it really any better in India, even in the past? Hasn't it all been going on forever? My friends and I were just sheltered more successfully. The poorer classes, the slum boys and slum girls—they didn't have exams like we did, their bodies were all they owned and their only source of pleasure. What about Navratri, the nine nights of dancing, ostensibly for the goddess? Garba let men and women dance in a circle, the still point of their orbit a full-color picture of Durga on her tiger. Raas dandia allowed vicarious contact, sticks on sticks, rhythmic, four taps and you moved on. There was never any one-on-one dancing, not even between husband and wife. But the statistics were eloquent. The number of abortions in Gujarat spikes yearly after those nine days. The raas boys in glittery red bandannas doing the showiest leaps, making the most of their brief opportunity across from us—they wanted our attention, our admiration, our lust. They were doing a mating display, like any peacock or gaudily crested tropical bird. Durga had nothing to do with it.

What was that phrase Ronak used, when he first brought Amber over? *On and off.* I had heard enough about *on and off* to know both might have had other lovers in the off times. I would never know. These were not things he would tell his mother. I had always hoped Ronak's innate shrewdness, his selfishness, might guide him to an Indian girl. There was no shortage. I saw them at every local get-together, always someone else's daughter-in-law. Or else out shopping, ponytailed, sunglasses hooked in the blouse, chic backpack with an Enfamil bottle in the side pocket, pushing her toddler in the shopping cart. Fresh out of their residencies, new mothers, working part-time . . . there were hundreds of such Indian girls, in Chicago, in the Bay Area, all of Ronak's generation. They liked the same movies and the same bands, but he hadn't wanted one. Since his early twenties he would dismiss the Indian girls I pointed out. He called them "future aunties." In Amber, he found the perfect compromise. She was the good girl who would raise his children and devote herself to him—and the white woman, thrillingly foreign, parentally forbidden. His choice had its own logic. I felt I should have predicted it: how he alone would manage to have it both ways at once.

Sachin puts the children to sleep. He has an easier time of it than Mala. From Mala, Vivek demands songs and stories; Shivani plays with her mother's hair. Sachin simply lies there, a child in the crook of either arm, and waits. Most of the time he goes to sleep alongside them, as he does tonight.

So Mala kneels and unzips the red wheeled suitcase, which is full of wrapped presents, while I go to our stash in the walk-in closet. I stacked our presents against the wall. They are hidden by Abhi's Arrow shirts. On the shelves above them, I store my sarees in crinkly Asopalav bags. They remind me of the photographs in which I wore them rather than the occasions themselves. Old-fashioned albums, sticky background with a plastic oversheet, small envelope containing negatives stored in the back. Each negative the bookmark in a finished book. Mala used to hold them to the light, squint at our dark teeth and luminous hair, and declare, "Ghosts! Everyone's ghosts!"

I touch my old sarees and marvel at this country where silk can lie folded so many years and no moths find it. So

clean, this part of the world. Sterile, almost. Uncrowded by
people, uncrowded by bugs.

The saris stay in my mind as Mala and I place the gifts
around the tree. Ronak has already stacked his in a tower and
gone back upstairs. We mix our boxes with his, making something arbitrary but aesthetic with the different box sizes and
the three kinds of wrapping paper. Ronak and Mala have gotten Abhi and me two things each, even though they know we
do the tree and gifts for the children. Ronak wanders downstairs again as Mala is putting candy canes in the stockings,
which she has hung beneath the peacock-filigreed show plate
on our mantelpiece. He has gift cards. He slides them casu-
ally out of his wallet.

"You still get stuff for Shivani from Babies 'R' Us, right?
Or is she too big for that place?"

Mala cocks an eyebrow. "You're really asking me? You've
got three of your own, don't you?"

"Amber handles that kind of stuff. Kid shopping."

"You didn't ask Amber?"

"Is this going to be any use to you or no?"

"Of course. Nipples and onesies." Ronak shows no comprehension of what even I understand to be sarcasm. His
hand is still in midair. Mala grins. "Amber's a saint the way
she treats you. What'd you get her for Christmas?"

Ronak drops the card in the stocking. "Massage treatment.
One of those spa things. She likes that."

"Any guesses what Sachin got me this year?"

Ronak glances at me. He knows Mala's cuts at Sachin pain
me. The first year, Sachin had gotten her nothing—like Abhi
and me in our first years here, Sachin assumed Christmas,
like Halloween, was for children. Abhi had advised him to get
Mala "something special," and the next Christmas, Sachin
had purchased some earrings. He called Abhi over to record

him as he handed her the gift. The smallness of the box might have made the gift seem bigger, had not the Kohl's bag (receipt still inside) sitting on the couch armrest. We have coached him since. He has gotten better.

Ronak now senses a cut coming, just as I do. "Ooh," he says to Mala, as if he has just noticed her baby candy canes. "Can I have one of those?" She offers him one, and he plucks it playfully from her fingers and taps it on her forehead, successfully diverting her attention. "Thanks!" he says, and makes an escape upstairs.

I watch as Mala rearranges the gifts one more time, steps back, then unhooks a silver ball and a reindeer and switches their places on the tree. "Let's see it with the lights on." She plugs in the lights Abhi has strung on the tree. They begin to blink. She thumbs a small device along the cord, and the fifty nipples of white light hold steady. She assesses the tree, and I know what she is thinking: *When they come down the stairs, this is how it's going to look.* She stands on the couch to tilt the star atop the tree so it will face the approach.

She is stepping down onto the carpet when she loses her footing. Suddenly her body fills my arms. Her hard shoulder blades dig against my chest. I have not held her whole in a very long time. She is out of my arms immediately. "Sorry about that. Good thing you were there."

My breath is coming quick and shallow. "You have room in the bag now, right?"

She is distracted. She tugs her shirt to make it hang correctly. "Hm?"

"In your red bag?"

"Yeah. It's empty."

"Let me give you some things."

"What?"

"Come on. I want to give you some things."

I take her hand in mine as she steps down. I lead her upstairs to the walk-in closet, hurrying, her hand in mine the whole time. I begin drawing my old sarees from their stacks and laying them at her feet, like Ahmedabadi saree merchants reaching to their shelves and flinging silk after silk before mothers and daughters, everything brought out. Nothing has faded. Does she remember these? The creases stay, but the colors spill, spectacular and Indian, on the carpet's beige. She will never have occasion to wear them. She senses the panic in my giving. I cannot conceal my panic, alone with her there in the closet. Abhi's shirts are still clustered at one end of the shelf, and I see empty space where the presents had been. I get down my punjabis and old garba cholis with bits of mirror sewn in, and they are all unreally vivid under the bulb. My hands shake as I give her dress after dress, telling her she can send the blouses to India to have them sized, telling her they are all hers now. "Mom, stop," Mala says. "Tell me what's going on. Please."

Part of me knows the children will rush down the stairs just ten hours from now. We will beam at them and crouch to see their faces light up from below with each fulfilled desire. This is the wrong time. I should wait. I cannot wait. I give her everything, and after I have given her everything, I tell her everything. If I had set the sarees down in neat piles, I might have stayed silent or made up a story. With the sarees disordered, I cannot hold back. Ronak hears Mala's small frightened shout. He peeks through the door of the closet and shakes his head at us embracing. "More drama? Every time. Jeez, what is it with you two?" He assumes we've had the usual quarrel followed by the usual crying. He is about to turn and leave us to ourselves, but he senses in our faces and in the wild turbulence of silks, a rupture beyond reconciliation. His eyes fix on me alone. His hand goes out tentatively as if to touch my face, then retreats. "Everything okay?" Mala buries her face in my neck. Ronak kneels. One knee, then both. "Mom?"

PART TWO

FAMINE

Rameshbhai Kothari, a distant acquaintance, no one close, died in the scent of fresh cut grass, unhooking the bag from the mower. Today is his katha at the temple, the recitation of Hanuman's story from the *Ramayana*. It has come up on the same day as a wedding reception. *Brandon Weds Neelam*—I still have the invitation in a drawer with its filigree Ganesha. I checked yes to the reception centuries ago.

"Both will be too much," says Abhi. "All that traveling. The temple is forty-five minutes, the Hilton is downtown."

"I feel good. And the last scan was good. Mala showed it to her radiologist friend."

"The scan means nothing. It's how you feel. We need to pick one."

I decide on the katha—it won't last as long, and there will be less socializing to tire me.

The car ride north takes us on the highway. I see a small pile of gray fur serried with darker gray. It's on the white line, a few bits of the body marking its trajectory. Abhi steers the car around it, and I do what I always do when I pass roadkill, a quick jab of the ring finger toward the spot where it lay, then to my chest, an under-the-breath *Rama Rama*. I do this even when we don't happen to be driving to the local temple. I never think about the soul, only of the black beady eyes and the sound of its paws—a padding then a clicking, curious. No grass. The sense of having arrived in a clearing. And then the instantaneous shattering of every bone.

The temple is a low brick building that might have been a school. Lexuses and Camrys and Honda Accords fill its lot almost to capacity. We are late, but we are not the only ones. A man in shirt and tie is followed by two young children in jeans and sweatshirts; the mother, paused by the car as it blinks its lights and beeps, looks over her shoulder to check the cascade of her saree, then does two quick shuffles to catch up.

Inside, leather shoes and worn Nikes and beaded women's chappals crowd the entryway. Hanuman has already jumped. He is in midair, en route to Lanka. This is the *Sundarakanda*, the part of the *Ramayana* that tells of Hanuman's journey over the sea to find Sita, his capture, and how he broke loose after the Lankans set his tail on fire. The Kotharis invited some musicians from Detroit. I saw two Toyota minivans outside, the ones with the Michigan *Proud to Be American* license plates, SNGEET1 and TAALAM. The father sings, the two docile white-kameezed sons play tabla and harmonium. I imagine them unloading their instruments, the speakers and mics and cords, the empty SunChips bags and Hardee's straws and cups from the long drive. They wear saffron turbans pleated and fanned at the front.

By convention, this part of Hanuman's story is sung for the dead. All those images of breaking free, first from gravity, then from chains. Unless this part is really sung to cheer the mourners with monkey mischief. Every other part of the *Ramayana* is sad: Rama's exile, Sita's kidnapping, the war against Ravana, the gossip in Ayodhya after they get back, Sita's banishment. Even the reunions are ruinous. Rama reproaches Sita when they meet in Lanka. Years later, when their twins are grown boys and the parents meet again in Ayodhya, Sita wills a chasm in the earth to open and throws herself into it. No, only Hanuman's part would do to send off the dead—a divine monkey jumping off a cliff and soaring.

We have slipped off our shoes. I push them closer together with my bare foot, his and mine, so they huddle like rabbits. A few young children run past us. The men and women are segregated, men left, women right. I will have to sit apart from Abhi. He is waiting, surveying the seated people, some swaying back and forth. The elderly grandmothers roost on folding metal chairs along the periphery. He doesn't want to be apart from me, either. I touch Abhi's elbow.

"Everything all right?" he whispers.

I am about to tell him, *These musicians are good, find out how much they charge.* I change my mind. I nod, and we settle on either side of the aisle, far to the back. He sits lotus style and checks his watch. I start looking at people's faces, the backs of their heads, their clothes. The men's bald spots vary in size and glisten. The women in front of me have thick braids. I touch my own diminished knot. My hair was always thin and quick to shed, even before. I got that from my mother. I use the comb gingerly now. How hard I always tugged when it caught! Now I extricate the teeth patiently, listening, in the misty bathroom, as my brittle strands break. I fear each day that I will draw the comb through and come away with a whole tuft.

Some women wear punjabis, others, sarees. The one directly in front of me wears a saree. Her blouse is taut, beneath it, her flanks crease from their own weight. Her lower back, bare, shows the faintest black down. The fine hairs mark the course water would take down the skin. The Indian word for *overweight* is *healthy*. It's still a compliment there, or was, when we last visited. (Things keep changing; it was only after India became American that I started feeling foreign to it.) I am not healthy. I am afraid to go. The relatives would notice and comment right away. There's no etiquette there in this regard. My saree blouse would be off my shoulders were it not for six strategic safety pins. No matter. It's not feasible to go, not anymore. Abhi sets up a webchat sometimes. I see our relatives that way—sitting close, shoulders up, constantly glancing at myself in the box. We have nothing to talk about but distance and absence. Yes, we want to make a trip. Yes, it's been too long. Yes, yes, yes.

Abhi is focused on the singers. He is rocking back and forth. He is really following this. Isn't his mind wandering? Isn't everyone's? I look around. Everyone is focusing. I should focus. What is wrong with me that I'm not focusing? I don't know where Hanuman is, or even whether he has found Sita yet. I listen to the singsong a while, trying to pick up clues, trying to pick up recognizable words. This is not in Gujarati or even modern Hindi, which I can usually follow. It is Tulsidas's Hindi, hundreds of years old and rhyming, almost folksy, *kahu, kachu, naahi*. I am thinking about focusing, and this is keeping me from focusing. *You are in a temple. This is being sung for the dead. The gods are watching you right now. They know what you are thinking, and they know you aren't thinking about death*. Must I? I do all the rest of the time. It's only now, when I am supposed to, that I get some respite.

I wish, I do wish I had been pious all my life. Now it is too late. Would the gods even want me if I went to them out of fear? What if I admitted it was fear, would they respect my honesty and forgive me? The slinking, shamefaced motive, last-minute slokas and good-luck Ganeshas. They must be used to it.

I note the nooks for each of the murtis. As I do, I sense a

kind of cosmic shaking of the head. Does it matter that I don't have an aptitude for religion? That I have *always* noticed things and daydreamed most keenly when made to sit still during kathas, bhajans, holy talks? I glance at Abhi again, and he is staring ahead, rocking gently. My eye jumps to a little boy in a kameez: he looks bored, he drapes himself across his mother's lap for a moment, sits up and stares at the ceiling, pokes, pokes, pokes her arm. She is paying attention, too, and she bats gently at his hand. He dives forward onto her lap.

The singer up front has a tilak on his forehead. Button-down white shirt, slacks, black socks, and a shiny fat-dialed wristwatch that makes him periodically raise and wag his wrist—all this, topped with the holy saffron headpiece. Are his sons really interested in this performance? They don't seem to be enjoying themselves. One looks sullen, actually. Heels of his small hands on the tablas, fingers curled and twitching by reflex, a clockwork flat-palmed slap . . . It is their father who is visibly pleased, either with Hanuman's exploits or with himself. He likes being front and center, doesn't he? Like those friends of Abhi's who hold karaoke parties and rehearse their songs for days in advance, CDs of old Kishore Kumar songs, only the background music, done with keyboard and synthesizer. The vanity always comes in, even if the father says—as they all do, these holy artistes—that he's "offering the music to God." Does he make his sons play accompaniment? Or are the boys really pious, do they have something in their genes that makes them give up sleeping in on a Saturday morning? And if they have it, why don't I?

Look at the shameful things you're thinking. And in a temple. Focus. Focus.

Abhi finally breaks his concentration and turns to me. He smiles. I smile back, relieved. Now I imagine everyone's mind wandering, up in the air, a spool of kite string spinning freely from each head, the kites trailing streamers of memories, streamers of wishes.

People enter, leave, reenter during the course of the performance. It is like an Indian wedding ceremony: the gods being invoked up front, several rows of attentive watchers, and a restless periphery.

I think about the reception we are going to skip tonight. The wedding must be going on right now. As with Ronak's, first there is the church ceremony, then the Hindu one, then the reception. The hotel ballroom must be just about full— the white couples clustered in their suits and dresses, a cashmere throw for rare color; the Indian guests milling about and glittering in the soft lobby light, here a watermelon kameez with gold thread arabesques at the collar and chest, there a *sarara* sewn out of dusk. The little girls, decked out like Bollywood, chase one another with a clinking of bangles. Ronak's wedding had been the same. I remember looking out at the crowd during one of the pandit's longer Sanskrit rambles. Sparrows to one side, birds of paradise to the other.

If we stay until the katha is over, we will shake hands, hug, trade pleasantries and low murmurs about the deceased. There are too many people we know here. They will ask if I have been in India these past four months—no reply to the voice messages, and the phone never picked up. I will see even more friends and acquaintances at the reception. Maybe this can be practice. I want to eavesdrop more than anything. Conversations at home—with Abhi or with Mala and Ronak when they call or visit—have a self-conscious quality. The words deal with all the day's topics and happenings, Nikhil's first soccer practice, Shivani's new words, and so on, but the pauses are all about the same thing. Then Abhi looks at me, and his fingertips walk across the carpet. I nod, and he puts his weight on his hand and rises. I hear the crack of his knee. Our shoes at the door have shifted slightly, like feet in the working shallows of the sea.

"Best to get home in time," he says once we are outside, under a weak spring sun.

We have mastered little dishonesties. That way we don't have to admit our lives have changed, at least not when we don't want to do so. Indoors, during the day, we are frank and almost businesslike. *What do you need right now? Get me the Vicodin.* At night in bed, we are pathetic and tearful and stroke the outlines of each other's faces, temple to cheek to chin to abyss. Outside, though, we pretend, even to each other.

We have to pretend now. In the parking lot, on one foot as she shakes gravel from her sandal, is Naina Doshi. She and her husband, Kalpesh, are sneaking out early, too. She slips the sandal back on and hurries over unsteadily, arms up to embrace me.

"You look *fit!*" she squeals, aborting her embrace early to take a step, lean back dramatically, and look me over.

I put my hands on my hips and look down at myself. "I don't know. I've been doing what I can."

"Have you been living at the gym? What's your *secret*? And Abhishek bhai, look at you, so trim. Still swimming?"

"When I get the chance. You know, busy busy."

"Are you coming to Neelam's reception tonight? I am going to watch you both and make sure you eat. Dieting *khattam*. Over."

Her husband strolls up to us. "There's Einstein," he says, grinning at Abhi, hand out to shake. His accent is still detectable, as all of ours are, but he likes more than most to use phrases he's picked up from his children. He looks at his hand after he and Abhi have shaken. "I swear, my IQ just rose ten points."

Abhi clears his throat. "Tragic news about Ramesh bhai."

"Tragic, tragic," agrees Kalpesh. "He was so young, you know!"

"Just a few years older than us," Naina mourns. "What was he? Sixty-eight?"

"Sixty-six," I say.

"So young! We had to come pay our respects, even though we are terribly exhausted."

"We got in late last night."

"Costa Rica," explains Naina. "So amazing, the rain forests, you know."

"Naina went on that, what is it? With the cable?"

"A canopy tour, Kalpesh."

"Yes, canopy tour. Where you slide along the treetops. Very high."

"You have to do it. It's a must." She looks at my body again. "And especially now that you've got this swimsuit body."

I want to hide behind Abhi. She is still thinking about my weight. Is she jealous? I feel myself flush. Fortunately there is only a single awkward beat before Abhi speaks. "The wife did it, Kal, and not you?"

Kalpesh frowns. "With my luck? I would break my neck."

"He got sunburned the day before," says Naina. "We went snorkeling, you know, and he didn't use sunscreen properly."

"Like I said, with my luck. I had to sleep on my stomach."

"The whole room smelled of that aloe lotion. *Chee!* I had told him to wear a UV shirt. I even bought him one. Long sleeve. Still he goes in a T-shirt."

"I don't need that thing sticking to my belly. They're made of, of, what's that clingy, tightum-tight . . . ?"

Naina shakes her head. "It blocks ultraviolet light. It's a special cloth."

"What is it? You know, bicyclists wear those shorts? That Lance Armstrong? What is that cloth?"

"Spandex?" Abhi guesses.

"See? Einstein. This guy is Einstein. You win any big awards lately? I keep waiting to see your picture in the paper again."

"It's not spandex," says Naina, irritated. "It's a special cloth." She looks at me again. "Weren't you going to Alaska this spring? On that cruise?"

"We canceled it," I say.

"Oh? Why?"

"Problem with the schedule at work," says Abhi. "One of my partners had a family emergency. You know how it is."

"That's horrible." Kalpesh's face goes serious. "Did you get a refund? Was there enough notice?"

"Oh, yes."

"Full refund?"

"Yes."

"That's good. Let me tell you: Forget Alaska. There's enough snow right here in Ohio."

"Alaska is beautiful," Naina insists. "And it was a cruise. You know I love cruises."

"Was it a Desi cruise? Indian buffet, every day?"

"No, it was a regular one."

Kalpesh looks at me. "You two don't eat fish, do you?"

"No."

"Those cruises have a lot of fish in their buffets. I don't mind. But *her*."

"Chee," says Naina again. "Fish is smelly."

"Doesn't matter. I'm not going somewhere to see snow anyway. Never again. Plenty of snow to shovel right here."

"You don't shovel snow. You pay a man to come with his truck."

"That's why I slave all day. To have some guy shovel my snow, and to take *her* on vacations everywhere."

Naina looks past me. "Shanu!" she shouts. Another couple is leaving early. We do not know them. Naina sweeps past me on her high heels and embraces the woman. Kalpesh, taking a step in her direction, pats Abhi on the shoulder to break the conversation.

"See you tonight. We'll drop by, we'll drop by." With that, he moves past Abhi. "There he is, there's Warren Buffett," he says to Shanu's husband. They shake hands. It is easy for us to escape. In the car, my hands cover my mouth, and I shake. Abhi, who has pulled out slightly, puts the car into park.

"Are you crying? What happened?"

I take my hands away so he can see my laughter. He still isn't sure.

"Are you okay? Look at me. Look at me."

"She thought I looked *trim*," I say, catching my breath. "Abhi, she was jealous of my figure!"

Abhi shakes his head. "She is an *ek number ka* idiot, isn't she?" He grins. "Naina and the rest."

"Swimsuit body!" I mimic her. I make an A-OK sign, which is also the evil eye. "Absolutely swimsuit body!"

He guffaws, and now we are both laughing with the car half out of the parking space. We can't stop. Our ribs and cheeks ache. Soon we are crying-laughing and finally just crying until we are on the highway, where we go silent and stay silent. At home, we lie in bed holding each other in our dress clothes, which we throw later that afternoon in a pile at the back of the closet: his suit, my saree, never to be washed, never ironed, never worn again.

Mala and family arrive. This time they come for a week.

"You can't keep wasting vacation," I tell her after the embrace and the *how are you feeling* and the grandchildren's cheddar cheese Goldfish in two Mickey Mouse bowls. The kids, snacked up, have gone to the toys I brought out for them: Ronak's old cars and Transformers for Vivek, for Shivani the ball she kicks back and forth with Sachin.

"It's not a waste of vacation," says Mala. "How is it a waste?"

"Remember you were talking about Disney?"

"Yeah. We'd have put that off anyway. She's still young."

"But this is when they would love it."

"She's still young. Besides. This is where they *want* to come. You should have seen how excited they were. Naani's house, Naani's house."

I nod. "It is such a long drive for you."

"We let them watch *Nemo*." She sits back. "For the billionth time."

A pause. I run my hand nervously along the couch arm, ruffling the fabric dark, then smoothing it light again.

"What's wrong?"

"I could not cook last week."

"Not a problem. You know that's not a problem, Mom."

"I don't know where the week went. I don't know where any of the weeks go anymore."

"We can order pizza."

"Your father is always eating like that now. I have no strength."

I realize I shouldn't have said that. She is going to read too much into it. "You can't expect yourself to cook, Mom. Not with all that's going on."

"It is not natural for me."

I am not looking at her. But I can feel her staring at the side of my face, hard. "Can I help?"

"What?"

"Can I help?"

"The number is in Abhi's phone. Abhi will go pick it up. Or Sachin. You can stay."

"No. I mean, can you cook if I help you?"

"You mean cutting the vegetables?"

"Oh *God*, Mom!" She talks to the ceiling. "I'm not *that* incompetent, you know!"

"I know. You are a brilliant girl. I know."

"I can do other stuff. I never learned. Or at least not as much as I should have. But I mean, there are things I can do. You could sit and guide me."

She has come into my kitchen only rarely. Once, when she had a home economics class in high school, she decided she liked baking. She wouldn't eat what she had made, not more than half a cookie fresh out of the oven. She would give me the other half from her fingers, hot, hotter where the chocolate chips had melted. As she grew older, she had no time, and then no patience, and then no respect for the art. It smacked of Old World female subservience; it was a chore, as lovelessly done as the dishes afterward. I try to imagine how it would be with her helping me now.

"I never learned. I can learn now. Mom?"

"Yes?"

"What do you say?"

"There is nothing in the house. Everything is used up."

"Write me a list."

"You want to go now?"

"I'll get the pizza on the way back. Then for dinner we'll have what you and I make together. How's that sound?"

"Good."

"Great." She smiles at me. "I get to be the sorcerer's apprentice."

She goes to the counter and comes back with a junk-mail envelope and a pen. She clicks the pen three times quick.

"Rattle off what you need."

I sit back and imagine my refrigerator and my pantry. I close my eyes. This is not what I am used to. I do all the grocery shopping for the house.

"Let's start with produce."

"Ginger," I say. "A lot of ginger. Maybe five whole roots." I go through it fast; it is my antiemetic.

She writes.

"Tomatoes . . . the cooking variety. You know those? They are kind of thicker, rounder—"

"I know cooking tomatoes, Mom."

"Okay."

"What else?"

"Onions. White. At least two. And two limes. Not the organic ones, those are more expensive for nothing. We have lemons I think. Cilantro, of course. And maybe bring grapes, too. Vivek likes grapes, right?"

"V, if I bring grapes, will you eat them?"

Vivek's truck pauses under his hand. "Yeah."

"You want the purple ones or the green ones?"

"The purple-flavored ones."

"All right, purple grapes for V."

He looks up suddenly. "Wait! Not with the seeds!"

"No seeds, got it. What else, Mom?"

I go through the store in my memory, aisle by aisle. I keep my eyes shut so I can visualize it exactly and not forget anything. The menu decides itself as I go: black beans, palak paneer, cucumber raita. As I say each ingredient, the finished dish implies itself and draws other items off the shelves and into my imaginary cart. Mala has started a second column. Some of the things I say I already have in the house, but I desire fresh cumin, fresh fennel seeds, even fresh salt, not three-weeks-unbreathing spices in the dark of my cupboard. It is wasteful of me, I know, so I press several twenties into Mala's hand. She resists, but not too forcefully because I am weak now. A little persistence on my part, and she takes the money. The back of the envelope is covered in pen, the second column packed smaller and smaller at the bottom right, fitting in as much as possible before the end.

That afternoon—in the smell of empty pizza boxes, the side panels untucked and the coupons left stapled to the cardboard—we start.

Mala comes down wearing a tank top. I remember, when she was a teenager, when I forced her to learn some basic dishes, she used to complain how hot it got around the stove. Now that she's not wearing sleeves I see the ancient scar on her upper arm. Centuries ago, when she was four, she reached up and pulled a pot of tea off the stove. I used the rear burn-

ers almost exclusively for three years after that and still prefer
them if I have a choice. To this day I turn all pot handles to
the twelve o'clock position even when there is no one else in
the house. The tea had splashed the floor, mostly; the pot
itself, bouncing off the stove edge, left that red slat on her
shoulder. I remember the scene afterward. Brown drops clung
to the nearby cupboards and the oven. Black tea-grounds
soiled the linoleum over a startling distance, like the spill
from a knocked-over houseplant. Thankfully she had been
wearing pajama pants, or her pale legs might have been
scalded by the splatter. She hadn't pulled the pot directly onto
herself. She had tried to move it aside for me, onto a neighboring unlit range, as she had seen me do every morning. The
heavy pot leaped at her off the high ledge. I had been washing
my hands across the gulf of the kitchen floor. I turned around,
and it had already happened. If she had been standing a little
to the left . . . if I had waited at the stove instead of washing
my hands . . . How efficient I liked to be, no time wasted,
every minute used. *Let me wash last night's ice cream bowls
while the tea's heating.* I was rinsing my hands when the milky
tea frothed, rose, rushed to the brim.

"Mom? You all right?"

"Let's start."

"Wait." She has brought something folded. Two matching
aprons. I never wear one, but I will today.

"You like them?"

"Of course." Was she planning this cooking adventure
before she came? "Where did you find them?"

"I passed them in the store, and I got them. Cute, eh? With
the teddy bears?"

"Which one do you want?"

"You pick." She holds one flat on each palm.

"Red."

"Here."

"You're sure you don't want the red?"

"I'm sure, Mom."

We put them on. We are both skinny now, mother and daughter. The ties at our waists could wrap us fully around and knot in front. But we tie them in the back anyway and let the long ends dangle.

We begin with knives and okra, speaking of Vivek's time at the Montessori school and Shivani's new words. She is saying *chocolate milk* and, of course, *Dora, Boots, Backpack*. I am happy about this. I know Mala had been worried, though she had no reason to be. Children speak when they are ready to speak. I had told her this and so had the pediatrician, but Mala was impatient because the daughters of Rachna and Sima, her two close friends, started speaking well before Shivani. We dice the potatoes, and I watch Mala's fingers. A cut this early might turn her off, or at least spoil the afternoon for her. Now that we are here together, I want to keep going. I want to talk to her like this for as long as she will stay. With cutting boards before us and a meal to be prepared, this is not a self-conscious heart-to-heart, taking place during time we have set aside to have one. The attention is off the words for once, and that inattention is sunlight. The words grow free and crack the pavement and cover the bricks in green. We talk about Rachna's marriage to Sohum for a while, and Mala takes some pleasure in telling me how hard their daughter is to discipline. They have to hide their pens because she's obsessed with writing on the couches. Then Mala shrugs and says how not everyone can be like Amber's kids, "all yes-ma'am-no-ma'am." We start talking about Amber. The more we do—about how Amber is far too strict with the boys, how Ronak needs to stand up to her more, how Dev has finally grown out of his stammer—the closer she feels to me. It is not cruel of us. Is it? If Amber were upstairs or had just stepped out, that would be different. But she is far away, and Mala is right here, opening up, telling me what she thinks, sharing stories from her last visit to New York. I know she loves Amber and Ronak and their boys. I love them, too, no question.

"So what happened back at Christmas?"

She stops cutting. "Hm?"

"You know. At Christmas. Ronak came home without warning. Amber wouldn't answer her phone. Were they fighting?"

She shrugs and starts cutting again, but the motions are suddenly subdued. Nothing like when she had been telling me her stories. "I don't know."

I watch her fingers. "You know. You're just not telling me."

Her voice is quiet. "I don't know."

"Okay."

In the silence that follows, I regret how the mood between us has broken.

"They're fine now," Mala says at last. "That's all that matters."

"It was probably just a fight."

"Yeah," she nods. "Probably."

Another silence.

"Are we done with this?"

"I think so."

"All right." She begins scraping what she has cut into a tighter pile. I do the same. "This is it. I'm going to cook. You tell me what to do, step by step."

"I don't feel very tired. I can do most of it, Mala."

"No, no, no," she says. "I'll never learn that way. Same as with procedures. Watching is useless. You have to do it."

She washes her hands and brings a chair from the dining room into the kitchen.

"Sit there," she says, "and tell me what to do."

I smile. "Mala, I can't just sit here."

"If you don't, you're going to get up and do it yourself."

"I am not so ill. Look at me. I feel good. You made me feel good."

"Mom, you're strong, you could do this in your sleep, I know. But I'm trying to learn."

"You already know some things. You made masoor ni daal last time we came. You made that wonderful raita . . ."

"From a cookbook. Shredded cucumber and store-bought yogurt. I want to learn the real stuff."

"Sachin will be happy."

She grins with one corner of her mouth. "Sachin will be ecstatic."

"Good."

"I want to do this for me," she says defiantly. "And—with you."

"Good."

"You'll sit still, then?"

We are connecting again, I can feel it. I sigh and roll my eyes, the way I have seen her sometimes do, and say, again like her, "I guess."

"So." She opens a cupboard and bites her lip.

"That pan. No. The one next to it . . . let me see . . ." Some things I only know Gujarati words for, but she knows the words too from hearing them so often. "The sansi is in that drawer. Put the gas on medium, about. Good. Let it heat up a bit. This is a good time to take out the cooker. We can get that started while we're doing the spinach. It's a good idea to get everything going. The whistle? I keep it in the drawer with the spoons."

On their second morning here, Sachin helps Abhi move the study upstairs so that I can sleep downstairs. I don't want this, but everyone decides it's too dangerous for me to keep going upstairs and downstairs, especially at night. They have watched me uneasily ever since that silly fall of mine in December—an honest slip of the sock, but try convincing them. Abhi has exhumed from the basement some ancient cardboard boxes from the year we moved into the house. He reinforces their bottoms and edges with duct tape. The name of the mover—are they still even in business?—takes me back. Abhi wanted the first-floor study because, he said, it would stay cooler, and he couldn't think in heat. That was his pet theory about blood flow and brain work: cold vasoconstricted the blood vessels at the skin, so more blood was available for thinking. The brain flushed and prickled. This was also why he didn't eat much at my table when he was seized with some idea. More blood to the belly, he believed, meant less to the brain.

Abhi packs my closet upstairs while Sachin transfers the study, whose contents are already meticulously stacked and labeled. This was a two-evening project for Abhi and it interfered greatly with his productive work. But he wouldn't let me do the packing for him.

Sachin's lankiness gains grace under a burden. The unexpected muscles show in his thin arms. He takes the steps two at a time, Abhi's books and journals stacked chin high. Moving, lifting, calling over to Abhi to ask where things should go, he is almost athletic. I haven't seen this quality before. But maybe that is when the virility in that kind of good man comes out, when the family needs it. Mala goes to help move things out of the study, but Sachin and Abhi both tell her to keep me company in the family room, where I am with the children. I see her stop to watch Sachin spring up the stairs and down. She doesn't drift back to me until she has watched him take the stairs a second time, arms full with an outdated PDR and a *Fundamentals of Neurology* and two thinner textbooks, both hardcover. She looks at him just to look at him.

Ronak is more muscular, but Ronak's body comes from years of day's-end workouts—with his weight-lifting gloves with cutoff fingertips and Velcro wrist wraps, slow hissing sets of curls while staring into the wall mirror, white cord of the headphones crossing his chest like a Brahmin's thread. He didn't give up those workouts, not even after the boys were born. Amber has that extra hour and a half every day to care for them alone. Because of his commute, Ronak ends up getting home about an hour before the boys' bedtime. Part of that time goes for his shower, part for his dinner. Abhi and I saw firsthand how their days went. (Not even for his parents' visit would Ronak break his fitness schedule; he was "in training," he insisted, though for what he never said.) The boys were in pajamas by the time he dried his hands after dinner. At Amber's order, they mustered on the couch to hear a story. The sun had almost set by then. The four of them yawned as the brave honeybees chased the bear all the way home.

Abhi wants to show me the "new bedroom" when it is done. I don't want to see it. He behaves as though it is a gift, but my world has shrunken by a whole story, effectively halved. I think of that room as the study, and I call it that without intending to. Mala, too, when she asks Sachin about it, says, *Are you finished with the study? Can we go see it?*

New bedroom makes it sound like an addition or a renovation, not what it is—an upheaval. The guest bedroom is the study now, and the study is the master bedroom. What used to be the master bedroom is where the upheaval is most evi-

dent. It has been gutted of its bed and headboard. The rectangle of carpet, at once unfaded and thickly dusty, is strewn
with paper debris and stray clothes and hair clips. I am too
tired and disheartened by the look of the room to tidy and
vacuum it. I see Sachin walking the vacuum cleaner up the
stairs, holding it neatly off the floor, not even rolling it when
he is level. "I'm going to get to this after dinner," he promises.
"It's going to look spic-or-span."

Mala, on another day, might have corrected that subtlest
of errors, "It's spic *and*, not spic *or*," but today she lets it pass.
We have made a quick lunch, nothing elaborate—I wanted to
show Mala some recipes she could put together when short
on time. She is buzzing with joy at working under me, and
when the dishes turn out, she puts the food on fresh plates or
in bowls, adds parsley or arranges tomato slices in a fan, and
says, "Ha!" Part triumphant, part astonished that she's tri-
umphed. I know she is proud when she takes out her phone
and snaps a picture of each dish. She presses some buttons
afterward; I think she is sending the photos to Rachna.

After lunch, Sachin goes in the backyard with Vivek and
Shivani. We see them through the window above the sink as
we rinse and stack. It's drowsy-sunny out and barely short-
sleeves hot, but Mala insists on sunscreen, so Sachin sun-
screens the children but not himself. Shivani sits on the deck
facing out and bounces her heels on the wood. The kite sniffs
wind and strains against its string, which Sachin keeps pinched.
I bought that kite over a year ago. The shape is a broad trian-
gle. Two large black dots stare out at me as if from butterfly
wings, orange and black imitating the widespread monarch.
Thick plastic and fat string soft on the fingers.

Sachin grew up in Ahmedabad where he is used to the
spry, lean, dispensable diamond-kites sold on the streets,
tissue-paper bodies on flexible balsa crosses. He is used to

hot-pink kite string coated with glass dust. You need to wear a rubber finger-sleeve or tape wound twice around a hooked finger. That kite string could cut skin. Kite flying on Utta-rayan is an air war between rival terraces. Sachin has a whole secret body of wartime knowledge. The salvage and refitting of downed kites. How to go slack when engaged, unspooling so your long sag of string saws through the attacker's lifeline. Also when to go taut—the frantic arm-over-arm ingather until the kite stiffens and sweeps skyward, slicing. Here the kite will fight no duels. Sachin tests the ribbing anyway and eyes the knots to see if he needs to retie them.

Vivek waits with the kite held in front of him; it is broader than his boy chest. The leaves stir, and the kite leaps out of Vivek's hands. Sachin pulls twice, and the kite strains a foot high, a foot higher, then takes a hairpin dive to the ground. They try again. This time, the kite boards a fuller, higher wind. Sachin feeds it string. Vivek and Shivani run to his side, as if they can judge the kite's true height only from its flyer's perspective. Their father waits out some of the kite's friski-ness, shortening the leash or giving it some play as needed. At last he tames it. A steady interval of flight. He brings the string down to Vivek. He shows both children how to hold the hand, index finger crooked to rest the line, the other fingers curled. They each raise a hand to mimic his gesture. Sachin nods. Vivek holds the kite for a spell, then Shivani. Son passes the string to daughter as carefully as candlelight poured wick to wick.

I was Shivani's age when my father died. I do not remember him except by the smell of mothballs. Two large metal trunks housed his clothes and effects. I used to steal upstairs to look at the clothes. I didn't cry. He died when I was two years old, so I didn't know him enough to mourn him. His shirts and socks seemed far more immediate than his unreachably high portrait, black-and-white and garlanded. Later, when I learned to sew, I restored the cuff button to a white dress shirt. (I'd noticed it missing as a seven-year-old and had not forgotten.) My mother never knew I visited this shrine of his effects until, by chance, in his less-often-explored trunk of books and papers (legal documents, a Victorian-era *The Tempest*, the Gujarati novels of K. M. Munshi), I found a yellowed diary. As a girl, I had been drawn to the glasses case in that trunk. I would hold those huge plates over my face and hope that someday my eyes would weaken to match his. As an adolescent, I realized that the true treasures might be among the books and papers, and sure enough I found the diary.

My hands started shaking as soon as I saw handwriting. What would I learn? Would he talk about my relatives? Would I read about myself? Would he record his delight at having one of each, a boy and a girl? Or would he write about the new infant screaming in the night, disturbing him at his work? I dreaded to know. I longed to know. Would he reveal himself too completely, flaws and all? I worried for my fantasy of him. I clicked the trunk shut and smuggled the diary to my room. And, by the dying window light, could not read a word of it.

It wasn't Gujarati. It wasn't English. The jigs and dots made me think of legal shorthand. Most of the pages were blank. He had written on only the first twenty-one. I spent a few days with the book, checking each page for a key to the code. I dwelled on his three drawings—a human head on the sixth page, a pair of sandals on the seventh, a bicycle on the eighteenth—as if they were mystical symbols. Finally I confessed to my mother how I had been rummaging. (I made it sound like this was my first time.) She didn't seem surprised. I begged her to decipher the diary for me.

"I can't read it," she said. "It is in Farsi."

I looked down at the diary with renewed fascination. "Why did he write it in Farsi?"

"To keep it hidden should it ever be found." She shrugged. "He never spoke it. Maybe he wanted to stay in practice."

She did not take the diary from me or tell me to put it back. So I kept it on my desk among my textbooks. I was in the tenth standard, preparing for the SSC exam on which my future depended. This was the exam that put my name bold-faced in the newspaper and eased my admission to medical school. I thought my father's diary, even then, a talisman. After my exams, I promised myself, I would learn Farsi and translate his words. Farsi: a natural choice for the language of a diary. His fellow Brahmins didn't care to learn it anymore; now that Britain ruled, they learned English. I would learn it. I would master it.

After the exam, though, I was too exhausted to take up a fresh intellectual project. My course loads didn't get any lighter the next year. Chores busied my weekends and vacations—I was a daughter first in my mother's house, and I had to make up for the months I had spent studying.

Not that my mother was stern or resentful. She herself had never gone past the seventh standard. Girls didn't take the SSC back then; they got married around that time, usually to men twenty or so years older. That was what happened with my mother. The shift in destinies between her and me was much more drastic than the one between me and Mala, even allowing for the difference in countries. During the school year, I did not help her cook. I had to study. She understood. She put no housework obligation on me. But for the rest of the year, I put the obligation on myself. I was like that. I am still like that.

When it came to Mala doing chores and learning to cook, I stayed hands off, just as my mother had with me. I trusted a good daughter would in time take on responsibilities. If she doesn't, the lineage breaks. An oral wisdom is lost—this book of women, this fifth Veda that guides the rice-offering, the milk-offering, the ritual oblation. The Agni is in us. The Agni is hunger.

I knew medical Latin would postpone Farsi forever. The summer after my SSC, I showed the diary to a local university professor, M. N. Ali, a very old gentleman in a blue Mussulman topi. Within the week, he dropped the translation off personally. Twenty-one pages handwritten became three, typed.

I wish I still had them. I would have transcribed them here complete. How did I let the diary and the translation leave my possession? To look away from such a thing, even for a moment, is to leave it sitting on a train platform. The move to college, exams, marriage, the move to America, the first child, the second child, some hectic India visits house-to-house-to-house, the family property sold, its treasure-trove trunks scattered . . . I feel I've ridden a single gust of wind to this far place and this late date. The swept-up papers are still settling.

My father had written about one incident in 1937. He had gone to seek treatment for tuberculosis in Bombay. He had cousins there. I don't know my father's relatives very well, and apparently neither did he. He was blood, though, and blood obliged them to put him up. Already the house was very full, the whole clan living under the patriarch's roof, sons and sons' wives and sons' children. There was a new baby in the house, and their guest was always coughing. The TB had advanced, he wrote, to three bloody handkerchiefs a day. He volunteered to limit himself to the open-air porch, where he could sit on the swing. The number of sandals dwindled in the mornings and swelled come evening, low tide and high. This accounted for the doodle he'd made of sandals.

In spite of the cold nights and mosquitoes, he slept on the swing so he could cough in peace. The milkman parked his bicycle and awoke him before dawn.

My father was not happy in Bombay. He took down the things his hosts whispered in the kitchen. The men would not talk to him for more than a minute or so at a time. Educated people had an idea of how tuberculosis spread by then; he suspected they were holding their breath the whole time. When he offered to go to a hotel, though, they wouldn't let him; he had to stay, they pleaded, this was his home, how could they let him go anywhere else? They feared the shame, he knew, of sending him off to a hotel. Word would spread: Madanbhai came to their house sick, and they wouldn't give him a bed. He was stuck there, fortunately only for three days.

I was not yet born. I was five months in the future. He wrote about the infant in the house, and that led him to think of me. He knew he would have to keep himself isolated from his newborn child. The doctors were recommending a high-altitude sanatorium near Mount Abu. (Streptomycin wasn't discovered yet; he just missed it.) I imagine him writing the words. His right leg pushes the swing while he rests the diary on his left knee. A spotted handkerchief peeks from his pocket.

The face he drew on page six was a self-portrait. He showed the eyes shut.

My imaginary memories are of my father as a young man. My real memories are of my mother. She is old in almost all of them. As I get closer to the age when she passed away, I realize how much like her I am. Mala and Ronak always loved to point out the similarities. We made the same hand gestures when we got excited. Our smiles were the same. There were a half-dozen other mannerisms I thought were just my mother's until my children pointed them out in me.

She, too, was intent on feeding everyone who came to her flat. And a flat of her own she insisted on having. The vast family house in Jamnagar had been sold years earlier to make room for the new India. Her building had started out a fresh pink, but one monsoon later, water damage wept gray down the walls. Television antennae came to bask and breed on the terraces like bold insects. In time these gave way to satellite dishes, which flowered and let down black tendrils. Every stairwell had its resident stray dog. The roads, I remember, were pavement one visit, potholes the next. Damp sarees waved surrender off balcony clotheslines.

By the time we sold it, our family house had gone rotten.

The grounds between the road and the house had been taken over by a carpenter. This carpenter, known to my mother only as Motilal, had lived apart from his family for two years. He spent long stretches of time in town, sent money home, and periodically returned to his village to father one more barefoot child.

My mother, her spine already wilting to a curl, had done her widow's shuffle from emptiness to emptiness. She called the carpenter to repair the legs of two chairs and a couch. Motilal saw the empty lawn and invited his family within the week, including his brother, his brother's family, and his brother's cows. One visit, I saw grass there; on my next, a year and a half later, the lawn was mud and dung. I closed the shutters in horror on a heifer's glistening, wobbly-jowled chewing. Dung patties dotted the brick boundary.

How had this happened? The story made me flush with guilt. It was I who had complained how the short couch leg knocked against the floor. I could have stuck a book under it before I departed. Instead I had left my mother with the critique that smarted every time she passed the couch. And so she called Motilal to the house.

Indian law, either the letter or the practice, made it impossible for us to evict the carpenter and his clan now that they were installed. The same went for the lodgers to whom she had let the upstairs of the house. Their rent had not increased since 1966. A month's milk cost them more than a month's rent. Up there, it was essentially someone else's house.

When the developer came to buy, each of these players—the carpenter on the lawn, the entrenched lodgers upstairs—had to be bargained with separately, as if they were owners. Both parties ended up negotiating a higher purchase price than we did. The negotiations stayed secret until after the signing. On that day, the lodger's wife came downstairs for

the first time in years. *So, how much did they give you?* She
made the descent in spite of the ratty cartilage in her knees. It
must have been quite painful for her, but that's how badly she
wanted to gloat.

My mother's new flat came to us in a clause of the deal the
developer offered us. It was worth about two lakhs in those
days; the flat is worth more now that the street is more packed.
The flat consisted of two rooms, a kitchen, and an occasionally
backed-up latrine with mud flecks on its porcelain footpads.
Ignominious lodgings for the widow of a London-educated
barrister, but she insisted on living there, alone.

My mother seemed to expect this diminishment before
the end. Her own father, also wealthy, had "gone mad" shortly
after his last daughter was married. Details were never medi-
cally satisfying; it sounded, from her wide-eyed descriptions,
like a schizophrenic break. But schizophrenia usually mani-
fests itself by age thirty, and my grandfather was easily sixty
when he stopped bathing and shaving, locked himself in an
upstairs guest room, and every night harangued a resident
lizard who only wished to sun beside his lamp.

Downstairs, meanwhile, a kind of slow-motion looting
began. Over several weeks, distant relatives, family "friends,"
servants, and eventually strangers picked out what they
wanted. Figurines, fixtures, pieces of furniture—from the
courtyard, they would shout, "Praful bhai! Can we have the
radio?" or, if they didn't know him personally, "Saheb! Can
we have the curtains?" They would wait for his irascible
shout, "Go on, take it, take everything, just get out of my ears!"
Get out of my ears was not an idiomatic expression. His con-
temporaries took it for proof of madness, and hence unfitness
to own so many beautiful things. Abhi claims the phrase might
express a schizophrenic's anguish at auditory hallucinations.
There is no way to know.

The story made me fear for Ronak. Had I passed something down to him? I soon stopped worrying on that account.
Ronak grew up shrewd and acquisitive from the beginning,
the opposite of his mad great-grandfather. After my mother's
diminished last years, I feared for myself, that I, too, living
out some family curse, might die impoverished in some
way.

The first day of one India visit, Abhi and I left our bags at his
eldest brother's house. Abhi's mother, also a widow, rotated
among her many sons, and she always timed the sojourn at
her eldest son's house to her youngest son's arrival. My
mother's flat was within walking distance of my own brother's house, but she lived by herself, as she insisted. We visited her the first evening for dinner even though we wanted
to sleep.

We made sure she had been given a ground-floor flat to
save her the ordeal of stairs. She left so rarely, though, we
might have done well to stipulate a unit one floor up. That
would have saved her—and us—the ordeal of rats. It seemed
the rats didn't notice her. They weren't startled into corners as
they were by other human footsteps. Maybe they were
emboldened, knowing they dealt with an old widow. Like the
vegetable sellers who rolled their carts to her window and
demanded fifteen rupees for three tomatoes.

Mala and Ronak, sullen preteen and teen respectively,
caught sight of a rat soon after they had touched their grandmother's feet in greeting. My mother spoke only to me, commenting on how much they had grown since she saw them
last. I thought back to a trip a half decade earlier—how ruddy
she had been, how much more happy fat she had carried on

the face and arms. As she was speaking, a rat cruised between some table legs and vanished into the kitchen.

Mala shuddered exaggeratedly; Ronak raised his eyebrows. They were having a conversation in body language about their revulsion.

"Take off your shoes," I told them.

"But—"

"You take off your shoes here when you go to someone's house."

"Swear to God we just saw a rat, Mom," said Ronak, in truculent American.

"It was *huge*," added Mala.

"Ronak, Mala, take off your shoes," said Abhi, removing his own with what looked like reluctance.

My mother was still speaking. I turned to her and leaned by her near-deaf ear. "I hope you didn't make too much!"

"What?"

"I said I hope you didn't make too much food! We just got off the plane!"

"Only the roti are left. I've done the dough. You can turn on the television. I'm making them fresh."

I followed her into the kitchen. I noticed her soles, black from the floor. I noticed the fissures at her heels. Her onetime rope of coconut-oiled, gray-silver hair had evaporated into a bright white halo with a pinky-sized ponytail at the back. She had no idea I was behind her. The dough was on a steel thali with a bowl over it. I checked the front room. Mala and Ronak sat cross-legged on the swing, looking uneasily over the edges of it, the way castaways on a raft might check for sharks. Abhi unzipped and lifted the dusty cover off the television, wiped his fingers, tried the power button. Lines rolled diagonally across a Doordarshan broadcaster. The

snow varied between squall and blizzard as he waltzed the
antennae and Mala reported, "Better, worse, *worse*, better,
worse . . ."

"Why don't you try another channel?" said Ronak.

"There *is* no other channel."

In the kitchen, a rat hurdled my mother's hand as, squatting, she clicked the lighter on the stove. Two stainless steel
bins sat on the stone floor beside her portable gas range. She
was no bigger than the fire-engine-red kerosene canister in
the far corner. I began to smell gas. The children would smell
it soon, too. Finally: flame. She tuned it to a crisp ring. A brisk
hand clipped the tawa onto the flame while her other hand
uncovered the dough and set the bowl aside.

I was at her side now, tearing the dough, racing to roll it
into balls while the tawa heated. She was still faster than me,
her arthritis gone. Decades vanished. The spheres she
sculpted were identical in volume. Little earths, flat at the
poles. Before I could get to it, she had taken up the rolling
pin, elbows out, putting her weight (such as it was) into the
flattening. When she swept the tawa magically out from
under, the rotli inflated, ruptured, sighed flat. No tongs; her
bare fingers snatched the rotli steaming from flame to plate.
She slapped it once and zigzagged a spoonful of golden ghee
over it, distractedly owning the miracle, like a writer signing
her book.

The same flat, six years later. The walls were darker with water
damage. More stray dogs loafed on the stairwells. Maruti
hatchbacks were scattered about now, not just Bajaj Chetaks.
More laundry on the balconies, more traffic beyond the gate.
The boys who once chalked wickets on the far wall had been
sucked into their bedrooms, where they did math problems

under cricket posters. The girls who had gone about in tight pigtails, wearing khaki school uniforms with maroon button-down sweaters in the winter, had graduated to jeans and kameez tops and the local Polytechnic. Abhi and I were at my mother's again, our first day back home.

Ronak and Mala didn't join us on that trip. Their lives had locked onto the rails of higher education and, soon afterward, their professions. They had no good reasons not to come, but they did have good excuses. It was easy for us, too, to say they had "no time," although Mala had three weeks between high school graduation and her unpaid research spot in a neurologist's lab. Ronak had called me— spring break at South Padre, winter break at Snowmass, always my phone—to clear a weeklong hiking trip to Arizona, followed by a road trip "just up to Nevada," as if he were independently wealthy. (Nevada. He didn't use the word *Vegas*.)

Abhi and I no longer pressed the children to accompany us on our India trips, which we had begun to make yearly as our mothers grew older. We felt that love of motherland could not—must not—be forced. Mala did, once, show interest in India, when a friend named Sarah got her excited about a nonprofit. But Sarah ended up not going. In any case, Sarah's nonprofit had fixated on vaccinating Bihar, which was far from our relatives. Bihar was a dangerous place, no better than Africa. Later we, or at least I, realized what should have been obvious: India was never their motherland anyway. It seems silly, in retrospect, that I grasped this so suddenly, crushingly, like the answer to a test question hours after I had missed it.

In my mother's flat, as always, we ate our obligatory first-night-in-India meal. I was almost glad Mala and Ronak were not there to see the flat or their grandmother. My own grandchildren weren't born yet, but I thought to myself, *Will I come* to seem this way to my grandchildren? Will I give off musty grandmother-odors and offer crème-filled biscuits of questionable age? Will they look at their dishes and wonder about my hygiene? Maybe I was already on my way. Mala and Ronak, when they visited, had taken to commenting how the house was getting old. They found what they looked for: the family room needed new carpet, the guest bathroom, new tile. I had not seen these things until they pointed them out. I defended the house's decay in their presence—but got estimates after they left.

My mother ate only after we had finished. She had to be free while we ate so she could monitor our progress and inter-rupt it with the customary insistent offers and, in Abhi's case, the uninvited ladle. When she did sit down to eat, she tucked her food to one side of her mouth and only chewed on that side. Abhi and I both noticed.

"Do you have a penlight?" Abhi asked me after she had finished.

I had one in my purse. I examined her; I was better at these everyday medical problems than Abhi, who had forgot-ten most of his medical knowledge outside neurology. If Abhi saw someone walking on a sprained ankle, his first thought was Friedreich's ataxia. I tweezed the splinters and iodined the scrapes of Mala's jungle-book childhood. I sat my mother down, pointed at her cheek, and asked, "Do your teeth hurt?"

She turned her ear to me.

"Why were you eating on one side? Do your teeth hurt?"

As soon as she heard the question, she sat back. "Oh, that. I bit my cheek, that's all."

I clicked on the penlight. "Let me see."

"Why do you want to look in my mouth?"

She was always resistant. She didn't wear a hearing aid for

the same reason. Abhi brought his face near my shoulder. "Let her check your mouth, Ma."

"I see Arvind bhai twice a year. He said it was nothing."

Arvind bhai was her doctor; according to my brother, her last checkup had been in November of the prior year. "Ma, how long have you had this?"

"A long time, a long time. He says I bite my cheek in my sleep."

"Let me see."

She dropped her dentures into her hand and tilted her head back. Loose neck skin stretched translucent over the flutter of her neck veins, then crinkled again when she opened her mouth. The old fluorescent tube overhead flowed right to left with fine ripples of flicker. Her face was bleached by its surgical light. With two fingers I lifted her upper lip clear of the gums. The motion stung then soothed a forgotten hangnail. I did not need the penlight to see. I drew away my hands and looked at Abhi. My mother stared patiently at the ceiling. Abhi nodded. Under the clockwise ceiling fan, my wet fingertips went cold.

I might have foreseen it. I often feared for her, but what I expected was a stroke or heart attack or broken hip. The habit—a smear of tobacco paste inside the cheek, every evening, for decades—was something I had thought harmless. Or maybe not harmless, but the least of many risks. She was so far along in years, why break her one vice?

Years later, when Mala became an ear, nose, and throat surgeon, she dealt with this exact lesion, squamous cell carcinoma. Her patients were work-boot-wearing, country-music men who swore by Skoal and once-pretty barflies whose lungs had gone to smoker's fishnet. How unlike that small, holy

woman! Yet my mother shared their coarse addiction. The girl
who came to sweep her floor passed a paanwallah on her way.
A clutch of one-rupee notes bought my mother her monthly
tin of tobacco.

Mala grew up to carve out halves of tongues and olive-
sized neck lymph nodes; I doubt my mother's cancer had any
bearing on my daughter's choice of specialty. Though I do
know she tapped the story for admissions essays and residency interviews. *So tell us, why ENT?* It supplied a personal
angle.

Abhi and I had taken that India trip to care for Abhi's
mother, who had suffered a small stroke. Instead we split up,
Abhi staying with his mother, me handling my mother's clinic
visits. She demanded that we go to Arvind bhai first—partly
out of social propriety (he was my third cousin), partly
because she believed in him. Arvind bhai, unrepentant, nodded sagely and told me she had been biting her cheek in her
sleep, he had told her to stop, but she hadn't stopped, and
now look. This was Indian medicine, where doctors were
infallible even when they were wrong. I got the name of a specialist, who confirmed what I already knew: even if she had
been younger and healthier, the lesion itself was inoperably
deep, inoperably spread out. There was nothing I could do.

I did everything anyway. Abhi and I didn't meet for days
at a time. I slept in my mother's flat—lay there the whole skit-
tering, cricket-loud night. I saw Ronak and Mala's logic in
preferring the flat board of the swing: it had no legs in contact
with the ground, so there was less chance of a cockroach
adventuring over you. I tried to ignore the midnight circus of
her rats—the scrape of a thali, the tumble of a pot . . .

Once I shook my mother awake at two in the morning and
demanded we stay at my brother's. She said no. "I want to
stay in my house," she insisted. What house, her house was

sold years ago, this was just a flat in the city. She said it was *her* house and that she had kept everything running these past years all by herself. She laid her arm over her eyes. A small mound in a white saree, but stubborn as a mountain. She wasn't going to move, so neither could I.

I shouldn't have asked, knowing her stubbornness. I had always urged her to come stay in America. I still see fantasies of that alternate life for her, that alternate death. On my first visits home, I used to beg her to let me book a plane ticket. The Western Lands felt magical and healing. If I could just get her there, I imagined, her hair might thicken and darken, her cheeks might fill out. I had seen them for myself, those grandmothers who came over. She could have been one of them: an old maaji in sneakers, brown cardigan over the saree, strolling past Bath & Body Works, the Gap for Kids, the food court. Bespectacled and otherworldly but covered by Medicare, paramedics never more than five minutes away. I fantasized about seeing her peel the stickers off Chiquita bananas—gigantic, yes, but not as sweet as Indian ones, she would declare. I could picture her sipping milky, cardamom-flecked tea, her Ritz crackers and chevda on a separate saucer. She would have had her own room on the ground floor—I imagined it sometimes when I went into Abhi's study: at once neater and dirtier than the rest of the house, a little patch of India, smelling of her, smelling of India, Parachute coconut oil in the blue plastic bottle, ayurvedic turmeric, mothballs, that luggage scent that never went away, her own stale body odor, gods and kumkum in the corner, a tiny incense stand (silver, blackish with collected ash), the hexagon of sandalwood incense sticks from the Indian grocer, pills for hypertension on the nightstand, cotton balls to stuff in her ears come winter, a quilt in a square at the foot of her bed. She would have folded clothes, she would have sliced zucchini for me, she would have watched the children and perhaps taught them more Gujarati than I was able to. I would have brought her bhajans, *Ramayana* recitations, Sanskrit stotras intoned with the ocean in the background. At first cassette tapes, then CDs, finally an iPod with everything on it.

Years more, ten years, maybe fifteen years more she might have lived. She might have retired to her room at seven like always and passed from half-sleep to nothing, propped on two down pillows, earbuds in her ears and the white cord vanishing beneath the blanket, blissful, the lamp still on at her elbow, Track 04 still playing, some spiraling alaap of Pandit Jasraj that would follow her soul through the chimney and up into the slate-gray Ohio sky. But she never agreed to come. *I want my own flat, I want my own place*, she explained. *And besides, a parent mustn't live in a daughter's house.*

At night, after everyone is asleep, Mala opens her laptop and sits in the glow. She starts to type, rapidly, as everyone of her generation does. It sounds like a small private rainfall. Our house has high ceilings and hardwood floors. Her key strokes echo. I can hear her from the study, where I am sleeping for the first time tonight. Maybe she is writing an e-mail to Ronak, giving him an update. Does he care to be told of anything but the big changes?

The ceiling of my days has been lowered by one flight. I wasn't looking forward to sleeping here. I regretted the night winding down. Sachin, who had made our cheeks ache with Gujarati jokes, put away the pistachio ice cream, and Mala rinsed the bowls and spoons. They went upstairs. Abhi and I went to the study.

Its dimensions felt wholly strange in the darkness. Twenty minutes into my sleeplessness, I whispered to Abhi, "I didn't want you to give up your study."

There was no need to check if he was awake. I had my head on his shoulder, and I could sense his body's tense wakefulness. "I haven't given up my study," he said. "I just moved my study upstairs."

"That room is half the size."

"I didn't use most of the room I had in here. It was empty space."

"It wasn't. It was space for you to think."

"This is the room I think in," he said, tapping on his head. "Besides, we were going to turn this room into a first-floor guest room, remember? If Ma or Ba had come to live with us, I would have transferred upstairs anyway."

"We talked about that years ago."

"So?"

I shook my head. "This has been your study for years, Abhi."

"I like it up there."

I lifted my head and looked at his face to see if he was lying. I can tell when he is lying; he does it to spare me sometimes. Like: *Of course they processed it wrong, they're going to pay for that scan in full*. He looked as if he meant it, but I could only see his profile by the flame-shaped night-light.

"The window upstairs, it looks out over the back. Just yesterday, I saw the neighbor's grandchildren on their trampoline."

I nodded.

"I think I'm going to sneak out to their trampoline one warm night and do some jumps."

I smiled. He yawned.

"Let's go to sleep, okay?"

Abhi, arm across my stomach, is pretending to sleep right now, here in the room where he used to come alive. He has started lingering until I fall asleep. His mind stays awake. He leaves when I steady my breathing for a minute straight. I have told him he can go right away, he doesn't need to lie next to me, but he says he wants to. He enjoys getting more rest, he says, he's fresher during the day. But I know he doesn't care about being groggy during the workday so long as his nights in the study have him at peak alertness. He can prescribe Sinemet or check a Babinski reflex on two hours of sleep or fewer. That can all be done on the auxiliary generator. It's brain-stem function for him. The main generator kicks on at midnight. His study burns white against a backdrop of sleeping suburban houses.

I slow my breathing. He starts to extricate himself. His arm goes weightless by degrees. He turns gingerly, watching how his movements transmit across the mattress. It's the way he used to leave for work on those kindergarten mornings when Ronak, scared of lightning or simply wanting his mommy, had shuffled into the master bedroom and come between us to sleep. (Even though she was the kid sister, Mala had no fears back then. Monsters, Abhi used to joke, were scared of her.) As he has done every night recently, Abhi stands and looks at me a while. Even though I am keeping my eyes shut, I can sense his gaze on my face. Its warmth makes me feel like I'm napping outdoors in the sun. He keeps the knob turned as he closes the door.

I try to sleep for real, but I can't. Abhi is upstairs now— the light on in his new study, his mind in low earth orbit. I go outside to where Mala is typing. She works by the dull light from the hall. Answering e-mails from work, maybe. I put my fingers on the switch, but I don't turn on the light. Should I ask her first? Best not to disturb her concentration. It is so rare for her, now that she has the kids, to get this kind of alone time. She usually checks her e-mail and the news before sleep. When I was a mother, I don't remember having anything I needed to catch up with. I never felt left out. Mothers now do; motherhood feels like pulling over and parking on the shoulder of a highway. I peer more closely at the screen. She isn't on the Internet, I don't think. The light from the screen illuminates a card from this afternoon. Three more are at her elbow. She sets it down and types again, her fingers moving while her head is still turned. I step up noiselessly (what do I weigh anymore?) to read the file name across the top: Mom.doc.

Mala turns. "Hey, Mom."

I smile and stroke her hair. "Busy?"

"Just taking some notes."

"Keep working."

"I'm almost done. Are you all right?"

"Yes."

"But you can't sleep?"

"I'll sleep soon."

Her hair feels like mine used to. She has many of her father's features, but this detail, at least, is mine.

"What recipe is that?" I ask.

"The dahl we made today."

I see what I have been doing forever only now that I can read it. What always felt like one reflex is really a sequence of small steps. It astonishes me that the dahl I have been making for the past thirty years can fill a whole screen with letters. It seems so important there, so permanent. But it's really just a cup of dusty-yellow mung beans soaked overnight.

"Do you need anything, Mom?"

"I'm just getting a glass of water."

"Are you sure you don't want the monitor?"

She doesn't say *baby* monitor; she's certain I would never say yes to *baby* monitor. Tonight, over ice cream, she proposed "the monitor" for the first time; she had gotten Sachin to make a case for it to me. She had probably coordinated with him, knowing I would be less likely to say no to him. A baby monitor! As if I would let my every toss and grunt be trans-

mitted upstairs in case I needed—what? A walk to the bathroom? "I'll be fine, Mala. I'm getting a glass of water."

"Okay. But if you kept the monitor, you could ask for it,
and we'd hear."

"I am okay without it."

At the refrigerator, I drink and pause and listen to her typing. The sound comforts me.

"Do you want water, Mala?"

"Sure, thanks."

I open the cupboard to get her a fresh glass.

"Your glass is fine, Mom," she says distractedly, picking up
the card again and setting it in her done pile, on the other side
of the laptop.

I know her. She will want two ice cubes. I set her water
beside her finished note cards without speaking. How satisfying it feels to set drink before thirst, food before hunger. I
pass the light switch again and rest my hand on it.

"Do you want the light on?"

"I'm almost done. Last thing is uploading the pics."

"The ones you took on your phone?"

"Yeah."

"The light will be better for your eyes."

"All right. Turn it on."

The brightness, sharp as a whistle, shatters the quiet. I use
the dimmer to restore some softness to the night.

"Good night, Mala."

"Night, Mom. Tell me if you need anything."

"Okay."

I turn to the hall that my shadow fills. Mala types another
line, then sips from my glass, her mouth where my mouth was.

In the study I still can't sleep. I look around. My bed is
where his desk was. His room smells of books. His walls have
no nail holes—this space is for pure mathematics, austere.

Uninterrupted planes. Abhi even kept the picture of me and the children propped on the bookshelf, not mounted. As a rule, he doesn't like paintings or pictures on walls. A Home Sweet Home plaque and three staggered porcelain wall-tiles hang in the kitchen because the kitchen is under my jurisdiction. The main room's vast walls are bare. It is where we entertain guests, or used to. Whenever we had someone over, I would see our blank walls through their eyes and complain to Abhi that we needed paintings or at least mirrors. He would shake his head and say the walls were beautiful the way they were. Why clutter them? He thought blank sheets of printer paper beautiful, too. Blank sheets of graph paper, even more so.

Before today's move upstairs, this study had been disrupted only once. After Abhi got his award, a local station asked to interview him for the ten o'clock news. He had fielded phone calls for several days prior to this, and six different magazines had done written interviews with him, but this was the first interest shown by a television station. When the crew said they wanted to do the taping in his study, he agreed right away.

The next day, two cameramen, keeping their boots on, set up their equipment. Soon a huge camera tripod was squatting in Abhi's sanctum like a gigantic insect. After a second trip to the news van, they brought a lamp on a pole, the sort used at photography studios. They had to tilt it through the doorway. Dirty-looking orange extension cords coiled on the hardwood. We kept staring at their boots, but it was too late to say anything. The soiling was done. The cameraman moved Abhi's chair so he was sitting in front of some books.

The local news had sent the doctor who did its health segments to do the interview, probably because Abhi was a doctor, too. It was the closest thing to a qualification anyone there could claim. We had watched Dr. Tim's segments for years. I had no idea his face was so pink in real life. It could have been from the sun, but the flush looked more like the kind that comes from smoking—Dr. Tim, who always warned how cigarettes cause lung cancer.

Before the taping started, Dr. Tim wanted Abhi to put the medal around his neck, but Abhi explained how one didn't generally wear awards of this nature. It wasn't done.

"That's probably true, but it would be helpful for the viewers to, you know, actually *see* the medal," Dr. Tim suggested, aligning papers on his lap.

"It's not from the Olympics."

"Sure, sure."

"I can stand it on the shelf behind me."

"That would be helpful—Chuck, is it in the shot?"

The cameraman nodded and leaned forward to speak quietly to Dr. Tim. "It's in the shot, but you can't see it. There's glare off the case."

"Maybe I can take off the cover?" said Abhi.

"Let's see. You know . . . why don't we take it out?"

Abhi brought out the medal, which had a ribbon affixed to it. Dr. Tim held out his hand. The cameraman and Dr. Tim tried different locations and finally set up the medal so that it dangled off the shelf. The case itself they used as a weight to hold the ribbon in place. I stood in the doorway behind the cameraman. Abhi touched a handkerchief to his forehead and scalp, where the light's reflection shone intensely white.

The medal was still swinging, pendulum-like. Dr. Tim told Abhi the interview would be edited for time and "flow," so he should feel free to stop and restart an answer if he wanted to; they would smooth things out in the cutting room. Abhi nodded and stilled the medal between his thumb and forefinger. When he let go, it began ticking again, side to side. Both Abhi and Dr. Tim waited before starting to record, staring until it hung still. The cameraman put up his hand and counted down with his fingers. The Record light went on.

Dr. Tim's demeanor changed. His posture improved. His voice took on the slightly high-pitched friendliness I knew from segments warning about processed sugar and fatty diets. He said a few brief things about how honored he was to meet Abhi. My husband glanced at me and nodded. Dr. Tim asked his first question.

"Can you tell our viewers a little bit about the Millennium Prize questions?"

"Well, in 2003, the Clay Mathematics Institute announced seven unsolved problems in mathematics. These were problems that have been hanging around, waiting for someone to provide a proof. Some of the problems were unsolved for centuries. Around 2005, I started working on one of the problems. I worked on it pretty regularly, and last year, I had what I felt was a publishable solution."

"And how much was the award?"

"Yes, ahem," said Abhi, flushing. I noticed he had not mentioned the award money. His voice went soft. "One million dollars."

"One million dollars! What are you planning on doing with all that prize money?"

"Well . . ." Abhi looked at the floor.

"Any vacations planned?"

"Not at the moment."

Dr. Tim nodded. "All right." He checked his notes. "Tell us: Were you always good at math in school?"

"I was good enough to get good grades. I certainly enjoyed it more than other subjects."

"So how did you end up in medicine?"

Abhi's shrug was more eloquent than it looked. It expressed everything: the passivity in the face of his father's profession, his title not inherited, but feeling that way, like the left-sided part to his hair. But the shrug also said *It never really bothered me.* People had trouble understanding how he had never felt constrained by his destiny. They thought medicine demanded absolute dedication, or at least sustained focus. But Abhi had excelled while in a state of perpetual distraction. It was as if he had read his textbooks using peripheral vision. On our coffee table, the *Journal of the American Medical Association* frequently sat under the *Journal of the American Mathematical Society.*

"Will you go on practicing medicine, now that you're a world-famous mathematician?"

Abhi smiled and shrugged again. "My life hasn't changed as a result of this. I really can't imagine my life without Neurology at this point." It was true: He had gotten the call about the award during morning rounds, had stilled the phone's buzzing when he saw it wasn't me, and resumed eye contact with the third-year medical student presenting a case. He finally found out four hours later, when he happened to check his seven messages. I hadn't found out until 6:30 PM that day because a complicated add-on consult had kept him late at work.

"So you have two passions, then: your numbers and your patients?"

Abhi, in utter innocence, said, "I wouldn't say that. My passion has always been one thing only, mathematics."

Dr. Tim looked at his papers and began again. "One of the most amazing things about this story is how you manage to be a full-time neurologist—and solve these daunting problems in your spare time. What's your secret?"

"It was only one problem I solved." Abhi spread his hands as if to show he was not guilty. "I think I can do it because I don't need a big lab or anything. Many of the attempted solutions sent in for the Clay problems are the work of amateurs, actually. Much of this is theoretical. I didn't need big computers."

A pause. "Can you explain, for our viewers, how you did what you did? How you managed to crack this particular nut?"

Abhi shook his head. "I don't think that's possible."

"Okay," said Dr. Tim. He looked at the cameraman. The red Record light blinked off. "Do you think you might be able to, maybe, summarize what you did? I'm talking about a very simplified version, for our viewers. Just so they get a sense."

Abhi scratched his ear. "That is . . . difficult. It's not something you can just explain."

He knew how difficult it was because he had tried with me, more than once. In his famous paper, he had written something beautiful and everlasting that only a few people on Earth could understand. And among their number was no one he loved. What he had written spoke of the universe but was not universal. All those years of secret exploration; at the end, a discovery, but one that was intrinsically secret. You could make it public and it would still remain secret.

"Are there any applications for your solution? Say, in technology? Engineering?"

Abhi scratched his ear again and looked at the camera to make sure it was off. "It's really a proof, you know. It's not a . . . it's really very abstract."

When he met mathematicians, it was no better. He was alien to them as well, the wealthy, well-spoken physician shaking hands with slouching unkempt professors and poverty-line grad students in jeans and tennis shoes. He had the absolute loneliness of the anomaly.

The interview started again. Dr. Tim, having gotten nowhere with questions about math, circled back to the other natural focal point of Abhi's story. How did he find the time? Was he really self-taught? And then he rephrased a question he had asked earlier. "Why didn't you decide to study mathematics in college?"

And this time, hearing it phrased this way—not why medicine; why *not* his true love—Abhi gave a different answer. "I felt I should do what was best, as a family man," he said. "There really is no job as rewarding as medicine, in every way. I am very grateful. It's very much a part of who I am now." And then, with a flicker of the eyes in my direction, unconscious I am sure, he added, "There was never an opening for me to be another way." Such an odd pair of statements, gratitude and regret in immediate succession. Dr. Tim did not register that oddness. He went on to other things. But I noticed it, and I felt a burning in my cheeks and neck. I knew what underlay that statement, even if Abhi didn't. If his wife had worked, if this had been a two-income household, he might have had more time. He might have given up the profession that wasn't his passion; he might have become a mathematician instead of a neurologist who solved a famous problem for a one-million-dollar prize. I remember looking at the boots of the cameraman and at the Rolex, platinum-heavy, on Dr. Tim's wrist. I know Abhi meant no malice. He might not have been thinking of me. In the segment that aired (one minute and twelve seconds, all edited), you can hear a small tap during one of Abhi's answers. That was me, resting my head against the blank austere plane of his study wall, blinking with sudden, bewildered, tearful guilt. Who might he have been had I not been me? How much better might he have been, if I had been better?

This is my room now. I have displaced him for good, haven't I? He did eternal things in here. I have turned it into a clock tower with no time left. There it is, on the nightstand, just plugged in—my merely mortal arithmetic, blinking twelve.

———

Abhi's mother grew immense in her last days. We bought a flat in Ahmedabad. It was important, to him and to the family (and maybe, had she been conscious then, to her), that she stay in *his* house. "My table, my house" was a fixation on Abhi's side of the family, too. Wherever we kept our luggage was the most privileged house, but we also honored the politics of meals, and in which order we visited families. A get-together at some common venue wouldn't do. The point wasn't to meet everyone at once; the point was to show respect by coming and eating. We had to plan our meals to make sure we had eaten at every elder relative's house before we left, ticking names off a mental checklist. The code also required that Abhi's mother be cared for at her eldest son's house. Our house in America was out of the question at this late stage. Our mothers began dying slowly at the same time. I stayed with my mother while Abhi brought his to the newly purchased flat. He and the most recent host brother transported and installed her like a piece of furniture. There: it was official now, Abhi was keeping her. His roof, his bed.

She could not thank him by then, near inanimate as she was. Inside her great girth hid a tiny girl-sized heart. Her coronaries were brittle, crooked, pinched in places. The deposits were everywhere: the arteries in her neck and belly, the big thumping aorta itself—her plumbing sparkled with calcium on the CT scan. Every so often, some fleck or chip would dislodge and swim to the tip of an artery. The spot of brain or heart just beyond, choked with blood, would smudge black. Little heart attacks, little periodic strokes; not enough to kill her. She lived months with a slight, marble-in-the-mouth slur to her speech. Later, her left arm and left leg turned to solid lead. Abhi's father had died early, but his mother proved indestructible. Even after the sagging left face, the failing kidneys, the fingertips pricked for sugar readings; even after the horn-rimmed bifocals could not read the *Gita*; even after the incontinence, yellow on white, sarees drying as fast as they were sullied, pulled in off the balcony to swaddle a mummi-fied parchment widow.

This indestructibility was its own curse. At first her body malfunctioned in small humiliating ways, error messages from the bladder, eyes, joints. The major strokes came only later. During those first years, her memory stayed inviolate while her mind peered over the side and observed the machine below going glitchy with age. It was much the same with my own mother. Our families were alike in that: The men died at thirty-nine, at forty-four, at forty-six. The garlanded photo-graphs showed black hair. The widows lived forever.

It was not a bad life, at least not for Abhi's mother, who had so many sons and stepsons—that is, so many daughters-in-law. She had been the patriarch's second wife. The groom had plucked the gray from his mustache. The bride had just passed the nymph stage. Over seven years, she bore five sons, something that seems scarcely mammalian to me. No epi-durals. Not even an Advil. Was she ever not pregnant? It is hard to imagine the Nehru-capped patriarch in the photo-graph grunting atop the wife still raw from the last child, splayed like an overripe orchid. But he did. The tally told the story.

Abhi's father had been just as prolific in his first marriage. The stepbrothers' wives were a few years older than Abhi's mother. (I remember being confused at our wedding—so many venerable old ladies, yet his mother ordered them about, *tu, tu, tu,* second-person familiar.) Their closeness in age made the rivalries meaner.

The new matriarch, the stepsons, and their young wives all lived together in the massive house that Abhi's grand-father had built. Bhola sahib, the father, had been a well-known judge. Even Abhi's mother called her late husband *Bhola sahib*—*sahib* tacked on to the affectionate diminutive of Bholanath. It felt natural when the family said it, but was very odd when I thought about it. I couldn't imagine an American family calling their father "Mister Bobby."

Bearing her husband so many male children earned Abhi's mother respect, even reverence. Superstitions rose around her—aging aunts and new brides came to touch her feet. Success in this one thing implied wisdom in all. From her cot in an inside room, no men allowed, she suckled her many toddlers. She kept nursing, I was told, until the youngest was five and during this time progressively absolved herself of all other duties. Her cot became the headquarters of the household. Orders issued from the room, and wives hurried in at the swing of a handbell like chambermaids to the invalid queen. And a queen mother she was, thirty-one years old, all-powerful yet curiously helpless. She drank milk to produce milk—prodigious liters, claimed the whispers—and never got out of the habit.

Who did this whispering? My sisters-in-law, behind their saree hems. Leaning close, they spoke in a whisper even when she wasn't in the house or the city. I had some inkling, when they lowered their voices, how people must behave under tyranny: nowhere relaxed, always furtive. It wasn't that they were afraid of their husbands overhearing; they told me nothing they hadn't yelled in an argument. It was *she* whom they feared even in her absence.

Hearing of Abhi's mother from Abhi, though, I could barely reconcile the two versions. To hear him talk, she was left a widow in a house full of grown stepsons and their wives. She was a minority in that house once her reason for being there—Abhi's father—was gone. And she had her boys; she feared how they would be treated, these vulnerable sons of the second wife. The house, once the wives started bearing children, soon had a schoolyard crowdedness. Struggles for space, struggles for resources. The men were well educated, well off, every stepson English-speaking—but the old village cruelty against the widow was only a generation back.

So she fought from the first day of her widowhood, demanding the larger, upstairs rooms for her sons. Her milk sufficed only for the two youngest; so, for her three elder sons, she demanded glass after glass, calling the boys into her room and bidding them drink. Her behavior seemed paranoid, but Abhi told me, very earnestly, that the wives diluted the milk, made their rotlis smaller, ladled them lukewarm dahl. The eldest stepson, whom Abhi called Motabhai, *big brother*, handled the running of the house, but she forced him to transfer two bank accounts to her name. The cash she withdrew she hid in three locations (known only to her sons, who were sworn to secrecy), and disbursed for bicycles, pencils, shoes—and expensive kite string on Uttarayan, so they could slice the kites of their cousins and stepbrothers. Abhi spoke of his mother tearfully, as if she were the Rani of Jhansi or some other warrior queen. Imagine her young, semiliterate, alone, he said. The wives would have made a housemaid of her, had she let them. But she hadn't; she had *fought*; and in time she came to dominate the household. Decades later, Abhi said proudly, when real estate was being bought up all over the city, Motabhai—himself stooped and bald by then, six years older than she was—traveled from Rajkot to sit before her and ask her permission to sell.

Always implicit in the stories told to me by the brothers' wives was unspoken resentment. As if every account of the old woman's pettiness were prefaced with: *Here's another thing you'll never have to put up with . . .*

I was insulated by distance, and the wives envied me for it. But I wasn't totally insulated. Abhi's mother had visited twice, both times in the eighties. Her second visit had coincided with an anomalously chilly Ohio May. Abhi knew she did not do well in the cold (it was *chilly* that May; it was never actually *cold*), so he bought her a ticket for the end of the month. Three costly, half-hour transatlantic phone calls had convinced her onto a plane. On her first visit, the overhead nozzle had kept up a hiss during her Frankfurt–Mumbai leg, and she had known neither how to shut it nor how to ask the stewardess. This time, she refused to fly Lufthansa and brought a scarf and two shawls against Air India's air-conditioning.

After tolerating the marathon flights, the putrid foil-covered navratan korma, and the lines in Customs, she made it to her son's city—and discovered the weather to be fifty-two degrees Fahrenheit with a strong breeze from the northeast. She experienced the temperature for about twenty feet, from the airport's sliding glass doors to the minivan. Yet the "ice," apparently, had gotten "in her bones"—a kind of psychological flash-freezing, irreversible. The complaint of cold lingered the whole trip. She kept her shawls around her through June's crafts fair and July's firecrackers, and at Niagara Falls in August. She scowled at Abhi's Nikon. In the van, we couldn't turn on the AC and we couldn't open the windows. When Ronak and Mala complained, we scolded them in Gujarati and dabbed our sweat in silence. The cold hadn't left her bones until she was back in India.

As soon as Abhi would leave for work, I saw what the wives were talking about. Her tea wasn't sweet enough, so I added sugar. She would take a slow slurp, fingers splayed under the saucer. Now the tea wasn't strong enough. I must make it again. A remark about Ronak's fingernails, about Mala's inability to sit still. Why didn't the children speak Gujarati? Was that normal here?

Her towel upstairs was leaving an itch on her. I offered her a fresh one, but no, there was soap "dried into the cloth"—I must soak the towel by hand in a bucket of warm water, and dunk and wring it by hand and let it dry outside, naturally. *By hand*, she made sure to repeat it, *by hand*, and added that the "girl" shouldn't do it. I should do it myself.

"What girl, Ba? Do you mean little Mala?"

Her face crinkled irritably. "The girl who comes to do the housework, of course."

"We don't have a girl for that. I do the housework myself."

"Even the dishes? Even mopping the floor?"

"Everything."

This puzzled Abhi's mother for some time. She had been expecting a "girl" to show up and do a couple of hours of housework, as in every home she'd lived in, and she had wanted to inflict some inconvenience on me. Maybe she expected two girl servants; this was America, after all, and her doctor son possessed infinite doctor wealth. I think she assumed I laid about as idle as a begum. Did her daughters-in-law assume that, too? When *they* had the luxury of ordering a maidservant?

I don't think she believed me until after lunch, when it became evident there were no slums to supply us a silent dark girl, no one to join her hands at a Happy Diwali coin from the mistress, no one who was going to wash my dishes or mop up the body lotion puddled—poured?—on the bathroom tiles.

My mother-in-law's weren't the assumptions of India's rich, either. The four sons who had stayed in India all drove Bajaj scooters to work. They were well-off but not wealthy. Assistant manager at a bank, two electrical engineers with the Gujarat Electrical Board, and a chemical engineer who worked for a fertilizer company. A certain family stinginess, inherited from their mother, kept their flats modest. Still, they were part of upper India, which as years went by only grew larger. Not the idle rich: the idle middle class. Their rupee went as far in the slums as our dollar went in the cities. On my last visit to India, the wives had stopped making rotlis; each one had a woman in her kitchen, a bai with thinly muscular arms who would steamroll a stack in fifteen minutes and leave. This bai was different from the one who made the rest of the meal. While the cooking took place, the wives watched television shows.

Those three summer months when I was in her power, she did her best to inconvenience me, and I was dutifully inconvenienced. Maybe it didn't feel like persecution because I knew it had an end. I wasn't her prisoner; I was being granted a tour of the prison, trying on the black stripes, having my picture taken in Alcatraz.

No matter how often I showed her what to do, she just would not drop her dirty underclothes in the hamper I had placed in her room. She draped them on the bar in the bathroom, next to the hand towel. There were wet footprints from her squatting on the toilet seat, water everywhere, the floor mat wet under the unwary sock. The toilet paper roll, thick and never used, sat swollen on the holder thanks to her old-country splashing.

More than once she had me make a trip to the Indian grocery for some emergent need like incense or Parle-G. Sometimes I thought to myself, *Here's a story I can tell.* I was pleased to have some stories of my own now—on my next visit, I could countercomplain. Once, I finished making rotlis, no dough left, the top ones cooling, the bottom ones still warm, the perfect time to call everyone, and she—who had watched me butter and stack them—declared she *must* have ghee on hers. I had to prepare another fistful of dough just for her, another three rotlis. Clicking the gas on again I thought, with detached amusement, *So this is why they hate her.*

Abhi knew his mother's tendencies well enough, and he monitored me for signs of conflict: the undue pause after asking him how his day had been, a refusal to sit in the same room, extralong we-need-to-talk eye contact. At night, he would ask me for a report. He didn't want to hear how she had done; he wanted to hear how I had done. Just to see, I floated a complaint. Sure enough, he didn't offer to say anything to her. Instead he offered pleas for tolerance on my end. They came out all at once (he had been storing them up, I suspect): it's only a short time now; she is used to living a certain way; I'll make it up to you after she's gone; she's getting old; it's an adjustment period; she treats the other wives far worse. And then the discussion ender, when I persisted: "Don't forget, this is my mother you're talking about. Okay? Enough."

I began to think of her, by the conclusion of that stay, not as a mother at all or even as an elder, but as a child. This was two decades before the strokes threw her back, physically, even farther—the inability to roll over or sit up, the drooling, the need to be wiped. Before she turned into an infant, I saw her for the child she was. Not evil, not cruel. Just bratty. Wanting attention and willing to make a mess to get it.

She issued her demands, but what she wanted had nothing to do with her daughter-in-law, although extracting deference carried its own pleasure. More than anything, she wanted constant demonstrations of her son's bond to her. By demanding more and more from the wife, she proved something to herself about her son: *I can go this far, and he still won't challenge me. I came first, and I remain first.* This is what struck me as most childish, the need for proof.

———

Abhi took care of her, but he wasn't present for the end itself. As we boarded the plane to leave India, he told me he knew it would happen soon, when he wasn't at her side. He couldn't guess how soon.

The phone call came while our bags, freshly unzipped, still made the bedroom smell of India. Four forty-two AM, the second night after our return. He knew the exact time; jet lag insomnia and the prospect of morning rounds the next day kept him aware of each minute. It was as if he had been waiting for the call. He was shaking his head, he told me, knowing the news even before he brought the receiver to his ear.

His brothers, all in the eldest brother's house, crowded around the green rotary phone. I could visualize the side table, the betel nut partly shaved in its silver tray, the niece's *Stardust* facedown on the couch arm. The connection was a good one, but both sides yelled, partly from habit, partly from the logic of the international call, longer distance, louder voice. In our cavernously dark house with its empty rooms, Abhi yelled *Hullo, hullo, hullo* into every pause and crackle. His yelling and their yelling kept back the grief, like torches waved at a feral animal. I hurried downstairs and picked up the kitchen handset so I could hear, too. Abhi's brothers were talking in the background, saying, *Tell him he doesn't have to come.* Abhi insisted he would. They all heard him and insisted he shouldn't, an almost panicked shouting at the phone—the journey was too exhausting, he would fall ill, it was too expensive, how would he get more days off? Abhi tried to speak into this stock-exchange cacophony but resorted again to a *hullo, hullo,* as if the voices were interference and he needed to reestablish the connection. His eldest brother, who must have calmed the others with a hand gesture, reminded Abhi that it was summer. The rites were scheduled for the same day.

There was no way he could make it in time. They would be out of their white kameezes and the ritual tilaks would be washed off their foreheads. I was upstairs again by this time, my arm around Abhi. He nodded at the impossibility and said nothing, his head on one hand, in grief or exhaustion. The other end of the line erupted in *hullo, hullo, hullo*. Abhi had dropped the phone and started shaking under my touch. His brothers hung up, assuming the line was dead.

PART THREE

SEEDTIME

It's not that there aren't fights. There are. They happen unexpectedly. Put me and Mala together for long enough, something will trigger it. I do not mind the arguments at first. They are like a new pain that takes the mind off the old pain. A fight with Mala is worth being able to forget, for a time, that I am Mala's dying mother. This one is about Amber. All I do is mention that she called. Maybe there is too much praise in my tone.

Mala doesn't look up from her chopping. "Amber called, hm? What did she say?"

"She was just checking on me. She had the boys get on and talk to me one by one." I smile. "You should have heard Raj. Have you heard him sing his songs? Amber sent us a video clip of him singing 'Old King Cole.'"

Mala looks up. "Really? When was that?"

"Just this week. Tuesday."

She nods and looks down. "Did Ronak get on the phone, too?"

I shake my head. "He was at work."

From here we go on to talk of other things. How Ronak works such long hours, how Mala's call schedule is going to get lighter now that they are adding a partner. The chopping is done, so we move to the gas range. Things have gotten going when she skips back to an earlier point in the conversation.

"Does she call often?"

"Amber? Very often. She's very conscientious, always checking up on me."

Mala nods at this. I realize that what I thought was curiosity and chitchat is really Mala investigating a rival, territorial. As if there could ever be our kind of closeness (a quarrelsome closeness though it sometimes has been) between me and Ronak's American wife. "How often does she call? Every day?"

"Not every day."

"And Ronak?"

"You're the only one who calls me every day."

"About Amber, you know, it's not like she's working. Why isn't she here more?"

I do not wish to defend Amber—at this point, I can tell it will annoy Mala if I do—but I feel I should point the facts out, at least. "The boys have school. And she wouldn't want to take them away from Ronak. He would miss them. They come as a family when they come."

"I would be here way more if I had the time, kids and all."

"I know that. But Amber isn't my own daughter like you. You can't hold her to the same standard. It's a long drive with three children."

"It'd be a long drive with two. I mean, it's not like she works and has that on top of everything."

"Are you angry with her?"

Her movements have gotten wider and more decisive over the course of our conversation. It's in the way she dumps the diced green peppers into a hot pan, then grabs the handle and shakes their sizzle; in the way her elbows come out when forcing my clove jar open. Just as I ask Mala if she's angry, she touches a hot surface. She says "shit" twice under her breath, shaking her hand. She sucks her thumb.

"Cold water," I say nervously, "cold water!"

"Relax, Mom. It's nothing."

"Put it under cold water."

She goes to the faucet. I hurry behind her, trying to see the burn. The worry makes my voice a little too loud. My next words come out more aggressively than I mean them.

"Do you see what happened? You can't cook while you are angry like that. You will always do something to yourself."

"What makes you think I was angry?"

"Let me see. Let me see."

"I wasn't angry."

I turn the pink, raw burn to the light. By reflex, I make a few quick, muted clicks with my tongue; she pulls back her hand, and I realize it might seem a tsk-tsk about her conduct and not pity for her pain.

"Let me get the ice pack."

We are soon sitting knees to knees, her hand in my hands, a towel between the icepack and her skin. I press and lift.

"I wasn't angry," she says.

The phone rings. We look at it on the table. She reaches over with her good hand. "It's Ronak." She brings the phone to her ear. "What's up?"

I can faintly hear his voice. "Mom there?"

"Yeah. She's right here. What's going on?"

"Are they there yet?"

"Who?"

"The guys I sent. They should be there. I just got off the phone with them."

"What guys?"

I hear a noise outside. It's either on our driveway or on the street just beyond the house. I leave Mala's hand on the ice pack and towel and investigate through the blinds. The sound was the slam of the ramp from a landscaper's truck.

"He sent someone to mow the lawn?" I ask incredulously.

Mala holds out the phone. "He wants to talk to you."

I put it to my ear. "What is this, Ronak?"

"Hey, Mom."

"Who are these landscapers?"

"You know how we'd been talking about coming over this weekend, when Mala and family were over? I was kind of sorry it fell through. I mean, I felt bad—I felt really bad, saying I'd come and then backing out, so I thought, what would Mom want?"

"Ronak, you know you don't have to get me anything."

Mala is eyeing the pair of landscapers busying themselves on the flatbed. Another pickup truck has parked behind them.

"I wanted to, Mom. I knew you weren't getting to garden this year. I'm having these guys do the whole front yard and backyard. And your garden."

My mouth drops open.

Mala looks at me. "What did he say?"

I am still listening to Ronak. "They're doing flowers, mulch, everything. And there's some really nice stuff they're going to do out front, too. I've gone over everything with them, but if you have something specific you want, go ahead and tell them. This is going to look nice."

I sit down with excitement and pleasure and above all a thrill: he thought about me. Ronak was thinking about *me*. I cover the phone and tell Mala breathlessly, "He's hired these men to plant my garden!" I speak into the phone again. "Ronak, how much will this all cost?"

"Please, Mom. Let this be my gift, okay?"

Mala is smiling and shaking her head. The coarse landscapers walk past our window in work boots and denim. One of them has a shovel on his shoulder. The others, in the driveway, are off-loading mulch.

"Ronak," I say, "I want to pay for part of this."

"This is an early Mother's Day present. Think of it like that."

"Let me have the phone," Mala says, grinning. Her hand is out. I give her the phone.

"Was this Amber's idea? Fess up."

"Look, can't I do something nice for once?"

"You know, while you're in this generous mood, I wouldn't mind a pool back home in St. Louis."

"Ha ha. Sorry, Sis, piggybank's empty."

"Run out of retirees to swindle?"

"Now Mala, you leave my retirees out of this. They're making sound investments on sound advice."

"Seriously, this is pretty amazing, Ronak. There's, like, an army out here."

"I told them I wanted everything done as quickly as possible. They shouldn't be there more than two days."

"You know this isn't a trade-off for getting your butt out here, right?"

"I know that, Mala. Jesus."

"Just checking."

"She happy?"

Pause. "Yeah. Ecstatic's more like it. She's watching them at the window right now. Palms on the glass, like a little kid."

"Good."

"You're still coming out here to see her."

"I know. Next month. This month wasn't good. I tried. It just wasn't happening."

"Next month. We're coordinating."

"Right. Next month."

Amber's parents moved to Pittsburgh late in life, after Don's company went under and he had to find another job. Their relatives were still in the Ohio area. So one Memorial Day weekend, when Don's brother Dave was hosting the family get-together, we were invited to their place outside Circleville.

This was early, right after Ronak and Amber had their first son, when Ronak was more willing to travel. By the time their third was born, he declared traveling with three kids, and all their paraphernalia, "more pain than it's worth." Abhi and I were a couple, and he expected us to visit his house in New York more often than he brought the family to us. The ratio ended up being our three visits to his one. This ratio did not apply to Amber's parents—he went with her to Pittsburgh every Christmas and every Memorial Day weekend, both very important holidays in her family.

That year, it had seemed appropriate to invite us, what with the grandchildren so close, but I suspect Ronak himself wasn't behind the invitation. He called to say we didn't have to go if we didn't want to, that he would make sure they "swung up" to our house for a day, but I told him I had already said yes. Abhi spent the long drive sulking. He wished I hadn't accepted. He claimed they hadn't expected us to say yes, but I said Dottie had phoned me personally, how could I say no? If they had sent the invitation through Ronak, I could have made an excuse. But to lie to her face?

"You were on the phone," said Abhi, shaking his head. "It wasn't to her face."

"I can't just lie to her like that, not outright. You saw the caller ID. Next time, you take the phone."

He fell silent and sulked for a few more exits, thinking, maybe, of some problem he was leaving unsolved in his air-conditioned study. He was only twelve months from finishing the proof that would put him in the news; he must have been able to see some outline of it. I do remember his constant impatience back then, his reversions to the temper of our early years.

The temperature, when we got to the cookout at 6 PM (far later than the time we were told), was still well over ninety degrees. The sun burned over the trees. We had to park on gravel among aging Buicks and Chryslers and a muddy pickup truck. We stayed inside, savoring the last of the cool air while the smell of sunscreen filled our car.

Outside, Amber's relatives seemed impervious to the sun. Her uncle had grown rich because he owned a plant that "rendered" chickens. *Render*, Abhi told me, was a way of saying *kill*. I could not stop myself from imagining the factory: a high-ceilinged warehouse, full of hundreds of calm, clucking chickens; then a hole in the floor would start to roar, a vacuum with a shredder inside it, and the birds would startle aloft like snow inside a paperweight . . .

Here, in the empty part of the state between Columbus and Cincinnati, Amber's uncle owned a large amount of land. This was his pond. Dave had sawed and sanded his own picnic benches out of raw planks. A dozen or so young nephews and nieces were taking turns on the family Jet Ski. The ones who were waiting did not stick to the shade, running about barefoot with giant green and orange squirt guns. One boy got ambushed as he dunked the gun's water barrel in the pond. He jiggled and raged as he screwed it back into place and took off for vengeance. Everyone's skin had changed color: some went pink, others gold. The boys were obese and buzz-cut with sagging boy breasts. I could trace them to their fathers in sleeveless shirts, guffawing on the picnic benches, the upper arm fat flattened against their sides. Abhi and I felt we were approaching a stranger's party until we saw Ronak, green beer bottle in hand, chatting with Amber's brother and manning the grill. Systematically he turned four reddish patties over to air the browned meat and black bars. Then he set the spatula aside for the tongs. A small girl was holding out her Styrofoam plate for a hot dog.

One of the women watching the Jet Ski, a small child shirtless on her hip, separated herself and hurried up to us. "Mom and Dad! Thanks for coming out here!"

Some of the relatives turned to us. Don and Dottie approached from farther off. Ronak turned at the grill and waved. Amber, Dottie, and Don, after the usual hugs and pleasantries, walked us over to Ronak, introducing us to two elderly aunts on the way. Ronak pushed the patties around a little and came over to hug us.

"Are you hungry?" he asked. "I made sure we got veggie patties, Mom."

The quicker we ate, the quicker we could leave. "Sure, Ronak. That would be good."

"Hey, Chuckie. Get me those Boca patties."

Amber's cousin pulled a red cardboard box from the orange Igloo. Ice cubes and Heineken cans shifted aside as his forearm rose dripping. Chuckie pinched the limp cardboard with distaste.

"Had to keep 'em cool somehow," said Amber. "But don't worry, they're individually wrapped."

"Sure." I felt odd speaking there. Everyone seemed to be happy to see us, at least those who knew us, but I still felt out of place.

"Dad? What are you up for?"

"Veggie burger is fine."

"You sure? You want to save room for the chicken? It's up next."

"Veggie burger is fine," said Abhi stiffly. He indulged in

meat sometimes, but he didn't like to do it in front of me. He feared I would judge him. I think Ronak knew this but in his excitement had forgotten. He had also forgotten, for example, that we did not like to see him drink beer.

Chuckie took an interest when Ronak made room for the Boca patties on the grill where he had been cooking beef. They were pale brown and partly thawed.

"What are they made of?" Chuckie asked, looking right at Abhi.

"Soya," said Abhi.

"What?"

"Soya, soya."

"Soy beans," Ronak translated.

Chuckie took another look and crinkled his tiny nose. "Beans?"

"You want to try one, Chuckie?" Amber demanded sternly. "They're pretty good."

"No way I'm eating that."

"Crinkle your nose again and you will. I'll see to it."

Chuckie hurried off.

"Isn't she great?" Ronak grinned.

"Chuckie needs manners, always has. I'm gonna have a talk with his ma."

"No, Amber, that isn't necessary, please." I feared that we would be the cause of discord in their family. I had not seen this no-nonsense side of Amber before, and I was a little taken aback. Just then Don brought over his brother Dave.

"So you're Roan's mom and dad! Welcome! Grab some food!"

"Mom, Dad, this is my uncle Dave."

"I'm the one they named your grandkid for!" After a long silence, he pointed back and forth, "Dave—Dev. Dave—Dev. Yeah?"

He was intentionally pronouncing them the same way. Abhi smiled and laughed. I took the cue and did so, too, noiselessly. Now what?

"How was the drive down?"

Abhi did the answering. "Two hours or so."

"Great day for a cookout, eh?"

"Yes, yes." Abhi, reminded of the heat, wiped sweat and sunscreen off his forehead with his thin forearm. The arm hair lay matted, swept toward his wrist.

"Y'all brought your swimsuits, didn't you?"

Abhi and I looked at each other, startled. "No, no we did not, I'm afraid."

"Don and I're 'bout ready to kick the kids off that thing," said Dave. He looked at me. "Y'ever been on a Jet Ski?"

I shook my head.

"Aw, God, you're missing out!" He looked concerned; I feared he would make me. "It is *fun*."

"Hey, is there any corn left?" Ronak asked Amber. "Mom loves corn."

Dave overheard and turned his head, birdlike. His wild gray hair fell forward over his creased forehead. "We out a corn?"

Dottie said in a low, discreet voice to him, "They don't eat meat."

Amber took a few steps to check one of the tables and shook her head. "It's all gone."

"Shoot," said Ronak. He knelt by a cardboard box beside the grill. It was full of lightweight husk-strips, yellow-green and hairy with fibers. His hand rummaged inside the box. "Yeah, I'm pretty sure that was the last of it."

"We should have saved you some," Dottie said mournfully, touching my arm.

Dave looked alarmed. "No problem, there's more. I'll get some. Hold on."

"It's not needed," I pleaded, raising my palms.

"Just a few minutes in the truck."

"Really, it's not needed." But Dave was off, digging the keys from the back pocket of his shorts. I turned to Amber, then to Dottie, who sipped from a Coke can. I felt worse when the truck started and Dave pulled out.

"He didn't have to go," I said.

"It's right up the road," Dottie assured me. "Do you like it this hot?"

"A little cooler."

"How's Mala?"

"She is doing her medical school."

"She must be so busy."

"Very busy, all of the time."

"But you must be so proud of these children of yours."

"Yes. Very much so."

"I was just telling one of my girlfriends the other day, you should write a book."

Dev began to cry. I hurried to Amber's side and put my hands out. She bobbed and sang, softly and in tune, "Momma's gonna buy you a mockingbird." She acted as though she hadn't seen my offer; she was wearing sunglasses, so I could not see if she had. Dev did not stop. I touched her shoulder, and she gave him to me. He did not stop with me, though I rubbed his back clockwise, which had always worked with Ronak. Dottie drank from her Coke can again as Dev grew louder in my arms. Of course he did; we saw Ronak so rarely, the infant was hardly familiar with me. Dottie came and rubbed Dev's downy head but did not offer to take him. "Someone's had a long day!" she said. Ronak had once told me how Dottie was no help to Amber. Dottie, according to him, was a very lazy woman. Amber came back with a pacifier from one of the side pockets of her mommy bag. I wanted to be the one who calmed Dev, so I took it from her hand and guided it to his scream. The nub pressed the tense tongue until the tension gave. My fingertip lifted when the plastic began to pulse. I should not have relaxed. Dev spat it out. Amber and I both moved quickly to catch it, but it bounced off my hand and fell in the grass, and after that there was no using it.

"I know what he needs," said Amber. I gave Dev back and he went quiet. Dottie's bland smile had not changed. Then Dev started crying again, which redeemed me. Amber carried him past the picnic tables to a private patch of green, grabbing a folded sheet from her bag as she passed it. She sat cross-legged with her back to everyone, leaned forward, and hid him under the sheet. Dev hushed and fed, small hand intrigued by the luminous white cloth. I watched her, alone with her child.

Dave returned with the emergency ears of corn. They swung two from each hand, like rabbits. The high dust began to thin and shift behind his truck, which had its front wheels in the grass now and panted in place. Abhi and I apologized again, but Dave knelt and said, "No prob, no prob," as he ripped the husks off the corn with a swift, concentrated violence. His arms were unexpectedly muscular, and his hands looked rough and dry as unsanded wood, and overlarge, too, as in those pictures of acromegaly in my old textbooks. I grew afraid. Was he angry at having to fetch the corn? I moved closer to Abhi. Dave stood up, laid the plastic-yellow uncooked ears in the space Ronak had made for them, and smiled at us. "There you go," he said. "Won't be ready same time as the burgers, though."

"These are pretty much done," said Ronak, spatula tilting one patty. "Plates are right there."

Dave told us to enjoy as he walked toward the pond. Don and Dottie, now that we had food, felt free to go off as well. Ronak slid the slightly ragged-looking patty onto a half of bun. I suddenly wished I didn't have to eat it. I wished I could limit myself to the clean, safe slices of limp tomato, the lettuce, the pale hoops and arcs of onion, the disks of sweet-and-sour sandwich pickle . . . what a happier, cleaner sandwich that would have made. I sat next to Abhi and lifted the sandwich and thought about the beef that had been cooked on the same rods. What juices and oils . . . what seepage must have come off those beef burgers and onto mine? Meat as I had glimpsed it before, in supermarkets, came to mind: pink, shrink-wrapped on a Styrofoam rectangle, label-gunned with a barcode and a price. Ground-up muscle, shaped into a palm-sized patty . . . what India's villagers did to cow dung was in America done to the cow herself. I ruminated on slum women forming black-green cakes between their hands and slapping them on a squat wall. My Boca burger sat between sesame buns, half covered by wet lettuce, tomato slice sliding on ketchup . . . I had bought veggie burgers dozens of times. I kept them as backup, good for a quick brunch when Abhi didn't want me "holing up in the kitchen." Yet they were deliberate imitations—in flavor, form, texture, look, down to the fake grill-marks—of something that revolted me. I wouldn't eat fake dung if they made it out of soy. But fake dead cow? I purchased it, I microwaved it on a covered saucer. And on that picnic bench, I was eating it. The mingled seepages merged, in my mind and mouth, the fake flesh and the true flesh.

Ronak, bringing the corn, sat down next to us to keep us company. Maybe Don had relieved him at the grill so he could be with us. Or maybe Ronak had asked him to take over so Amber's relatives wouldn't think he was neglecting us. He didn't have much to say. I put butter on the corn. At home, when I made corn, we rubbed each length with a lemon wedge dipped in chili powder and salt. All they had here was butter, salt, and pepper. Ronak was waiting for me to eat, so I did, all of both, but my dizzy distaste for the soy burger kept me from enjoying the corn. I looked down and discreetly picked the shreds from my teeth, my fingernail drawn vertically in the space between my incisors. I felt ashamed, as if my etiquette might be judged. I fought back nausea the rest of the evening. I was never so sustainedly nauseous again until years later. By which I mean, until now.

Ronak sat beside us until a new relative, later even than we had been, arrived to a small fluster of high fives and handshakes. This was Rob, I would learn later, the cousin who lived in Cincinnati. I did not learn whether he had a family of his own; he had driven up alone. Rob looked coarser than the others. He had not shaved, and he wore beige work boots under his jeans, even in this heat. Ronak rose and left us when he heard the others greeting him, a quick "I'll be right back" after he had stood. The green beer bottle, which he had kept off the table, in the grass at his heel, went with him. He stood outside the cluster of men, bottle in front of him, navel level. I saw his hand false-start for a shake then drop to his side again. Moments later he saw his opening and shook hands with the celebrity. To my surprise, they started talking.

"We shouldn't have come," said Abhi quietly, in Gujarati.

I felt the flush up my neck and cheeks. "I will say no next time, okay? We were invited."

"No. I mean for his sake."

I said nothing. Ronak was still talking. Rob said something that made him laugh.

Abhi turned his corncob past a pocked-black patch and carefully placed the next scrape of his teeth. He is very finicky about burned food. He spoke with the corn raised to conceal his lips.

"Don't keep staring."

"He is so many people," I said. "They are all bundled up in him."

Amber, seeing us unattended, buttoned herself and left her place on the grass. She took Ronak's seat and showed me Dev sleeping in her arms. By reflex, my hands swept the air over his sleeping face and rose as fists to my temples and opened. This was how to collect stares of envy off a child and gather them onto oneself. Envy works the ruin of what it envies if measures are not taken. Blessings bring risk. Amber was used to this old-fashioned, superstitious precaution of mine. When Dev was born, I tapped his cheek, as I had done Ronak's and Mala's, with a pinky-fingertip of kohl. One had to satisfy envy with a fake birth blemish. *Move on, envy, this one is flawed. Stare at someone else's grandchild.*

That night, back at home, I could not soap my lips enough. I brushed a long time. In bed, a single oily belch made the toothpaste taste vanish. Finally I knelt over the toilet and rejected it: the only meal ever served me by my son.

Amber visited us the first week in January, driving straight from her family in Pittsburgh. Ronak had not told her any earlier. Christmas Eve, when I cried and spilled it all, the tears and the words made me understand what Abhi's mother had felt when she rang her bell and picked haplessly at her wet bedding. The closest analogy has to be that: I was incontinent of tears, incontinent of secrets. How to clean this up without getting other people involved?

All four of us had sat on the bed. The original four, so rarely reunited. At one in the morning, squinting groggily at our sleepless high noon (we had the closet light, room light, and bathroom light all on), Sachin showed up in the doorway. I began again. We weren't ready to talk about Christmas morning and the presents until 3 AM.

"We cannot tell Vivek and Shivani until later," I said. "They have been looking forward to this for so long."

Mala nodded at Sachin. "We have to ease them into it."

Abhi said, "Children can always sense something is up."

I buried my face in my hands.

"But we will manage it," Abhi hurried to say. "We have come this far."

"I'm not calling Amber then, either," Ronak added quietly.

"Of course not," I said. "Let her and the kids have a normal Christmas over there."

"I mean, this isn't an emergency, is it?"

"You can tell Amber when the time is right."

"When will the time be right?" Ronak looked at me uneasily. He chewed a hangnail on his index finger. This was one thing we hadn't discussed. "Mom? Did they say . . . ?"

I shrugged and shook my head.

"So we don't have a time frame?"

Mala interrupted, her voice very high. "Tell Amber when you're all back in New York, okay? It's past three." With a glance she checked her wrist and touched her pajama waistband. She wasn't wearing a wristwatch or a pager; it was a confused reflex from the stress. Sachin sensed the same thing I did and held her upper arm, steadying her on the inside. "Look at us, we need to *sleep*," she said incredulously. "It's so late. It's too late."

Sachin nodded. He stood with his hand still on her arm. "Mala is right. The kids are going to wake up at seven."

Actually Vivek woke up at six thirty, Shivani a few minutes after. I insisted on handling the camera; I wanted no image of me, not even a glimpse while the photographer panned from one gift to the next. The video I took never leaves their bright faces, never tilts up to the three too-wise observers in the scene. There's one snippet of Sachin's profile as he kneels and stacks scraps of glittery red wrapping paper. Ronak doesn't look up as he scissors the hard plastic around some batteries and fits them in a sleeping puppy's back. He sets the puppy down, and I take the camera to its level. Its eyelids open. It lives.

We adults opened our presents hours later, off camera. It was really just part of the cleanup around the tree, which Abhi stripped and packed away shortly after lunch.

Ronak stayed through the New Year and called Amber as she was leaving Pittsburgh. She took an exit and merged west while still on the phone with him.

Amber's sons banged their boots against the outside of the house before setting them on the mat. Even Raj, who was only a little older than Shivani, imitated his brothers. Dev, the eldest, held a broken model airplane in his hands, both wings, one wing rotor, and the intricately etched, minutely stickered body. The boys gave us hugs on tiptoe and accepted kisses on their foreheads. We kissed them on their foreheads the way we had seen Dottie and Don do. Dev used to flinch and wipe away the cheek-crushing kisses we gave, but we hadn't stopped and changed until we saw the hello kiss he was used to.

Dev held up the model airplane. "Do you have any superglue here?"

Raj interjected, stammering with eagerness, "We, we, we, we need to fix it."

"Let's see what my Air Force Repair Shop can do," said

Abhi, taking his reading glasses out to see a wing's break site up close. He brought the rotor to the engine to see if it might click back into place and spin, but it didn't. "First tell me this: Did it get shot down over Iraq or Afghanistan?"

Dev said patiently, "It's a World War Two bomber. They flew those in World War Two."

"And it's *Aff*ghanistan, not *Uff*ghanistan," said Nik.

Abhi glanced up over his glasses, eyebrows high, as if startled at this information. He nodded. "So, Germany."

Raj pointed at the plane. "And, and, and my great-grampa flew those in the sky."

"Wow!" Abhi lifted the plane high and made it wobble and descend. "Help, help, the Nazis are shooting me down! Was your great-grandpa okay? Did he parachute out?"

"My great-grampa," said Dev, "served in the Pacific."

Amber stood very close to me. She had not yet fully detached from her hug. "Tell Dada how it broke, boys."

"Nik dropped it."

"No I didn't! Ma!"

Amber didn't raise her voice. "Dev." All three boys went quiet. "What kind of truth do we tell?"

All three: "The whole truth."

"So what's the whole truth? Dev?"

"We were fighting over the plane."

"No matter, no matter. Let's see what we can do, shall we?" Abhi turned to me. "Do you remember that little . . . that tiny screwdriver you used on my eyeglasses?"

"The drawer closest to the fridge. The superglue is there, too."

He went to get it, trailed by the boys, who kept to an orderly line. Amber turned to talk again, but I followed Abhi, and she stayed next to me. He began pushing some things around.

"In the tray with the scissors," I said.

"Found it," he said, holding up the repair kit and super-glue. He set them on the dining table. The boys climbed wordlessly into the other chairs and observed him. Amber and I found our way onto the couch for hushed words. I asked her how much she had told the three boys.

"I haven't told them anything, Mom. You can see. I wouldn't have let them come here without making you cards, if I'd told them."

"Why do they think they're here, then?"

"They think it's a surprise."

"When are you going to tell them?" She put her hands on my hands. The contrast between our skins startled me. "Do you want me to tell them?"

"No. I think . . . we need to ease them into this."

This was the phrase Mala had used. They had been talking. That was only right; they were both mothers with children to safeguard against too much knowledge too quickly.

"You're right, Amber. We can take our time."

"And you would prefer to have them like this, right? Not knowing?"

Had she thought of this on her own? Did she know me that well? It couldn't be. She must have talked to Ronak and Mala. They had told her I wanted the family over without this pall, so she was giving me her three boys as I longed for them, care-free, no shadow. I stared at Ronak and Amber's children. Amber parted their hair on the left, unlike Ronak's because he now combed his straight back. When he combed it like that, he looked even less Indian. Maybe Latino, you would think, or a particularly handsome Iranian; quite a few friends used to tell me, even when he was a boy, that he didn't look Indian. They meant this as praise. I had always admired the sharply drawn features of half-white, half-Indian children. An

all-Indian child who looked like Ronak's boys would have been
thought very beautiful indeed, back home—such fair skin,
such light eyes, he will grow up to be a film star! But knowledge of one white parent changed the way you saw the beauty.
It seemed foreign, and you didn't compare the child to Indian
children. Your eyes picked out in the face what was Indian
(the nose, the deep-set eyes) and what was white (the jawline,
the cheekbones). You parsed the beauty. Or I—I parsed the
beauty. Usually just for a split second, when I saw the boys
after a long absence—which way are they going? Is there any
trace of us left? With Dev and Nikhil, I would say no. I would
not think them Indian if I did not know who their father is.
Ronak's good looks had that disadvantage: he brought no indis-
soluble Indianness of nose or chin to the mix. Raj had something of Ronak in him. But so had Nik at that age, and he had
lost it by five. They became more Amber as they grew older,
and not just on the outside.

"Mom?"

"Yes?"

"Is everything all right?"

I nodded. I wondered how hurt she would be if she knew
my thoughts just then. Could anyone love anyone if our skulls
were clear glass? "What will the boys eat?" I asked. I was more
able then—the spread was less and the first injections were a
week in my future.

"We stopped by at Hardee's an hour ago. I hate giving
them that food, but the boys were getting ornery."

"An hour? They might be hungry again. I made my veggie
lasagna when I heard you were coming."

"I doubt they're hungry. Boys?" They looked at her. "Anyone hungry for lasagna?"

Dev and Raj murmured "No," already distracted by Abhi,
who was laying a careful trail of superglue along the wing.

Nikhil gave a *blech*, pointing his finger in his mouth. This made Amber say his name; he shut his mouth, but he didn't look at her.

"They did eat a lot," Amber apologized.

"Did you eat? Can I get you a piece? It's very fresh."

"Um . . ."

"It's very fresh. And very healthy—squash, zucchini, spinach. I used light ricotta."

"Sure, I could probably eat a piece."

"Only if you are hungry."

"I'd love a small piece, Mom."

"Abhi? Do you want any lasagna?"

"I am contributing to the war effort," he said, his glasses on his nose. "No time for a break when the Germans are on the march."

"The Japanese," Dev said impatiently.

The fluted pasta corners had not been cooked through properly and were dry and hard as plastic. I cut Amber a soft piece from the center. I microwaved it twenty seconds so her tongue would know it was fresh. I had kept it bland for the boys but I knew Amber liked spicy, so I offered her the crushed red pepper shaker and the grinder for black pepper. She agreed to some orange juice. Her forkfuls were slow to rise. She chewed slowly. I realized she was as full of burger as the boys but eating for my sake. She even showed an interest in the recipe, meatless though it was, lasagna that wasn't really lasagna. When she was done, she sipped her orange juice and watched Abhi. He was trying to figure out how to reaffix the rotor to the wing engine in a way that would still let it spin. For the first time I can remember, I bent down and kissed Amber's brown hair, something I did naturally to Mala.

Amber stiffened briefly. Her glass paused at her lip. She turned and beamed up at me with a joy and gratitude whose intensity was startling, almost disproportionate—a simple press of my lips! She had seen me kiss Mala that way in the past, I think. I did it absentmindedly sometimes, if I happened to find Mala sitting. The habit had originated in her high school years: she would be bent over calculus or American history, and I would visit her with a bowl of grapes and a kiss. Amber I had never kissed that way, not until that afternoon—such a small morsel of affection, but it made her rejoice. I never should have starved her.

The time Mala and I spend now, in the kitchen, is sometimes sweet, sometimes bitter. The day after the landscapers arrived to work in the backyard, Mala and I go from tenderness to argument without intending to. I am about to drop some cumin in the dahl when Mala stops my wrist.

"Wait, wait," she says. "How much are you putting in?"

My fingers are pinched together. I turn them up slightly. "This much." I drop it in.

"No, Mom, wait. I need to know how much that was."

"Why?"

"So I know for the future."

"It doesn't matter how much exactly." I pinch my fingers and open them again. "This much. You use your sense."

"I don't *have* a sense." She points at the notepad she has at her elbow. "That's why I'm writing all this down for myself."

"Write down 'some.'"

"'Some'? How much is 'some'?"

"Write down 'a pinch.' Even cookbooks use 'a pinch.'"

"Cookbook writers aren't as neurotic as me." She picks up the stacked plastic measuring spoons and holds out the smallest one. "Here. Sprinkle the same amount into this so I can see, at least."

I do, even though I feel silly doing it, and the grains barely fill the depression. She makes a notation. I roll my eyes. "Are you going to measure it in micrograms, Doctor?"

"If I could, I would." She sets down the pen. "I want to get things exact."

"However you make things will be right."

"I don't want right." She takes up the ladle and stirs. "I want exact."

She keeps stirring, maybe so she doesn't have to look at me.

"I want *you*."

I want to hug her when she says that. I hold back. I see she does not like the heat. I tear a square of Bounty off the roll and touch her forehead.

"There is a fan in the basement," I say.

"Oh, I'm fine. This is nothing."

"It gets hotter when you have so many flames going. But it goes quicker."

She blows upward through the corner of her mouth, and her hair skips off her forehead. "I know. How did women cook in India?"

"It could get bad in the summer. But there you don't notice so much."

"No?"

I shrug. "You can get used to something there that you could not bear here."

"How about when you've been here a while, and go back?"

"You cannot bear it anymore."

"I bet," she says. "Like the way men treat us."

"Who has treated us badly? No one ever treated us badly. You were a princess when we would take you there."

"I mean, in general. The way men treat women. Having to cover your face and all that stuff."

"It was just the way. Now no one covers their face. And it is no nicer of men here to expect women to show their bodies off."

"That's one way of looking at it, I guess." She stirs the dahl. A thumb's length of dark cinnamon stick swims to the surface in the ladle's wake before going under again. "But what about cooking?"

"No one cooks now unless they want to. They all have servants and Maggi noodles there."

"But in the old days. It's not just hot. It's *lonely*. If I didn't have you here, I'm pretty sure I'd be lonely."

Is she thinking of the years I stood at this gas range, the children upstairs or at practice, Abhi in his study? *I was never lonely*, I want to tell her. *I should have been, but I never was.* She is still reflecting aloud as she taps the ladle and sets it in the bowl.

"And having to do this for the men every day. No frozen meals, no eating out tonight because you're tired or don't feel like cooking. That's how it used to be. It's servitude, is what it is."

I feel a flush creeping up my face. "It may have been that way for some. But I know for a fact that it can be different."

She looks up in alarm. "Wait, Mom—you know I'm not talking about *you*, right? Or us? I'm generalizing. And you're right, I shouldn't generalize like that."

"It can be the opposite. Complete opposite. When I cook, I am the giver. The husband, the son—he comes to you with a bare plate. All empty inside. The man is the receiver."

Mala raises an eyebrow; she has decided against backing down. "Or the *taker*. Giver and *taker*."

"Only if it is not a gift."

"If you *have* to give something, day after day, it's hardly a gift anymore."

"If there is love, then it is a gift."

"Why can't we call it what it is? You can do a chore with love. You can do that chore while full of love for your family."

"It is not a chore."

"I'm not saying *chore* in the bad sense. I'm saying it literally. A routine thing you have to do."

"Do you want to stop? Do you want to go rest? I can finish this."

"Mom, please. That's not what I meant."

"This is play for my left hand!" I have translated verbatim, in my rising anger, an old Indian expression I would have used if I were speaking Gujarati. It sounds awkward. I switch into Gujarati, and I am suddenly freer. "I can finish this. You can go upstairs."

My shift to Gujarati is an escalation. Mala knows it well. I do not want to shout. In another time, before my illness, she herself would have begun to shout. But I am already exhausted by my indignation, and she drops to one knee beside my chair and presses her lips to my hand. "Forget I said that, Mom. Forget the whole thing. I'm sorry." Dying is a kind of royalty. I stroke her cheek. She waits, looking up at my face in the stovetop light. The pressure cooker whistles, and she rises.

It had gone through my mind when I was taking care of my mother. It must be going through Mala's. *I need to do this, or I am going to feel guilty later.* That is what it is like for us good daughters. Not just guilt over the past, but fear of future guilt. Daughterhood has one natural resource, and that is guilt. Hourglass sand blows over events and words and, a million years later, there are guilt deposits, black guilt anywhere you sink a drill. So much burning out of something buried so long.

Old quarrels; forget them. But there are new quarrels, too, things Mala asks that she wouldn't if she didn't feel newly close to me. One afternoon, without preamble, she pauses a carrot on the slope of the grater. By now it bears a nib like a calligraphy pen's.

"Why did you give it up?"

She starts grating the carrot again, then lifts the grater to check the pile of shreds below.

"Give up what?" I ask.

"Medicine."

I swallow. This is not something I expected. Does she know it still hurts? Decades, and it still makes me flush with shame. "They did not let me past the exam," I say quietly. (*They did not let me past* is far easier to say than *I failed*.)

"You could have taken it again. After we'd grown up a little."

I shrug.

"Was it Dad? Did he tell you not to?"

I shake my head.

"You shouldn't have given up. You could have done it."

"I did other things."

"You're brilliant. You're just as smart as Dad."

"I did things."

"Well, cooking and cleaning. I mean—"

"There is nothing wrong with cooking and cleaning."

"Don't get mad. Please don't get mad."

"I am not mad."

"Yes you are. Look at you. Mom."

"I am not mad. I am just saying there is nothing wrong with what I have done with my life."

"I wasn't saying that either. I was just asking *why*."

"Why this *why*? Why does *why* matter?"

"I'm sorry. This came out wrong."

"I am fine."

"I—I wanted you to know I think you're brilliant."

I stare at her. Anger. I feel my healthiest in months during my anger. I forget everything. I actually feel strong. "You don't think I'm brilliant, Mala."

"I do."

"You don't."

Anger helps me stride out of the kitchen—and abandons me on the carpet. I sit, instantly exhausted, on the couch. Mala turns off the gas and rinses her hands. She is helpless in the kitchen without me.

I am in a sulk. I know I am in a childish irrational sulk, but I can't help myself. I don't like knowing she sees that old failure when she looks at me. I do not want my humiliation anywhere in her memory. How will she respect me? Respect, respect: I sound like Abhi fifteen years ago, always shouting at the mute children for respect. I shouldn't have gotten angry. My heart knocks my ribs in the after-excitement. I felt shame and showed anger. I shouldn't have done that. Part of me knows this one is my fault. But a bigger part of me wants to see if she will come apologize. That is childish, too. I wait. She comes. She sits next to me.

"I'm sorry. I shouldn't have brought that up."

"I know you are thinking the question, Mala. What else do I have, other than cooking and cleaning? Ask me."

"You have plenty of other things. You've read more books than . . . than anyone I know. And the garden—"

"What else do I have? Ask me."

"I don't want to ask you that."

"Ask me."

She rubs her temples. "What else do you have?"

"*You.*"

She shakes her head. "You were really storing that up, weren't you, Mom?"

I feel out of control. I am pushing her to see if she will ignore my outburst and stay close. I want to pull out of this conversation and repair us. So I say, "Don't talk to me right now. Go somewhere. Go," but this makes me sound even angrier—like I don't want her anywhere near, when really I want to protect her from the foulness inside me.

She is still shaking her head. "God. I never knew you had so much anger."

"Me? I have anger?" My voice is not holding up. Fresh anger and fresh shame melt together in an old, recognizable sadness. But I am still talking. "You are the angry one. All the time. You are angry. At everyone."

Even my Gujarati has broken down. I cannot bear the touch of her arms around me, or the way she presses my sobbing to her as if I hadn't been the first to argue. She feels guilt, maybe, that she brought this up. I wish a single question did not have the power to do this to me. I am overreacting. But my emotion is real and it measures what it measures. Mala murmurs as she holds me, and I want to be angry at how she dares put herself in this calm, consoling attitude after she has stirred me up this way. But I need her compassion as deeply as I need air. I wish it didn't feel this good to be held by her. I wish my sickness hadn't made me this dependent, even if she is my daughter. I want to be the compassionate one. I used to hold her during *her* crises. Her first C on a chemistry test. The meanness of other young girls, the sleepover that happened without her when she knew she was a topic of discussion. The time in medical school she totaled the Accord and staggered from the wreck marveling at her intact self and had the police drive her to her Histology final. Her despair at being single. I had consoled her, always, but now she is consoling me. I am grateful, and I am indignant. In time, as she kisses my scalp through my thinned hair, the gratitude overpowers everything else. I sit humbled in the embrace of my child. I nuzzle into her and go quiet, resisting nothing, drained. My cheek rests on her collarbone. My tears are on her neck.

Just when I settle into a new rhythm of days, I hear the click of luggage nubs against the hardwood. Sunday afternoon shines on blithely. The luggage comes downstairs, carried two pieces at a time. Then the handbags, the grandchildren's cartoon-colorful backpacks, the bags with snacks and bottled waters. Time to go. These are the things the parents have been packing upstairs, both cell phones diligently charged from the same wall outlet, Saturday's sunscreen-smelling clothes quarantined separately to wash at home. The departure has never left their minds. I am the only one who has gotten used to having them around. I grew shorter- and shorter-sighted all weekend, seeing no later than Saturday no matter how close Sunday approached. They got the next day's boarding passes online while I was still promising the grandchildren Neapolitan and Cookies & Cream, "but only after dinner."

The grandchildren and I live exclusively in the present. Saturday is Saturday. Sunday morning is Sunday morning. So for us, zipped luggage descending the stairs is a surprise. The children cry. They don't want to go home. They don't want the weekend to be over. I wish I were young enough to do that; it's what I feel, after all. But I am mature, so I nod and check the clock on the microwave; yes, it's time, don't be late.

Flight or drive, it's no use pleading. The times are there on the creased printout. Or else the drive's first leg has to be coordinated with Vivek and Shivani's after-lunch nap. The thinking is practical. The parents' need to leave hastens their farewell hugs.

Shivani is in her car seat. I tap the van window for a smile. I screen my temples against the tinted glass and make a face at Vivek. After the van pulls out, a window slides down so a hand can wave. The hand pulls in, the window slides up. All four profiles have turned toward home. Then the van is gone, but for a few beats afterward I am still waving. Abhi and I cross our arms and shuffle back into the house too big by two rooms again. Abhi turns on the television, but in vain. Not silent is not the same as full.

I still take care of the mail. My daily expedition is to bring it indoors. I open and sort it and pay the utilities and credit card bills. Abhi insists he can do it all online, just a few clicks on the tablet he carries around the floors now, but I don't want to let go of mailing our payments. The stamp may be a cracked bell, but up its edge is the word *FOREVER*. At some point during my overlong day, sealed indoors against the too-hot Ohio summer that quite recently was a too-cold Ohio spring, I pile the credit card solicitations and home improvement deals with the weekly SuperSaver circular; the utility and Amex bills with the bank and Scudder statements; the medical journals with the CME conference flyers: Alzheimer's in Maui, Sleep Medicine in Tampa, Cerebrovascular Thrombolysis in sunny San Diego.

I have a fourth category, for Abhi's mathematics-related mail. For years there was nothing at all. For six months, it filled its own bin. Since then, the mail has petered off. Intermittently, Abhi gets envelopes from strangers in faraway universities. These are separate from the e-mails, of course, and their attachments. Because he is (or was) a fellow amateur, other amateurs tend to send Abhi copies of the Unified Field.

I sort the occasional manila envelope from an obscure professor in Hungary or South Africa, addressed using small, closely packed capital letters. They never spell his name wrong.

Four times in May, I noticed the thin envelopes that meant payment for publication. I held each to the window light and could make out a check. The fourth check was from the London Mathematical Society.

"You've been doing a lot of good work recently, haven't you, Abhi?" I asked him when he got home. "You're getting papers published everywhere. London, too, I saw?"

He nodded as he unlaced his shoes. "How was the day? Did you do okay?"

"You aren't telling me the good news anymore. You used to tell me every time you got something accepted."

"Don't worry about those mailings."

"I still care. I still want to know if you are having more success, Abhi."

He slid one shoe over the heel, then the other. "Of course, I don't doubt it. I'm just saying you can put it in a pile. I can take care of it."

"Why didn't you tell me such good things were happening?"

He hooked a finger in his tie and loosened it. "It's a very long process. It gets read, it goes to peer review, the professors take their time. It comes back, they read what the professors said about it . . . It takes time. That is work I did last year. They only got back to me recently."

"The London Mathematical Society, Abhi! Isn't this a big thing?

"Yes."

"When did they get back to you?" My voice, involuntarily, fell. "December?"

"January."

"It wasn't a good time."

"No."

"I wouldn't have minded celebrating. It might have cheered me up."

He shrugged. "It didn't cheer *me* up."

"Well, now you can be cheerful, right?" I asked as if something had changed between January and June. As if things hadn't gotten, in their own slow humiliating way, worse. "Abhi? Can't we celebrate tonight?"

His sunken eyes turned to me. He stood abruptly to change the mood.

"How do you want to celebrate?"

"I don't know."

"We can sit on the recliner together and watch *Chupke Chupke* again."

I smiled. My hands came up and clapped two noiseless claps. "Yes! Can we do that?"

My smile didn't make him smile. My shrunken face must have crinkled strangely and clashed with his memory of my smile. He looked away.

"You don't have to finish something, do you?"

"No. Not at all. It's been a long time since we last saw it. Let's watch it tonight."

Having ice cream or sparkling grape juice to celebrate wouldn't have worked, now that I neither hunger nor savor, so we saw the movie instead. We were rewatching all our old comedies, one a week, cycling through them a second time. I like going back to the old Hindi movies. Abhi is indifferent. He watches them to be with me. I know I am taking up his time, but by now it is a ritual. He catnaps on me, then works in his study into the early morning. I am not soft anymore, although I am his pillow. I make sure I laugh without shaking my shoulders. I stay very still from the neck down. My face, ghosted white by the screen's light, periodically tilts back, and my lips peel away from my teeth.

After Mala's weeklong visit, I decide to let people know.

It is a project. Abhi sits next to me holding the handset and an old-fashioned spiral-bound notebook where he has scrawled the numbers of our circle. I tell him we should only call family and let the news spread on its own, but he has more liberal notions of who deserves a call. Not just every family in India; not just the local friends with whom we had dinner parties and after-dinner card games. Our old, once-a-year friends in Tennessee and the Bay Area all, in his opinion, would do well to hear my voice. "They are going to call you anyway when they find out," he says.

"I know, so let them."

"Who knows how things will be two months, three months from now?"

So that is the time frame he has in his mind. "Big news travels faster than that."

"But it doesn't travel that fast *uniformly*," Abhi says, waxing professorial as he does when he wishes to convince me. "People get left out. People get missed. These are our people." He points at the book. "At least people like Dhimant bhai."

"We haven't gone to Virginia in six years!"

"I have the book out. This is the morning. Let's just take care of everyone and get it over with. Then if you want to leave the phone off the hook for a while, fine."

"Why call Virginia?"

"Let's do the India calls and then see how we feel."

"Dhimant bhai is your friend. He is not my friend."

"Wait a minute. He is a family friend. He helped me in

New York when I came here for the first time. I stayed in his apartment for two months."

"At least start with the India calls."

"If your friend Kalyani had this going on, imagine how you would feel finding out from some third party. Just over dinner at someone's house . . ."

"This is going to be more exhausting than you think."

He is already dialing the international code. "Let's take it one call at a time."

"Who are you calling first?"

This is a petty point, but he is dialing his own eldest brother, and I want the first India relative who knows to be my brother—even if only by minutes. Abhi aborts the call without arguing, licks his thumb, and flips to my brother's number.

The calls take hours, as I predicted. I had put off this strange obligation for as long as possible. I am a shy person, and there is nothing so public and look-at-me as spilling one's mortality in a living room three thousand miles away. The closest relatives in India suggest flying over to help. They are well-off, but they are not rich; two families have daughters with weddings coming up, and I do not want them tapping into their savings. I claim I will ask if I need them to come. I point out how Mala stayed the week with me, and how both families are visiting next month. *I am taken care of here*, I tell my brother. It makes me feel very proud to say that. I get to show them all: Look, here in America our children are close to us, too. I raised them right. They are caring for me in my time of need.

I dread telling the cruise-loving Nainas of our circle most of all. I fear my chitchat-and-potluck relationships will break under the weight of my news. I don't want their awkwardness, their visits, their feelings of obligation. But everyone, includ-

ing Naina herself, reacts as I imagine myself reacting to a
similar phone call. Their shock and grief are genuine and full
of urgency. The wives offer to bring meals. Calls come in over
the rest of the day as word spreads locally. Abhi has trouble
remembering which family he has promised which evening,
so he starts a database on a scratchpad, the days of the coming
weeks listed in columns. Soon each day has a dash and a
name.

They offer to drive me to appointments any time I need.
They offer this sincerely, but who would take up such an
offer? The meal is different. It can be made and dropped off
at their leisure. But a ride I don't want. My friend's day would
have to be built around my two hours. I would bring my odor
of mortality into her car, her mind, her morning.

The visits begin the day after the phone calls. They all
want to help, my book club friends, my dinner-party doctors'
wives, my house-key and houseplant neighbors two blocks
over—and they all want to know. Has it spread? When could
I first tell that something was wrong? What was the first thing
I felt? (Prompting, I am sure, the inevitable thought: *I have an
ache there, too, sometimes . . .*) What did the doctors say? How
are they treating it? And then the question never verbalized
but ever-present, the one they ask every time their eyes flick
over my wasting body. How long?

Sometimes people write these things in a book. I have so
much trouble answering the questions I am asked, maybe I
should write a book. That would give me distance. Everyone's
eyes would be on the words, not on me. I could hand over a
copy and say, "It's all in there. Read it later. Talk to me about
something else for a while."

I would still hold some things back: how many injections,
how many pills. The brooch and earrings on the oncologist's
nurse practitioner, her face smeared flawless with foundation

that contrasts with the aged, big-ringed hands that take down my answers. The oncologist showing me and Abhi the scrolling images of an abdomen scan, pointing out exactly what is new and what has grown.

Whoever read it would think, in frustration, where is it? Where has it spread? How long do you have?

I would have my answer ready, if I chose to answer. This is not a book about dying. This is a book about life.

Milind Shah used to invite us to the karaoke parties at his house. I was no singer, and no amount of polite clamor could stir me from the couch. I would sip Diet Sprite and eat salted cashews from the crystal bowl. Couple after couple would insert their CDs and present what they had rehearsed. Abhi had a good singing voice—Milind and the other couples would never accept a no from him. Besides, it was proper for at least one member of a couple to perform.

Abhi hated these parties, but Milind—Mel—ranked extremely high in the hospital administration. (Back then he was chief medical officer; recently he has risen even higher.) We had to go. Abhi never attended things he didn't want to attend, except these karaoke parties. On the drive there, I would try to console him. "There's actually no audience at all," I said, "except me, because I'm not there to sing. Everyone else is a singer, which means they are either nervous about their performance, or they're up there, singing. Or they're wondering how they just sounded. Really, you could be singing in the shower."

This didn't keep Abhi from his ice-cube-crunching irritation—interrupted, I confess to my amusement, when he had to get up and sing some benign old Mukesh song. Abhi's voice sounded best when he sang Mukesh.

> *Kal khel mein*
> *Hum ho na ho*
> *Gardish mein taare*
> *Rahenge sadaa*

"Tomorrow I may or may not still be in the game, but the stars in the heavens will remain forever . . ." Abhi's resentment would fixate on Milind-Mel, who enjoyed his karaoke parties immensely and expressed his good mood with lively, crowd-pleasing Kishore Kumar songs. At the end of each evening he would turn serious and sing a long, classical geet, during which he would roll his head wildly to match the intensity of his alaaps.

"That? That's just amateur humming," he would say afterward, collecting the compliments. "By the way, Kishore Kumar wasn't classically trained either, you know. Manna Dey, Yesudas, the other classical singers—they looked down on him. But he had a natural command of the ragas. It was in his blood."

Over dinner, when Milind presided, the men's conversation would turn to investments, the market, bonds, Treasury bills, inflation rates, what the Fed was going to do. They asked Abhi's opinion. With Ronak working in Manhattan, Abhi must have some kind of insider knowledge, yes? Abhi always disappointed them. They could not believe his utter disinterest. They thought he must be holding back the tips he got from Ronak and secretly making a killing in the market.

How alike they all looked, sitting under the chandelier. Balding, prosperous Indian physicians in late middle age, polo shirts, khaki shorts, the children grown and off living distant lives. Identical. No indication, on the surface, of Abhi's secret life, of his abstract breathtaking inner world, where mathematics had the same relationship to money as poetry did to news.

Abhi ran into Milind in the doctor's lounge the day he heard about my diagnosis. Milind expressed his shock and such while continuing to smear cream cheese on his bagel. While Abhi gave him the details—when we found out, what the prognosis was, what the scans were showing—Milind bit into his bagel and kept nodding with cream cheese at the corners of his mouth. "He must have been catching a quick breakfast, Abhi," I said in Milind's defense. "He must have had patients to see."

But Abhi was full of indignation he hadn't been able to express at the time. He described in detail Milind's breakfast. "Then *Mel* asks me whether there are any clinical trials. And right away looks down to choose a banana. I am still answering, and he starts *peeling* it."

"Don't be so sensitive, Abhi. If you approach people like this, no one will be able to say anything right."

"He is completely . . ." Abhi put two fingers to each temple and crushed his eyes in frustration. "Completely *inside his own head*."

I nodded. "Some people are like that. They have trouble imagining how other people see things."

"That's what it takes to get ahead in politics the way that man has. You have to have a big ego."

"What else did he say?"

"That he and Kamala want to pay a visit."

"Oh," I said, looking around uneasily. The mess had quickened as I slowed down. Rice Krispies were crushed into the tablecloth. The hand towels stank of sour damp. Ants had formed a long thread stretching across the kitchen floor to an ancient sticky patch of maple syrup. Paid and unpaid bills littered the counter as well as a sloppy stack of junk mail I had

not yet trashed. Abhi offered often enough to hire a maid ser-
vice. Sometime soon, I knew, it would be inevitable. But not
yet. I could do it, but I needed time. I started calculating how
quickly I could get the house clean or at least tidy. "Did he say
when?"

"He's going to call."

We heard nothing from Milind for a week.

It is Saturday. He calls. Are we at home? They want to come
over to give me a gift.

He is only a few minutes away. This could mean anything
from five minutes to twenty-five minutes, but in any case, it's
not enough time to make the house clean. I am on the couch,
propped on my three throw pillows. A book sits on the floor.
I have not read more than five pages. Occasional sweeps of
nausea make me feel like I'm reading in a car. My hands rest
on the blanket. The knuckles look very bony. I hide them. It's
not as though they are going to shake my hand. I hear the
doorbell. Abhi's welcome is muted, no pleasantries, no rise of
voices in hello. There is disease in this house, and disease has
its decorum.

Milind's wife, Kamala-Kim, comes in first. She bends low
over the couch to put her hands on my shoulders, a symbolic
substitute for an embrace. The purse on her shoulder falls
forward and rests on my chest. It is small and lightweight. I
am surprised. My purse grew full during motherhood, a kind
of separate pregnancy, and never wholly lost the weight.
Milind joins his hands, as if the occasion is religious, and
keeps his distance. His face is serious—in its classical-geet
mode. The murmurs begin. Kamala kneels beside my couch,
her penned eyebrows high. They both have a *Hello My Name
Is* sticker on their chests.

"Were you attending a conference?" I ask.

Husband and wife look down at the evidence. "There is a community health fair going on," says Milind, "over at the recreation center."

Kamala nods. "We like to help out. Blood pressure checks, advice about diet and exercise, that sort of thing. Mel gave a talk."

"Really? What about?"

Milind clears his throat. "Basic stuff. It had a clever title, though. 'These Boots Were Made for Walking: Making Regular Exercise a Part of Your Life.'"

"Is that a saying?"

"I think it's a song, right?" Kamala looks to Milind.

"Frank Sinatra," he says. "Tell me. Has music been a comfort to you, in this trying time?"

"Yes. And reading."

"Reading is good. But there is nothing, no*thing*, like music." I nod.

"We brought you some CDs." Milind lifts a small bag with two plastic CD cases in it. "I went through my MP3 collection and burned you all the bhajans. The one I labeled *Volume 2* has some gems of Rafi at the end."

"Rafi had some beautiful religious songs," says Kamala. "Like 'Man Tarapat Hari Darshan ko Aaj.' Even though he was a Muslim."

Milind raises his hand and turns his wrist and closes his eyes, head softly rolling, a face of mystical ecstasy. "Music transcends these divisions. Caste and creed. It trans*cends* them."

"It does, it does," I say, glancing at Abhi, who is sitting on the armrest at the far end of my couch.

"Can I get you something to drink?" asks Abhi. "Water? Juice?"

"We had lunch at the health fair," says Milind. "What have you been listening to? Bhajans?"

"Yes, among a few other things."

"You know, we talk about this and that and science and whatnot, but music heals us at a deeper level. I tell my patients that. It is medicine administered per os—by ear."

"Kamala?" Abhi asks. "Water, juice, anything?"

"Oh no, I'm fine as well."

Milind stares at me as if seeing my sunken face for the first time. He purses his lips and nods to himself. "I should come over some time and sing some bhajans for you. Would you like that?"

"Of course, Milind bhai. But you are so busy . . ."

"I am not busy now. And even if I was, this takes priority." He is kneeling by me. He glances a few degrees to his left and says, to no one in particular, "Is there a chair?"

Abhi brings over a chair from the dining table. Milind pushes away the coffee table so he has enough room for the chair and his own presence. Kamala sits on the love seat at a right angle to my couch. Her husband has his eyes closed and is readying himself. She looks at her watch.

Milind begins a low hum. "I have not rehearsed," he says, "so you must forgive my mistakes."

Abhi takes the seat next to Kamala, his body leaning away from her, his head on his fist, his gaze fixed on the far end of the house. Milind begins singing, full-voiced, no adjustment in volume made for the close quarters. He does have talent. Not even Abhi could deny that. The eyes stay shut, meditative. He begins a filmi song from several decades ago, again by Rafi. The lyrics talk about Radha dancing—tirikita toom, tirikita toom, ta, ta—and Krishna playing his flute. The tune is as chipper as classical gets, but the song has Radha and Krishna in it, so maybe it is appropriate. Extempore alaaps add gravity. After Milind finishes, I say, "Thank you so much," but he is concentrating, as if he has a word on the tip of his tongue.

Finally he lifts a finger. "And there's also this, in the same raga . . ."

"Mel," Kamala says. "She must be tired."

"This is music," he answers, irritated. "It is relaxing. It is the opposite of tiring." He looks at me. "Are you tired?"

"I am not the one singing, Milind bhai. As long as your throat is—"

Milind starts a prefatory alaap. This segues into a bhajan. When he is done, he says, "You see how they are identical? You see?" But it sounds nothing like the first song, at least to me.

I nod. Abhi stands up and says, "Mustn't overwork your voice, Mel."

Milind touches his throat. "I am speaking at a dinner tonight on a new diabetes drug."

"Best of luck."

"It's at the Savoy Park Steakhouse."

"Mel, Kim, thanks for stopping by. We won't keep you."

"No, no. It has been my pleasure to share what I can." He points at the CDs in the bag and nods at me. "You will find great comfort in these CDs. Books are helpful, but music is music. Let that be the one thing I leave you with. Music is music."

Kamala rises, then kneels at my hand.

"It must be so hard," she says, shaking her head at me, "so lonely. What with your children so far away." Her eyes fall to the carpet. "I tell Ankur all the time, What if something happens to us? L.A. So far away. It's just a flight, he says. But still."

"The children come very often—Mala, every weekend she has off."

"How are Mala and Rahul holding up?"

I am about to say *Ronak*, but I stop myself. She is trying. No need to reveal how little we really know each other. "They are both coming over this weekend, actually."

"You must be so excited!"

I smile. Kamala leans forward and makes a kissing sound in the air beside my cheek. "Keep smiling, okay?" she whispers. She stands and tugs her purse back up, onto her shoulder.

Milind keeps a hand on Abhi's arm. I can hear the confidential wisdom he imparts.

"In the beginning," he is saying, "you take part in life, you laugh and cry. But toward the end, if you are wise, you become a witness. You become detached. You witness your own grief from the sky, you know? Like God."

It feels good to say my children are coming to see me. This is what I tell the loneliness when—five hours since Abhi left, five until he gets home—the loneliness asks why the house is so quiet. I answer *afterglow* or *anticipation*. Mala comes often enough that I can say that, with or without the grandchildren. After Kamala's visit the weekend comes quickly. Mala's minivan is suddenly in our garage, both doors slid back and the rear door high. Abhi pulls in behind her, having fetched Ronak's family from the airport.

When everyone is here, it's the same as if no one is here. I cannot focus. Vivek and Ronak's three boys play tag, thumping upstairs, thumping downstairs. They dissolve into squeals and laughter at the moment of tag, then go quiet suddenly as the running and chasing starts anew. The hair at their temples slicks down with sweat. During their rare pauses, they throb like space heaters. I feel I could warm my hands at their flushed cheeks. Shivani, still a little shy in big gatherings, stays with her father. Ronak gets her to sit in his lap by showing her a Pixar movie on his phone. The central conversation is him talking to Mala; Sachin listens closely, leaning forward, elbows on his knees, left foot bobbing, eager to charge into the pauses.

Amber sits quietly, in a silence without anxiety. She monitors the children and simply says a name if she wishes to stop a behavior. Dev, when he hears "Dev," stops jumping off the chaise for the rest of the afternoon. I am on that chaise under my blue microfiber throw; he climbs on it and jumps off without seeing me. Amber is the one Abhi talks to when, periodically, he emerges. There are enough people in the house that he can retreat unnoticed. Everyone is distracted. They don't notice his absence the way they don't notice my presence.

Not that I am reproaching them. I like basking in the family noise. I like how the hours go by, how baths get delayed and everyone's in their pajamas well past eleven in the morning, how lunch is late, how even Amber's children get their nap times thrown off in the general excitement, how the words *ice cream* get said instead of spelled aloud and suddenly all the grandchildren are demanding it. I don't even mind the random tantrum, Mala kneeling and shouting and making it worse, Sachin scooping up Vivek and going upstairs for a time-out. I don't mind Raj screaming for the small stuffed elephant that's been in Shivani's hands all morning. It's best I am too weak to pick him up and promise to find him an identical one at the toy store; Amber never liked it when I did things like that. She watches him cry for what feels like a long time but probably isn't.

This is how she trains them. I remember being in their house when she was teaching Dev to sleep by himself in the crib. She used to watch the clock and go in at intervals, some technique she had read in a book. All three of her children slept wherever she laid them, even with daylight through the blinds. Her husband drank from my breast until he was three years old and slept in my warmth until he was five. He had his own bed, but he never stayed in it past midnight. I remember his skin smelling of Johnson & Johnson's from the night bath

I gave him. I would hover my lips over his hair and savor the tickle. I always slept badly. He would toss and kick. Abhi used to flee for the recliner downstairs. I did not mind.

Both families, Ronak's and Mala's, begin solemnly at my side when they arrive, asking for updates, getting me water, having the kids each give me a hug. I tell the children to play, play, and I turn the conversation to other things than me. After a few minutes, my encouragement works. The conversation shrugs off the sick mood and becomes animated, freer. The grandchildren ask to put their shoes back on and play outside. Mala, always wary of sun exposure (more so than Amber, who burns), tells them to wait until the backyard falls under the shade of the house. So they play tag indoors. On my chaise longue, I settle into the noise like a bath.

Now, a few hours into the weekend, they speak of things that have nothing to do with my health.

". . . This is the time," Ronak is saying. "If you refinance the house, do it now. But there's no hurry. The rates aren't going anywhere."

Sachin nods. He likes hearing Ronak open up about money matters. Finance to him is esoteric wisdom, and Ronak is among the initiated, if not the elect. "They say I can get less than four."

"Easily. This is a historic time." Ronak waves his hands expansively. "Historic."

"Thanks to some historic blunders on the part of the banking community," says Mala. She is always needling him about the financial crisis; it is in jest, but only partly.

"I wouldn't call them *blunders*."

"No?"

"*Blunder* is too generous. It sounds like they didn't know what they were doing."

"What, then? *Crimes?*"

"Maybe that's shooting to the other extreme. They were making money, which is what they were supposed to be doing. The right word is kind of in between."

"It's okay, Ronak. You're not in front of a congressional committee."

"And I never will be. I had nothing to do with that whole part of it."

"Nothing?"

"What I do is in a completely different department. It's like, let's say the cardiologists get caught doing something shady, like cathing people who don't need it just to make money. You don't blame all the doctors in the hospital. You don't blame the ENTs and family practitioners. You blame the cardiologists and leave it at that."

"Well, those cardiologists are gonna have to ramp up how many caths they do, because there's no money in seeing patients anymore."

"You mean the Medicare cuts?"

"That's only the beginning. That's just the first few nips from the piranhas. We're waiting for the feeding frenzy."

"They've got to save money," says Sachin, "so they do it by paying us less."

"Doctors usually don't have to deal with this kind of uncertainty. It used to be the one good thing about medicine."

Ronak stretches. "Uncertainty's everywhere these days, Mala."

"Everywhere but JPMorgan Chase."

His stretch relaxes abruptly as he lets out a one-note laugh. "You guys'll eat well. I wouldn't worry."

"Maybe. Maybe not. The golden age is over. We'll be like the doctors in Britain soon."

Sachin smiles. "That's not so bad, as long as we can work their banker's hours."

"What about the free dinners from the pharmaceutical companies?"

"The spouse has to be a doctor if they want to come. All those fancy dinners we went to with Dad, they're gone."

"Well, what about the pens? You still get the pens, right?"

"Nope."

"You're kidding. They don't even give out pens anymore?"

"Not one measly ballpoint."

"That's cruel."

"That's medicine in the twenty-first century."

Ronak glances at Shivani. "You going to tell her to go into it?"

"I'm not going to tell her anything. She can be what she wants."

"It's still the noblest profession," Sachin insists. "It's still a good profession. You help people."

This is one of those Sachin comments that no one can argue with but no one can wholeheartedly support: factually right, but wrong for the mood. Ronak and Mala exchange a look. Mala is disillusioned with medicine in a way that Sachin isn't, even though, as an ENT, she makes three times his family practitioner's salary. Medicine, like anything else, has diminished by comparison to finance. His third year out of college, Ronak was making more than Abhi's attending neurologist salary at Ohio State. Ronak took a shortcut to wealth that exacted no weekends and no house calls. He escaped Mala's drudgery-decade of medical school, residency, fellowship. She did best in English as a student, yes, but what kind of job would English get her? She could read books in her free time. She needn't major in it . . . We had not *pushed* her into medicine. We *suggested* it to her, mainly because we could. When it had been Ronak's turn, we had asked his plans, received shrugs and mumbles, and waited until he told us. With Mala, we knew advice—was the advice itself pressure?—might have an effect. But she chose her profession herself.

The two eldest cousins, Vivek and Dev, have approached Amber. They know that her yes or no is inflexible; convince her and the others will follow.

"The kids are asking about the pool," Amber says to no one in particular.

Suddenly they all turn to me as if asking permission, even Vivek and Dev.

"Go, go. It's a hot afternoon. It's a shame to keep them indoors."

"You sure?" Mala asks.

"Yes. I'll stay here, of course. The nurse is coming."

"I can stay behind."

"No," interrupts Ronak. "I'll stay behind."

"No one has to stay behind."

"Someone should stay to get the door."

"I can get the door, Mala! And besides, your father is upstairs."

"I'm staying behind with Mom," says Ronak firmly.

"Ronak can stay," seconds Amber. "I can go in with Raj. Dev and Nik are fine in the water."

The two boys have been watching this conversation carefully, waiting for the right time to rejoice. Dev gives Vivek a double high five. "Waterslide!"

Abhi comes downstairs, rubbing his hands. He has the excited, relaxed air of having finished long work on something. "Sounds like we're planning an outing, eh?"

I want to capitalize on his sociable mood. If Mala speaks first, she may apologize for the boys' noise and tell him he needn't come—she always assumes her father would rather be alone. But I sense he is on a break. "You can go if you like. Ronak is staying home with me."

"Ronak? You don't want to go have fun?"

"I'm fine."

"The kids would love it if you go, Pappa," says Sachin. "Come. Do you have a swimsuit?"

"Second shelf, left side," I say.

"I think I will come splash around. What do you say, Vivek?"

Vivek returns Abhi's high five. "I'm going to wear my Transformers swimsuit!"

Ronak absents himself from the preparations, snacking on Cheez-Its from the box Mala left on the counter.

"You guys need me?" Ronak asks Sachin, who is frantically searching for the pair of red sunglasses that will calm Vivek's tantrum.

"Oh no, everything's under control. Thanks for keeping Ma company here." Sachin looks at me.

"Good times," says Ronak.

The general shouting goes mute behind child-locked doors and tinted windows. The minivans pull out; I wave good-bye and am on the couch before the garage door groan has ceased.

Ronak approaches me, his phone out. He sweeps and taps the screen, then tucks earphones into its jack.

"I've got something for you."

"What is it?"

"The *Bhagavad Gita*. It's set to music with this full orchestra. Dad said you would like it."

"Sounds interesting."

"It's awesome. I listened to a bit just now, it's really great. Here." He tries to tuck the earbuds in my ears.

I put up a hand. "Why don't we talk, Ronak?"

"Sure. Sure. What about?"

"I don't know."

"You don't want to try listening to this? You'll like it. It's really holy."

He holds the earbuds out plaintively at the level of my chin. Babies get binkies in the mouth. The old get holy music in the ears. "Okay."

He eases the earbuds into place. His hands at the sides of my head feel like an embrace stopped short. The music is too loud. I look up at him to ask him to decrease the volume, but he has already turned to fetch his laptop. He points at the chaise, speaking so I can hear him over the music. "I'm right here if you need anything. I'll just be on the computer."

I pick up the gadget and try to find the volume. Ronak, settled into the chaise longue, sees me fiddling and says something. I take out an earbud.

"You know," he says, "you can surf on that while you're listening."

"I want to turn down the volume." I press something. The screen changes completely.

"There should be a button on the main screen."

"The screen is gone."

He sets his laptop aside with a sigh and scoots from his niche. The Sanskrit, belted by a church chorus with an intermittent string section in the background, deafens my right ear. I pull out the other earbud. He finds the correct screen and brings down the volume.

"This is the main screen, okay? You can surf, you can play solitaire, anything you want."

I accept the thing in my palm and nod at its columns of icons. Ensconced again, Ronak hooks himself into headphones of his own, and his head starts bobbing forward and back. He still moves his lips when he reads, a habit he had as a child. You would not notice unless you looked very closely. I watch his fingers tap a private rhythm. His feet are crossed, one ankle settled in the cradle of the other. The one on top is bobbing. A music I cannot hear has colonized his whole body, head to

foot. I look down at his phone. My eye falls to an icon at the
bottom with a small red dot in its upper right-hand corner.

Mail.

I wonder. I shouldn't. But I wonder. I touch the icon. The
screen changes.

Can he tell? Does he have the same window open, or
minimized, over on his own laptop? Can he see my activity?
No. He will only be able to tell if I change something. And I
won't. I will just have a look and back out.

I wait. It takes only a few seconds, but they feel like a long
guilty minute. Then I am in. His e-mails are all there, two at
the top boldfaced, the rest not. I scroll the list. The names
speed up and slow down and stop. I check for women. I want
to know. Older. That is when. December or November. That's
when their fight happened. I keep going back. There are hundreds of e-mails for every month. He is so busy, so connected.
A lot of bland American men's names. A few Arab-sounding
names give me pause, but he seems to be doing business in
Dubai and Abu Dhabi. I won't read the mail itself. I just want
a name. The name will tell me what I need to know about the
indefinable coldness between him and Amber. February. Come
on, hurry up . . . January. No mails from Amber. Of course
not; they probably did their fighting over the phone. December. I slow down. I stare at each name. All work-related—
people with banks in their e-mail addresses. He is shrewd. He
would delete them.

I pause. I rub my eyes.

Do I really believe my son would do such a thing to his
wife? Only Americans do that to their marriages. Not us. But
his generation—they are all Americans now.

I press the garbage can icon. I am rooting through his garbage now. Trash.

Most Indian mothers think of the girl as a calculating

woman and her son as a boy, baited. My unlucky boy—even his lust is naïveté. Yet I never thought this with Ronak. From the beginning, I worried for my American daughter-in-law. At Christmas I had thought, *What has he done to her? What has he done that she has exiled him from her family's house?* Whatever it was, she forgave him. No surprise there. He had a showstopper to start his apology, didn't he? *Mom just told me she's dying . . .*

Trash. There are hundreds more e-mails here. A woman's name. Jenna DeVine. Who is this? A coworker? A secretary? I bring the phone closer. "Singles in your area! Manhattan area sing . . ." I shake my head. The e-mail is boldfaced; it slipped through his spam filter, and he deleted it without reading it. Another woman's name. I can't believe I am doing this. I press the square button that says Inbox. I scroll up and down. Everything is as it was before. Back to the innocuous screen full of icons. There. I focus on the Sanskrit being sung in my ears. He will never know. Neither will I.

The nurse is not a hospice nurse, or at least we do not call her that. She is here to chart my vitals, draw my blood, and ask questions. I told the oncologist I did not need someone to check up on me, but he said it was part of the specific research protocol. All the visits would be paid for. Abhi added sternly that we would do everything the protocol specified. He is always tense around office visits, even though he accesses my scan results ahead of time and discusses them with his oncologist friend from San Antonio, Sunil Joshi. (He and Sunil went to medical school together; I suspect Abhi called him as early as November, when I still didn't want anyone knowing.)

The doorbell rings, and I worry that Ronak didn't hear it. But he has uncrossed his ankles; he plucks out his earbuds and sets the laptop and pillow precariously on the armrest.

I hear the front door open with the quietness of strangers meeting. Ronak leads the nurse to me and sits at the foot my couch, his eyes on her. She is younger than the nurse who was here last time. Only her eyes are old, set deep in what is otherwise a girl's face. Her accent sounds eastern European, maybe Russian, so this fits, this mark of a past in the eyes. I watch her profile as she inflates the blood pressure cuff. She asks questions off a questionnaire, followed by a checklist of potential symptoms, fatigue, yes, sleeplessness, sometimes. I rate my pain, assign it a number as if I know what ten feels like, giving it a three. Last comes the rubber tourniquet on my forearm, the near-horizontal slide of a needle, and three test tubes turning a heavy human crimson. My blood always shocks me with how dark it is.

The nurse is done with the visit in about twenty minutes. Ronak asks her no questions while she is beside me, but I hear them talking in hushed voices as he walks her to the door.

"I didn't catch your name," says Ronak.

"Lisa."

"Ah, Lisa. Ron. Thanks for coming out here and helping out with my mother."

Something gets said that I don't catch. I move to the foot of the couch so I can hear better.

". . . It keeps patients from having to go into the hospital for these kinds of blood draws," Lisa is saying.

"It's a big help. It's tiring for her to have to go to the hospital, at this point. Look, can I offer you anything to drink? A snack, maybe?"

"Thanks, but I'm all right."

"I couldn't help noticing your accent. May I ask where you're from?"

"Ukraine."

"I thought so. I actually took two years of Russian in high school."

"I see. Do you still speak it?"

"Spasiba."

"Ah, you're welcome."

He says something longer in Russian.

She laughs. "Your accent is actually very good," she says, sounding genuine.

"You know, you look awfully young. How long have you been a nurse?"

"Two years."

"How did you pick this kind of nursing?"

"This is more of a transitional thing. I am saving money to go back to school. Are you in medicine?"

"Finance, actually. But everyone else in the family is. I'm kind of the black sheep."

Lisa laughs again. "Finance is nothing to sneeze at!" The expression sounds odd spoken in her accent.

"Why do you want to go back to school?"

"I want to do pediatric nursing. Maybe intensive care."

"I can see you doing that, I really can. Has it been a busy day for you, Lisa?"

"Not too busy. Just steady, you know, appointments through the day."

"Do they have you driving all over the place?"

"It's not so bad, usually. But my next house is an hour away."

"Lisa, let me get you something for the road. A bottle of water at least."

"Water would be nice."

"I think we have a few cold in the fridge."

He goes into the kitchen while she waits. I push the silent earbuds back into my ears. From my couch I see him bending in the light, not finding the water.

"On your right," I say softly. "In the door."

Ronak is heading back to the nurse when he stops and says, "Can I grab my phone?"

I unplug the headphones from the jack, glad I restored the screen. He takes the phone and goes back to the door.

"Thank you," says the nurse. "You're very kind."

"Lisa, my sister is here, too. She may have some questions for you. Is there a number where we can reach you if we need you?"

"Sure."

She says the number. He repeats it back as he types it in. Then he asks, "Is this your cell phone?"

"Yes. Or you can call the central Home Health number and ask for me."

"Hey, thanks for all your help, Lisa."

"My pleasure. Thanks again for the water."

"No problem. Drive carefully, all right?"

"Sure. Thanks."

I hear the door close. My son sits back in his niche in the chaise, the notebook open on his lap, the earbuds in his ears. He has forgotten the phone in his pocket. I watch him in silence, the cords from my ears meeting, coiling in my lap, ending in a bright blunt pin.

Late that afternoon, Mala and I start cooking. Amber and Sachin keep the children upstairs. I am often surprised at how easily Sachin and Amber talk to each other; they strike me as being in disjunct worlds, their only similarity the family they have married into. They don't talk if there is someone else to talk to, but when there isn't, they are like old friends reunited. Right now, over a cacophony of music-playing press pads and boys shouting at the Wii (Abhi bought a whole game system for this visit), Amber and Sachin are having a long conversation about Indiana Jones movies.

Mala is making rotli, so I am here to ball the dough for her and give her company. She has gotten very good at the mindful repetition of rotli. Seconds of inattention can roll a seam into the dough or pock the underside black. But circle after circle becomes sphere after sphere. I worry about what she thinks during this phase of it; there's no creativity involved and nothing to learn, just the brisk execution of a task. She does not complain, and I could not take over, at this point, for more than a few.

Ronak is flipping TV channels: black-and-white jackboots stomp to sinister orchestral music, followed by a gray-haired veteran whose testimony comes in subtitles I can't read from my distance. Girls dance in a music video, flash flash flash, each camera angle and close-up lasting less than a second. He stays on this channel a little longer than on the others. Then a dark-haired, slightly overweight woman pours two whispers of sherry into a sauce pan. Ronak brings out his phone; someone has texted him. He starts typing something back.

Sachin has skipped down the stairs.

"Come on, Mom," he says playfully, "Mala is stacking hot rotli and you didn't call me down?"

Mala smiles and grabs the swelling rotli off the flame with her fingers instead of the tongs she has used until then. "Here." She sets it on her growing stack, slaps it, and picks up the margarine stick, its paper splayed apart like a shirt with its top buttons undone. She holds it down for two eyes and pulls it across for a smile.

Ronak finishes texting and strolls over.

"You know, this is pretty amazing, I have to say."

"What is?" asks Mala without looking over her shoulder.

"You cooking. I'm seriously impressed."

"Mala is a wonderful cook," I say defensively.

"I know. Like I said, I'm impressed."

"All right, this really isn't the time or place, okay? I mean, even *you* should see that."

"Mala," Ronak says, sounding hurt. "I'm being serious here. I love that you two are doing this. And Amber was telling me about your cookbook?"

Mala checks over her shoulder to assess his face. She decides he is sincere. "Yeah," she says. "I've got, like, forty recipes at this point."

"You haven't seen it?" Sachin asks Ronak, taking a bite of his second fresh rotli. "It's a masterpiece. Pictures and everything."

"Just simple pictures. I took them with the phone."

"She's being modest! It looks professional. She's writing everything up. Wait here. I'm going to get the computer."

"You can finish what you're eating. Don't go upstairs just for—"

But Sachin has already stuffed the rotli steaming into his mouth and left the kitchen. He sprints upstairs and comes down with the folded MacBook on his palms like a waiter's tray.

"What's the file name? 'Cookbook'?"

" 'Mom,' " says Mala quietly. "It's right there on the desktop."

Sachin finds the file and scrolls down so Ronak can see our recipes and the corresponding pictures. Ronak starts scrolling, pausing on a recipe here or there.

"You put a lot of work into this," he says.

"I didn't want it all on note cards. This way I have all the recipes in one place."

"Amber would love this."

Sachin nods. "Has she seen it, Mala?"

"We talked about it, but—"

"Can I get this onto my thumb?" Ronak asks, sliding his keys across the counter. He left them there next to his wallet. His key chain is his thumb drive. I am about to say yes, please do; Mala is, I realize, about to say she would rather he didn't. Right then a beach ball bounces downstairs, fleeing an avalanche of boys. Shivani takes the stairs more slowly, hand on the banister, as cautious as Mala was reckless at that age. Once she sets socks on the floor, she starts running after the boys. Amber is the last one down. Ronak's thumb drive flickers its blue light, drinking. In a moment, the whole file has crossed over.

Sachin points at the screen. "These are all the recipes Mala has collected."

Her eyebrows rise in delight. "We were talking about this!" She scrolls. "Photographs and everything. Wow."

"I'm getting it for home," says Ronak.

"You know, Mala, you should have this printed out in color and bound. They can do it at Kinko's. It'll be like a real book."

"I'll look into that," Mala says without turning. "I'm still adding stuff, tweaking stuff. It's a work in progress." Her voice drops a little. "It's going to be a work in progress for some time yet."

"Make sure you e-mail me the final version when you're done," says Ronak.

Amber nods at the screen. "I'd love to make these dishes."

"We're lucky guys!" Sachin smiles at Ronak.

"You know, I need to take down my grandmother's recipes. She knows all these old German desserts and things."

She stops scrolling. "Did you make a table of contents, where you list all the recipes?"

"Like I was saying, it's still a work in progress. Nothing's alphabetized or classified yet."

"Is there one for chicken biryani? Nik won't eat hardly any Indian food, but he loves chicken biryani."

"That isn't in there," I say.

"Mom doesn't cook meat," Ronak explains. "You knew that."

"Right. Of course."

"You can cook the chicken separately and put it in with the rice," I say. "There's a recipe for pulao in there. It's the same thing. Add chicken and it's chicken biryani. *Biryani* just means *rice*."

Amber nods. "Look, can I help out in here? I fear I haven't done a thing all afternoon."

"You watched the kids so I could do this," says Mala. "That was huge."

"Let me at least set out the plates."

"I'll help," declares Sachin, and does. Ronak, caught up in the sudden mobilization, finds himself spreading a stack of bowls across the dinner table, counting spoons from the drawer, catching ice from the dispenser in a glass pitcher. When he is done, he remembers to eject his sated drive from the computer. The sum of my theology has been preserved on an inch of plastic, to be grabbed off a hook on the way out, to dangle from the ignition, to be stuffed into a jacket pocket as all four car doors lock at once.

The visit is going well until I make the mistake. I do it right before they leave; I make a happy trip end unhappily. Everyone is careful not to ruin things and then I ruin things. It happens

by accident. I try to get myself milk to quiet the burning in
my stomach.

It is three in the morning. I don't want to wake anyone.
Mala is sleeping next to the children. Abhi has come to bed
late, as he always does, and has just fallen asleep. I knew I
wanted milk, or at least water, when he came to bed. I should
have asked him then but I didn't.

I navigate the hall by moonlight and the night-light. My
eyes are adjusted well enough. My hand finds the hallway
light. I turn it on. The night-light in its shin-high socket blinks
off. Are the glasses in the dishwasher clean? I usually know,
but Mala and Amber finished up because I was tired. I had
gone to the couch and stayed half-awake, half-asleep. Did
they run the dishwasher before they came upstairs?

I hold a glass up to the light. When my hand and eyes rise,
the dizziness surges. I hurry and set the glass upside down in
the rack, and it makes a sound too loud for what I have done.
I get my fingers in the rack and ease myself to the floor. The
glasses and bowls rattle, but not too noisily, I think. The clat-
ter feels distant. My ear can't judge. I am on the ground. Did
I just fall? Let me sit a while.

I sense the glow of more lights coming on behind me, and
the pounding of feet on the stairs.

"Mom!"

Mala's loose hair swishes over my face. Her breathing is
frantic and shallow. She is shaking me.

"Mom!"

"Stop," I murmur, putting my hands on her shoulders.
"Stop."

"What happened?"

In quick succession, Sachin, Ronak, and Amber all arrive
in the kitchen. They stare at me from above.

"I had to rest."

"Did you fall? Did you hurt yourself?"

"I had to rest," I say again, directing the words past Mala to my new audience. "Go back to sleep."

Sachin kneels next to Mala. "Ma," he asks in Gujarati, "do you feel pain anywhere?"

I flush. He called me "Ma." I feel elderly, asked this question in Gujarati.

Amber murmurs something at Ronak's elbow, and Ronak nods.

I answer Sachin in English. "I got a little dizzy. That is all."

"Why were you out here?"

A grandchild starts crying upstairs. The cry is contagious. Mala looks at Sachin, Ronak at Amber; in a moment, it is just me and my two children. The crying upstairs peters off grandchild by grandchild, then stops. We are silent until it does. Meanwhile Ronak sits down next to me with his back against a cupboard. Mala, her arm around me, whispers urgently, "Why did you come out here by yourself?"

"To get something to drink."

"What was Dad doing?"

I say nothing. Ronak holds up a finger. "Listen." We hear a soft, rhythmic scrape of breath over throat.

"*That's* what he's doing," says Ronak, with a bitter smirk.

"He has just fallen asleep," I say.

Mala closes her eyes, striving impatiently for patience. "You can wake me up, you know. You can wake me up."

Ronak mutters, "You can wake *him* up."

"Why should I wake him up? I can get a glass of milk by myself."

"Is that what you think, or is that what Dad thinks?"

Mala glares at Ronak. "This is not the time, all right?"

"No?"

"Go back to sleep, Roan."

"She's down here on the floor, and he's in there snoring. Isn't it exactly the time to bring this up?"

I feel anger on my cheeks and forehead. "He was working until late."

"Yeah. Up in the space station."

"Ronak."

"Sorry. In the study. Are we forgetting that he does this mathematics thing because he wants to? That he's doing it for himself?"

"Why bring this up, Roan? Why?"

"He needs to pull his weight."

"Right now, of all times. With her like this."

"With me like how?"

"Mom—"

"With me like how? Let him say what he wants. We are all up now. No going back to sleep. Let him talk."

All of this is happening in increasingly hoarse whispers. No matter how much anger I feel, I am still worried about waking Abhi and the grandchildren.

"Nothing," says Ronak sullenly. "Bringing up anything is just a disaster. I open my mouth in this family, and it's a disaster, every time."

"Roan, come on."

"Just keep the status quo, just keep the machine running for him, and it's all good. And thanks for the backup there, Mala. Especially when *you* were the one who brought it up in the first place."

Mala shakes her head, but she is not looking at me.

"What were you two saying about your father?"

They stay silent.

"I want to know. What were you two saying behind his back?"

"Look, Mom," says Mala. "We're worried about the week-days. The weekends, one of us can make it here."

"You don't have to come on the weekends. Who said you have to come, ever?"

"We want to come."

"That's why we're here, Mom. We want to be."

"I have your father to take care of me on the weekdays."

"Right, Mom, but how much is he *around*?"

"What do you want him to do? Quit work? There are copays, you know. There are deductibles. What is happening to me, it isn't free."

"Why don't you come stay with one of us?"

"What will your father do?"

"He can stay here and come—"

"I am not leaving your father alone. I am not leaving this house."

"Okay," says Mala, palms out. "We didn't mean perma-nently."

"I am not leaving this house."

"Okay, okay," Mala keeps repeating. "We had to ask."

"Amber's at home," Ronak says quietly. "She says she would love it if you came to stay a while. And at both our houses, mine or Mala's, you could have the kids around you every day. Just think about it."

"You don't want to come here, I never said come here. It is inconvenient for you. I know. I know. I don't need you."

"It's not inconvenient," sighs Mala.

"And you *do* need someone."

"Ronak, listen to me. I have your father."

"Right. That you do."

I cannot tell if this is sarcasm, so I study his face. Does he know how much like his father he looks? "Ronak?"

"What?"

"I have your father. He is so good to me. He pays so much attention to me. All the time."

Ronak does not look at me. He unfolds his legs and stands up wearily. "Of course he does."

Mala helps me to my feet. My body is slack in her embrace, though inside I am tense and raging. "All right, Mom," she whispers. "Slowly."

I stare at Ronak. "What do you two say about him?"

Ronak opens the refrigerator door. "Did you still want your milk?"

"No. I don't want anything from anyone."

"Jesus Christ." One frustrated shove shuts the door.

"Okay," breathes Mala at my ear.

"What do you two say about him?"

"Let's go, Mom. I've got you."

"What do you two say?"

My body. I think about what has been taken from me, what remains, what functions, what doesn't. But I try not to dwell on all that. I don't want to flatter the suffering by photographing each symptom and giving it a caption. The details are at once trivial and humiliating. Like: I nearly fainted going to the bathroom this morning. Opiates can do that to a person. This was during the week, so no one was home. I sat down, started urinating, and went dizzy and nauseous and sweaty all at once. I dropped my head between my knees to get some blood to it. That didn't work. I knew what to do. It's a maneuver I have. I lifted my shirt, dropped forward off the toilet, and pressed my stomach to the cold tiles. If Abhi had found me there—facedown on the bathroom floor, pants at my shins, sweat on my forehead—he would have called 911, even if I told him not to with my own firm voice. I looked like a catastrophe, like this was it. But I was in control. I waited while my heart slowed down. I savored the cold of the tiles. I could feel my aorta pounding inside my abdomen; I hadn't felt that since my skinny girlhood.

I sat up, as refreshingly harrowed as if I had vomited. A surprising lot of urine had wet my thighs and underwear. I

felt the pants bunched now between my ankles. I wet a wash-
cloth, cleaned my skin, cleaned the floor. I changed. I walked
to the couch. Here I am. I could write a book about this slow
sloppy business of dying. People do. I am not one of those
people.

I am never more alive than when family is with me. Even
if it is Mala without the children. Vivek has kindergarten now.
Mala is spending extra days with me, tacking a Thursday–
Friday or a Monday onto a weekend. Her partners accommo-
date her. I hope she is not building up too many debts. She
will have to pay them back later, when days off are less precious to her. Their nanny knows about the "situation" and has
agreed to extra hours.

This coming weekend, only Mala is supposed to come.
Sachin is staying in St. Louis to take care of Vivek and Shivani
by himself. I marvel at his devoting his whole weekend to the
children. Four PM Friday, when he picks them up, until 9 PM
Monday, when he picks her up. Mala's tone on the phone
sounds as if it were a natural arrangement. "He understands,"
she says flatly.

On Friday around noon, I am busy imagining a menu for
us. I have run out of basic dahls and subjis; I am moving on
to parathas with potato bits in the dough, and the delicate
fishing-out of jalebi from a basin of hot oil. I write down the
supplies we'll need. I have had two weeks since her last visit,
but I put off this happy task so I wouldn't grow impatient
with the remaining days.

This is when I get a phone call from Ronak. My pulse races
when I see his name on the caller ID. Usually Amber's name
shows up when a call comes from their house; she is the conscientious one. Ronak himself is calling, from his own phone.

"Ronak?"

"Hey Mom. I've got good news."

This is the same voice and words he used three times before to tell me Amber was pregnant. I sit up and brush aside my grocery list. "Yes?"

"I've got a surprise to tell you about. You and Mala. I've got to tell you both."

"What is it?"

"I said, it's a surprise, Mom."

Something in me still hopes. "Are you and Amber . . . ?"

"No. God, no, Mom. Isn't three enough?"

"You don't have a daughter."

"Okay, it's not that. But it's a good surprise. I've got to tell you both."

"Mala's flight gets in at seven. Or you can conference call."

"I'm telling you in *person*."

"You arc coming?"

"Tonight. I'm hopping a flight. I want to be there."

"What is it?"

"Listen. Can't you wait, like, seven hours? I'll see if I can arrive around the same time as Mala."

"It's going to be expensive, booking a flight at such short notice . . ."

"I'll use my points. If my arrival time's later, I'll just take a cab from the airport."

"Oh no, Ronak, I don't want you taking a cab."

"Dad will appreciate it, trust me. He's not going to want to make a second trip. Most likely I'll get onto something that times out right."

I am overjoyed and confused. "See you . . . tonight, then."

"All right. Look, I've got to go. I'm at work."

"Okay. Love you."

"Love you."

After he hangs up, I sit with the phone in my hand. He didn't ask me how I was feeling, but that's not what bothers me. My condition so monopolizes the beginnings of conversations, I'm pleased to see it passed over for once. Rather it's that phrase, "hopping a flight." If it's so easy for him, why doesn't he do it more often? Why does he need some big news in order to hop a flight? I call Abhi to tell him.

"Amber's pregnant," Abhi says right off.

"I asked him. He says that's not what it is."

"Then I don't know why he's coming. He said it's a surprise. Maybe he bought you some expensive gift."

"What do I want? I don't want anything in the whole world."

"Well, you want his company, don't you?"

"Yes."

"Then think of that as the surprise."

I call Mala next. She is at work, too. Maybe that's why her voice is hushed and her initial silence is long.

"He's coming *tonight*?"

"Did he tell you?"

"No." Another pause, during which I suspect she is checking her phone. "He hasn't texted me, either."

"What do you think the surprise is?"

"He probably bought you something big."

"He said he wanted us both here."

"Well then, he bought you something big and wants me to know."

"You don't think Amber is pregnant?"

"Amber isn't pregnant, Mom."

"You sound very sure . . ."

"Amber isn't pregnant. That's not what it is."

"Okay."

"Guess we'll see him tonight, then."

"I miss you, Mala."

"Miss you too, Mom. Hey, look—"

"I know. You're at work. You have to go."

"I would talk more if I could."

"I know."

"I'm literally at a nurse's station right now. I really can't—"

"I know."

"*Mom.*"

"Just come. Your father will pick you up. Ronak will probably get ahold of you once he has his flight time. If he forgets—"

"I'm texting him as soon as I get off the phone with you."

"Okay. Love you."

"Love you."

Ronak's flight is due to land forty-five minutes after Mala's: a
short enough delay so they would not leave without him, but
long enough for Mala to feel the wait. Ronak called Abhi earlier to insist he pick Mala up alone; she called a few minutes
later insisting he wait for both. Abhi suspects some sibling spat
from the tone of voice, and he knows Mala is the one not to
cross. The benefit of Ronak's borderline indifference is that he
doesn't hold grudges, which means we don't have to worry
about being forgiven. Mala would be hurt if we sided with
Ronak.

Still worse, his flight is delayed by half an hour. I stay in
touch by cell phone. After a certain amount of waiting, you
have to follow through to the end; otherwise, the time you've
waited is wasted. I drowse on the couch and miss the call that
says they're driving home.

The garage door awakens me. Ronak carries Mala's luggage
from the car into the hallway. I get to see him as he dresses
for work: tie, gelled hair, dress shoes, thin black socks. It must
have been a long day for him. He has come for me, bringing
only the duffel bag he takes to his workout. He comes to
embrace me. I smell old coffee, Right Guard, faded cologne:

not entirely unpleasant, the smell of wealth, and exactly the way his father smells after work.

Mala sits down beside me.

"So out with it, Ronak," she says.

Abhi sits on the end of the chaise, arms crossed. "He hasn't dropped one hint the whole ride home."

"Let me run upstairs and shower."

"Now you're going for a shower! This better be good, Ronak, because you're really hyping it."

He shakes his head. "I think I've built this up without wanting to. It's not that huge. Let me just freshen up a little. I've been in these clothes since six AM."

He takes the duffel bag and goes upstairs. In his absence, we speculate. Mala is convinced he's brought me a fortune in a velvet case, but I tell her jewelry would be absurd. He'd be slipping rings on the hand of a skeleton. (I don't say that out loud, of course.) Abhi has no idea what it is—Ronak has never done anything like this before. Abhi confesses he called Amber, who also knows nothing.

Ronak returns, hair wet, in his Umbro shorts and a T-shirt. Now I'm seeing him as he looks when he goes to the gym. He sits back on the love seat and puts his hands comfortably behind his head.

"All right, Ronak," Mala says. "Talk."

He resists a smile. "Why don't we talk tomorrow morning? I'm a little tired."

Mala throws a pillow at his chest. He hugs it and laughs. "All right, all right." He grins. "Here's the story. I was in the city, and I was talking to this woman at a party. About the cookbook you're doing."

Mala looks at him and waits. Finally she says, "Okay?"

"You know how I had it on my thumb drive, right?"

"Right. For Amber."

"So I was talking to this woman, and she said how she loved Indian food, and that the book sounded interesting."

"Was she Indian?"

"White. Anyway, I went down and had Kinko's make a color printout. High res, glossy paper."

"I was planning on doing that myself."

"You should. You really should. It looks great."

"It's not done yet, Ronak. And there're things we may have to change. Right, Mom?"

"It's not done yet," I say. I do not want it to be finished, either. Ever.

"Where is it?" asks Mala.

"Listen. This woman."

"You just *gave* it to her? That's Mom's cookbook."

"Hear me out. She's a literary agent."

Mala can sense, faintly, the coming news; she smiles an almost suspicious smile. "What were you doing chatting up a literary agent? You haven't read a book since high school."

Ronak shrugs. "It's New York, you meet people."

"Okay. So?"

Now he is coy. "So what?"

"What did she say?"

A feigned, offhand air. "Oh, she showed it to some people she knows." He tosses the pillow she threw in the air and catches it. "You know. People who publish that sort of thing."

Mala looks at me, then back at Ronak. "And?"

"She thinks she can get an offer."

"And?"

He takes out his phone. "Let me show you the e-mail." He hands it to her.

"You are kidding me." She leaves her mouth open. She expands the screen and shows me the number.

Ronak closes his eyes and lowers his head in a small, mock bow. "Mom? Your thoughts?"

"That's a lot of money," I say, "for some recipes."

"You're not kidding."

"Why would they pay so much?" I ask.

Mala gives a one-note laugh. "God, Midas touch! How are you so good at wheeling and dealing, Ronak?"

"Why would they pay so much for recipes?"

"That is the number she believes she can get. You know how unusual that is for a book like this? If you agree to a few things, you're going to be famous, Mom. You're both going to be famous."

"For my recipes?"

"Well, not just the recipes. It's the whole story. That's what keeps it from being just another cookbook. She was saying a book like this does a lot better if there's, you know, back-story."

"What story?" I ask.

"You know, the story." He gestures at me, at Mala. *"This."*

Mala hands him his phone.

Ronak watches us, sensing he has done or said something wrong, but not entirely certain what it is.

"What do you mean by 'this'?" Mala asks quietly.

"You know. Mother, daughter."

"Mother, daughter, what's the story there?"

"You know, you two were, well, not the best of friends, at least not all the time, and then things change and, like, you guys bond over . . . food. It's a great story. It's heartwarming."

"You told the agent all this? About us?"

"They're in a business. You have to have something special in your pitch. A hook."

"You told them about Mom, didn't you?"

"Look. How many friends do *you* have in advertising? I

went over the whole thing with Rakesh Gupta. I did breakfast with him even though I can't stand him, and I laid it all out. He said if I left out the part about Mom, it wasn't much of a hook. The book, as he envisioned it, would be a kind of book-club memoir for women, plus a cookbook. The story part first, then the recipes. That would be the hook."

"The *hook*. God, that word. That *word*."

On the other side of the room, Abhi, who has been listening with his arms crossed, stands. "You three sort this out. I will be upstairs."

"Wait, Dad, can everyone hear me out? It's not like we were keeping this a secret. We kept it a secret for pretty much forever because that's what Mom wanted, but it's not a secret now."

"You three sort this out."

Ronak turns back to me and Mala, but our faces must clash greatly with what he dreamed on the plane ride over.

"Abhi," I say, "wait. Sit here. We are all four of us here. Okay?"

Abhi returns to the place where he was sitting. Ronak is shaking his head, a faint incredulous smile on his lips.

"Is this real? You guys are *angry* at me for trying to do this?"

"Not angry," I say, sitting forward in alarm.

"*Angry* isn't the word, Ronak. *Morally appalled?* Maybe that's it?"

"All right. I should have cleared this. I didn't know you felt so proprietary about Mom's recipes."

"That's not it. It's not that you sold a book. You sold—the story. You went and told some stranger about Mom."

"Mom and you. Why don't you admit that? Mom and you."

"You know, what if it does get popular? What if people do say, aw, what a sweet story—mother and daughter reconciling over good old-fashioned ethnic cooking. Is Mom supposed to what? Do appearances? Go on TV?"

"First of all, chances are, it will never get famous. These things usually don't, ninety-nine point nine percent of the time. It's just that we've got a chance here, enough of a chance that a publisher might gamble on it." He points at his phone. "*That's* what you're seeing. Right there."

"Yeah, but what if hundreds of complete strangers are suddenly talking about our private lives?"

"It is private," I echo her. "It is all so *private*, Ronak."

"Even if we did write about ourselves—"

"Mom's written articles before."

"We're not putting Mom through this! I don't care how much money they offer, this is a stupid idea!"

"Look, by the time this thing is even . . ." He doesn't finish.

Mala crosses her arms and sits back. "Finish that sentence," she challenges.

Ronak purses his lips. "You know, I try to be a part of this thing you two have, I try to be a part of it . . ."

"Finish that sentence."

"I should have just let you two have this. I was stupid to try and be a part of it. This is your thing, Mala."

"Finish. That. Sentence."

Ronak swallows and shakes his head.

Abhi stands up. "Enough. We all need to separate."

"What Ronak was about to say," Mala says loudly, enjoying the kill, "is that by the time this thing is even published, Mom won't—"

Ronak leaps off the couch. I stare for a moment in panic. "Ronak!" My cry misses his back. I hear his feet go rapidly up the stairs.

"Everyone relax, relax," says Abhi in an even voice.

I feel prickles up my neck. Will my boy leave? Will he call a cab, get a rental car, drive home in the middle of the night? Or change his flight to tomorrow morning instead of Sunday? I should have defended him. Why didn't I? He was trying to please me. I get off my couch. I step on a splayed novel as I race after him. Mala shouts, "Mom!" Abhi and Mala stay to either side of me. Abhi begs me to please, please calm down. I hurry past them to the stairs and lurch forward to climb, clumsily, like an animal long standing on its hind legs giving up the pretense. Palms and feet thud stair and stair. My movements have never been so narcotic-sloppy as now. Can he hear me? Might he think I have fallen? If he hears me, he doesn't come out of his room. I call his name again. He had to have heard that. He doesn't come. In his room, he is doing what I feared: kneeling beside his duffel bag and stuffing into it his dirty clothes.

I tumble to his side. My knee bumps the duffel bag askew. I pull his clothes out onto the floor and slam my hand on the bag. He shakes his head, his face calm, trying maybe to offset my wild-eyed stare.

Don't you dare go. Not like this. I don't say that. I don't have to.

I see Abhi in Ronak's profile, except his eyes and eyebrows, where I see my mother. Such a face. My husband and my mother. Everything beautiful to me is preserved there young. I kiss his face. I begin on his cheek. I grab the stone of his expression and reclaim it with my lips.

He is so many people now, all of them so different from me, but there was a time when he was contained, whole, in me. I have this right. I keep kissing him. So hard I admit no space between us. My nose flattens on his temple, his fore-head, his shower-wet hair. He flinches when I go too close to his eyes. He doesn't jerk his head away, but he leans away from me a little. I hold him and keep claiming him. His hair is cold and smooth under my lips. I work around to his face. My hand goes to the back of his skull and cradles it, steadies it. I kiss him the way I used to when he was a toddler and I would pin his wrists together with one hand and cover his face. He would laugh and struggle, then grow more and more frustrated until the laugh became the beginnings of a cry. I would let him go just in time; his almost-cry would switch back to a laugh, and he would wait for me to do it again.

I kiss my son. But even as I do, and feel the sobs fluttering under my ribs, there's part of me that thinks, *Why aren't you crying, too? I am your mother and I am dying.* And the kissing becomes spiteful, interrogative. *What do I have to do? Doesn't this love I am showing you override all quarrels?*

So when he turns and holds my face to stop me, nodding, his eyes shut, murmuring, "Okay, okay, Mom, okay, okay," it's a vindication, a triumph. I rise up on my knees; he crouches on his. I am above him; I hold his head to my chest.

He submits, shaking in my arms. I have broken through to the old Ronak, which is to say, the young Ronak, weak as he once was, when I was all food and drink to him. When he would push away from his father and call to me. This is how powerful I used to be. When he got hurt and cried, I used to hold him. Like this, like now.

In the morning, Ronak is on the treadmill in the basement. I hear the belt's unlubricated whine and the thump of decade-old tennis shoes he salvaged from the garage closet. He needs clothes. I go upstairs and lay out clothes for him the way I used to: a running T-shirt that used to be baggy when he was younger, briefs from the drawer, a pair of Abhi's bright green scrub bottoms. Mala is waiting at the table nursing the half glass of cold skim that is her breakfast. Abhi joins us, and we eat in silence. Finally Ronak makes it down after a quick shower, his cheeks flushed with the workout, which he started at five in the morning. He must have woken up and been unable to fall back asleep.

"Look," I greet Ronak, "all four of us. Like old times."

I try to ignore the arguments and tears of last night. I fell asleep with my cheek on his cold wet hair. He must have carried me downstairs to my bed. I do not remember.

Ronak opens a cereal box. I have set out a bowl and spoon for him.

All four of us. There is sweetness when both families are here, but I cannot focus. Now I can focus. The sweetness is different, from an earlier time, Ronak and Mala still in high school, especially with Ronak in his old running shirt. *I Run Therefore I Am.*

They pretend. Maybe Abhi told them to, for my sake.

"How's Shivani liking Montessori?"

"She really looks forward to it. I thought it was going to be bad."

"No tears?"

"No tears."

The carpet brightens. The blinds rise, and it is a sunnier morning. The breakfast table is populated with the English muffins I used to buy back then and the glazed strawberry Pop-Tarts Ronak liked. Abhi reads a real newspaper instead of his iPad.

Abhi peels a grapefruit. "Did that new partner join, Mala?"

"Two weeks ago."

"You said she was plastics?"

"No. Peds."

"You said she was Indian, right?"

"No."

"Wasn't her name Ramalingam or something?"

"That's her last name. Her first name is Jocelyn."

"Having a peds specialist will bring all kinds of new business to the practice."

"That's the plan."

"Sinuses and whatnot."

"Yeah."

The fat returns to my face, my arms, my hands. The ring does not spin so easily on my finger. We had different couches then, but they were in the same places. The past is not all idyll. There—that is where Ronak sat while Abhi scolded, *You are absolutely not allowed to drink; this is the final warning; no one in this family has ever been a drunkard!* That word, *drunkard*—Abhi had no idea it wasn't in use. Cut off that last syllable and it was just *drunk*, the right word. Keep that last syllable, and it spoke of an English-medium secondary school in India. His rage antiquated itself in the saying.

The pretense breaks when the silence lasts too long.

"I've been keeping a diary," Mala says quietly, looking at Ronak. All her anger is gone.

Ronak looks up from his bowl.

"I can make something out of that. For the book."

"I already e-mailed them. It's off."

"Ronak . . ."

"You were right last night, I was being stupid. It's off."

"Who would want to read it anyway?"

"Yeah."

Abhi clears his throat. "Does anyone want toast?"

Equilibrium is restored. I watch Ronak. I think what it was like for him back then. He grew up with darker skin and a strange name. He picked up how to talk and what to like and who to be, but he couldn't pick up the right color skin. So he changed what he could, which happened to be everything on the inside. He watched and mimicked. He scavenged phrases off the television and the school bus, remembered, reused them: *jeez-o-man, puhleese, suh-weet*. We didn't speak that way at home. Home was a bubble. His parents roamed safely inside it, a meek species, herbivorous and physically slight. No wonder our rage struck him as silly. A meek species. Thriving, yes, if thriving meant three cars and five bedrooms. But native? Never.

The toast jumps, and Abhi hooks it from its slot with a fork. He returns to the table.

Final warning. How often he gave those. But Ronak always knew the grounding would never be enforced, the car key never confiscated. How often Abhi's scoldings switched direction. *You coddle him! You protect him! He is your doing!* I didn't mind. I liked being responsible for as much of him as possible. There was so much I wasn't responsible for: his speech, his walk, his taste in music. His taste, too, in food. I wanted more of Ronak in my name. If the flaws, then the flaws.

Mala. "What did Amber say about Thanksgiving?"

"It's a go."

I put my hand on his forearm in excitement. "She doesn't mind?"

"Course not."

"And her parents?" Mala asks.

"We've spent the past three Thanksgivings in Pitt. They've got nothing to complain about."

"I'm doing the whole thing here."

"Looking forward to it."

"She knows there's not going to be turkey, right?"

"Yeah. No bird."

"Do the boys know?"

"They're not crazy about turkey either."

"But they are used to it. I mean, there's tofurkey, but—"

"You can keep it Indian."

"I'm going to use the cookbook."

"You should print a copy out. Just to see how good it looks."

"It's not done yet."

"I know, I'm just saying, it looked nice."

"It's not done yet."

Mala is still working on the same three fingers of milk. What she takes aren't sips. I suspect she tilts the glass just to let the milk touch her upper lip before setting it down again. It's only a few months now that my arms have been thinner than hers. We never worry about how boys will turn out, do we? Not in the same way, not with the same intensity. But the daughters, the daughters we watch from the day they are born. Some families try to be traditional, dressing their girls in the full Arangetram getup, one set of fingers pinched, the other flared, bee and flower. The daughter a bird of paradise there in the Sears Portrait Studio. Traditional music, traditional dance—inoculation against the club scene and the college party with its filthy futons and red plastic cups. Some families are Bollywood: six chirpy film soundtracks in the dash's six-CD changer, and tickets to the stage show dhamakas full of singers and stars fleeing the Mumbai summer. Some homes are Hindu, and when they buy the graduation Civic, they go to the temple to have a coconut broken on it. But some homes are nothing in particular. That was the home I gave Mala and Ronak. A nothing-in-particular home. Or do hand-carved elephants on the end tables count? But one thing all our families have in common: we watch the daughters.

Ronak leaves on Sunday morning. I prevail on him to take two granola bars, two apples, and a Ziploc full of chevda for his journey. I know he thinks it is silly to stock up for three and a half hours, especially when he will get soft drinks and pretzels on the flight, but I am not refused such things anymore. Mala is sweet and quiet; she volunteers to drive him to the airport. I wonder aloud to Abhi, after they are gone a few minutes, what they might be talking about.

"Who knows?" says Abhi. "Depends on whether she is feeling nasty or not."

I am surprised to see him taking Ronak's side. I am even more surprised at my own reaction. "What did you say?"

"Sometimes she gets nasty for no reason."

"Mala? She's sweet."

"One moment she's sweet, the next moment she's mean and nasty. I think of poor Sachin when I see her like that."

"Abhi, that is not fair to her."

"You know her. Why are you defending her? *You* see the worst of her."

"Who acts the same way all the time? Can't she act out what she feels when she's at home?"

"Mala acting however she feels is the problem. Ronak has at least straightened up in how he talks to us. Your daughter just says whatever comes into her mind."

"Abhi!"

"You will see. You'll say the wrong thing, and she'll get nasty with you, too."

I shake my head. "You're wrong." I pick my book off the floor and slam it on my lap.

I am careful all day, wishing dearly we might prove Abhi wrong. And we do. Mala exhumes a dusty box of checkers from the basement, and the serrations are still crisp around the pieces. They come alive after more than a decade. We start bringing up all the old board games, Monopoly, Clue, Aggravation. Remember how Ronak used to throw a tantrum if he lost? Operation, after a pair of fresh Duracells, is still operational, its red-nosed pudgy patient still staring up in faint panic. I take the tweezers and extract his Wish Bone, his Broken Heart, his Writer's Cramp. I end up beating a surgeon trained in ossicular reconstruction. The new Wii is upstairs, but Mala and I prefer these diversions. Risk, Parcheesi, Hungry Hippos. We play and play.

That night she is typing again, and I am sleepless. I do not want water, but I use the excuse to come out. She closes her screen as she turns to me. I take it as an invitation to sit. She pulls her mug of hot chocolate close and wraps her fingers around it. The heat must hurt her hands, but she doesn't show any sign of pain.

"What were you writing, Mala?"

"Nothing." Then, realizing how this sounds evasive, she adds, "Just answering e-mails."

I nod. It is not long before she tells me what she has been thinking about.

"There were those months," she says, "when you and Dad were taking care of Ma and Ba."

"It was strange. It happened at the same time."

"You were taking care of your mothers."

"Yes."

"Where was I?"

"You were in school, Mala."

"No, I mean, what was I doing?"

"School. It was a busy time."

She shakes her head. "Why wasn't I there? Where was Ronak?" She is shaking her head and staring through the steam of her drink. "They were my grandmothers. They were dying."

"You were busy."

"With what?"

"They were in India, Mala. There was nothing you could do."

"I don't think I even cried."

I don't know what to say to that. Maybe I could tell her the truth and say I had never imagined her crying. Or would that make her feel worse?

"It was my grandmother, and I found out, and . . . you called me, remember?"

"You were sweet to me. You were very sweet."

"I consoled you."

"You did. You said such sweet things to me. I still remember."

"Yeah, but I wasn't crying, Mom."

"You hadn't been to India in years. You hadn't seen them for years."

"How is that okay? That my own grandmothers died within a few months of each other, and I didn't cry?"

She sets the mug on the table but doesn't take her hands away.

"I feel like, like I've done this horrible thing in my past . . ."

"Ma and Ba were proud of you. They would ask about you."

". . . And I didn't know it until now."

"We showed them photos."

"For God's sake, where *was* I?"

Her hands slide away from the mug. They are shaking. I reach and steady them in mine, and the heat in her palms is sharp and startling and does not fade. We stay like this for a while. But my hands do not wholly calm her. After her next sip, she says, more steadily, "I guess they were kind of unreal to me."

"They were so far away."

"It's no excuse."

"It's partly our fault. Your father and I should have made sure you saw everyone more. How many times did you even see them face-to-face?"

"It's not your fault. It's just that they were unreal to me."

I do not know what the young mean when they say this word, *real*. I remember overhearing Ronak once, right after he got engaged, on the phone with his old high school friend Philip. *The problem with that city is, none of those women are real. Amber is just real in a way they aren't.* I know it is good to be real. I want to be real. I ask her, "Am I unreal?"

"How could you possibly be unreal to me, Mom?"

"I feel unreal sometimes."

"You're more real to me right now than my job or even my husband and kids. It's been that way for months."

"No. Don't say that. It's not right."

"You are all I think about. Coming back here and being with you."

"Mala, Mala, do not get too deeply . . . I am not permanent. They are permanent."

"It's too late for that, Mom."

"Focus on them."

"You went to India for months to be by your mother. This is the same thing."

"You were out of the house by then. You were grown."

"I should have gone there with you. That was my grand-mother. And if not for her sake then at least for yours. I should have gone."

She takes a sip of her hot chocolate. I can tell it has lost its taste for her. It is just heat now, and fading. She slides the mug away.

"Remember what Ronak said about us writing our story?"

I remember what she said just yesterday. *No one would want to read it anyway.* I shake my head and sit back. "He doesn't understand. It would be so embarrassing."

"So what, we fight sometimes. Everyone fights some-times."

I point at the shut laptop. "Is that what you were doing? Writing about us?"

"No. I was just writing some things for myself. To myself. Abstract stuff."

"What were you writing? About Ma?"

"No."

"About me?"

"I was just thinking. Nothing specific, just ideas. What if someone wrote someone else's life, from that person's perspective?"

"Like a biography?"

"More like an autobiography."

"But isn't an autobiography written by the person?"

"That's what this would be. The writer would try to see everything as her subject sees it. Everything. Even herself."

"Like in a novel?"

"Like, imagine me writing our story. I'd talk about us, only I'd be doing it from *your* perspective. Not mine."

"To do that you would have to get inside my head. That would be embarrassing!"

"No. It wouldn't, not at all."

I glance at her laptop. "You aren't going to write about me, are you?"

"When do I ever write anything?"

"Your essay won first place. Remember, when you wrote about Martin Luther King? Did you forget?"

"Mom." Mala laughs. "That was in eighth grade!"

"It was a beautiful essay. I still have it in a folder. You wrote so many stories in high school."

"You keep that stuff?"

"I do. I keep all of your things from that time."

"Where are they? In the basement?"

"No. Upstairs."

"Can we see it sometime?"

"Why not now?"

She helps me upstairs. Mala stops outside the walk-in closet. I realize it is where I first broke the news. This spot in the house retains the trauma for her. I take her hand and lead her inside. I find the boxes and pull them out. Her old zigzag coloring-book pages are talismans of innocence. I have not

saved everything, but I have saved a lot. I show her a red pen
"A+!!!" atop a geography quiz, a paper-clipped stack of report
cards, ecstatic scribbles in Teacher Comments sections, Perfect
Attendance certificates, art class fingerpaints on a paper plate,
a Thanksgiving turkey made out of fanned popsicle sticks,
and finally her old book reports and essays in outsize cursive.
I have them in plastic slipcovers. We pass them back and forth,
reading choice sentences aloud and laughing.

That night makes me forget. I can still say too much, ask too
much. Mala came on Friday night, so she arranged for Monday off. She is there to drive me to my appointment. We are
silent for much of the ride, groggy from having stayed up so
late. Finally I ask her.

"So you keep a diary?"

"What?" A defensive reflex. "Yeah," she says, more quietly.
She keeps her eyes on the road.

"Do you use one of those blank books?"

She shakes her head. "The computer."

"Was that what I saw you writing last night?"

"Yeah."

"That's not safe, is it? Anyone could click on it."

"You can lock files. You can hide files. There are things
you can do."

"Do you write in it every day?"

"No time."

"When did you start writing it?"

"I don't know. College. I write off and on."

"Do you write about me?"

"Good things, Mom. Don't worry."

"Then can I read it?"

"No, Mom, you can't read it. It's private."

"But you told Ronak you would make it the story part of the cookbook."

"That's not happening, remember?"

"I know."

"We decided not to."

"Right."

She checks my face and turns back to the road. "Did Ronak say anything more to you about it?"

"No."

"When you were holding him?"

"No."

"You sound like you don't mind the idea anymore."

"It was a bad idea. We are not like that. We do not talk about ourselves in public."

"That's what I thought. Then why are you bringing up my diary?"

"Why? Mala, I am your mother. I am curious what you think, what you feel."

"I tell you what I think. Even if you and Dad don't always want to hear it."

"I want to know about you."

"What about me? You know everything."

I pause. What point is there in being dishonest now? We have never been this close. We have never been this open. "I want to know about you before Sachin."

She looks at me through the corner of her eye. "You mean my love life?"

"Yes," I say softly—and then the shame of my admission comes over me. I try to make her understand. "It is none of my business, I know. But it is such a big part of someone. With Ronak, at least—"

"You think I'm keeping secrets."

I say nothing.

"Your son is the one with secrets. But *he* gets covered in kisses. I can do everything right, and you'll invent things I did wrong."

"Not wrong. Nothing is wrong. But if you had someone, if my own daughter loved someone, I can't imagine never knowing."

"Mom—"

"It is all over. You are happily married now. Why is it so hard to open up to me? Do you think I will judge you? After all this time, when you have two beautiful children?"

Mala shakes her head. Three times she taps the bowed-back curve of her palm on the steering wheel. Very lightly; it is not anger, it is annoyance. I should have stayed quiet.

"You want the dirt on me, Mom?"

"Don't say *dirt*. It is not dirt."

"Here's the dirt. There was no one. All through high school, all through college, all through med school, residency, everything. I don't attract men. And if anyone ever showed interest, he would hang around me a while, and either I wouldn't like him, or he wouldn't like me, and that was the end of the great forbidden romance, every time."

Her voice shakes toward the end. She is telling me the truth. I flush.

"I'm not even sure, Mom, what kind of shame I'd have preferred. The shame of having had some guy in secret, which would be shame in front of you and Dad and all our India relatives, and, I guess, God, or *this* shame of never having had an actual boyfriend. Never having bowled a guy over with my looks or my personality or my anything."

"What about Sachin?"

"I love Sachin."

"He is the one you bowled over. He is the one."

"Speaking of shame—"

"How can you be ashamed of such a wonderful husband?"

"I am *not* ashamed of him!" Her voice has risen in volume. Red light. She brakes a little too roughly. "It's just that I . . . I actually *did* the arranged marriage thing. Me alone out of all my friends. I mean, even my cousins in *India* are doing love marriages. But me, I married the guy my parents found for me."

"What is wrong with that?"

"Exact same caste, from the exact same part of India, with my parents knowing his parents from way back. The whole arranged marriage thing, which I had so many problems with since I was a kid—that whole system turned out to be *set up* for people like me. I would have never thought that growing up. Never. You want to know my secret? My secret is, I really *am* this person through and through. My past really is me taking exams and me renting romantic comedies. Are you happy? Is that secret dirty enough for you?"

I look out the window. We drive in silence until the next red light. She brakes hard again.

"Your daughter did everything right. Became a doctor, married Indian, had the babies."

I nod.

"So next time, when you're deciding which child's face to cover with kisses, keep that in mind. I. Did. Everything. Right."

After her outburst, Mala is silent. After her silence, she is sweet.

She asks me to direct her to the parking deck even though she knows how to get there. Her hands on my elbows are gentle as she raises me from the passenger seat. I can walk by myself, but she stays close and eventually holds my hand, like a little girl. She is repentant. I hold no grudge. How can I? When I have her grown-up little girl hand.

She signs in and fills out the clipboard pages without asking about my medications or allergies. She knows all of them. I am here to have the fluid drawn off my belly. I know what to expect. I have had this done twice before. A gentle-voiced technologist in a teddy-bears-with-stethoscopes scrub top squirts clear jelly onto my domed abdomen and smears the jelly around with an ultrasound probe. The screen is mostly dark. The dark is the fluid that's accumulated in me. It looks like a third pregnancy—my navel is like Mala's now, an outie.

A Sharpie makes a mark on the downcurve of the dome. The doctor, in a plain blue scrub-top over his shirt and tie, numbs up the Sharpie mark with a thin lidocaine needle whose sting dulls and keeps dulling until it becomes a little crater of numbness. I remember Ronak grinning after a dentist's visit, tapping his face in fascination. *Hey, Mom, my cheek is still dead!* The small sting makes me oblivious to the big sting, the thicker needle sheathed in plastic that dives an inch into the fluid. The needle comes out while its tube sheath stays inside me. What emerges is not blood but a fluid that looks like apple juice. The nurse connects some plastic tubes to a vacuum jar. The yellow races along the tube and finally the jar begins to fill, noisily. The fluid, drawn out hard by the vacuum, froths. This is when I look away. Until then I feel fascination—look, that is my ascites, look, that needle is actually inside me—but when I hear the fluid rush out of me, the sound reminds me of a man urinating in a quiet house.

Today is the first appointment when Mala has been present. She holds my hand the whole time. As soon as I lay my head back, no longer wanting to see what's going on, she starts talking. Last time, the technologist, who had to stay to supervise the drainage (the doctor had left with a kind pat of my hand), talked about her dogs. I do not know what collies look like. Today I have Mala. Eager to make up for raising her voice in the car, she talks about Vivek and Shivani. Her voice is louder than the draining fluid, whose jet changes timbre as the jar fills. With her hand in mine, I don't mind the gurney and tube light. My five-months-along belly deflates. The technologist, freed from the obligation to chat, turns her swivel stool and browses an old *Good Housekeeping*. She looks up when my tubing is ready to be switched to a new jar. Mala keeps talking until I am all drained away. A jar and a half total. The radiologist comes in, scribbles *1.5 L clear yellow ascites*, and leaves. Without any prompting, Mala bends to kiss my hand. It is easy to forget her brief anger on the car ride over. I do just that.

On the way home, Mala takes a sudden turn into the supermarket without touching the brakes. An oncoming car speeds past us, horn blasting.

"I need to get some things," she murmurs, half to herself. "Can you come with me?"

I am lighter now that the fluid is gone. I could walk beside her without help, but it is nice to feel our fingers lock. The supermarket doors part. It has been weeks since I have come here. Coriander bundles lie freshly misted from the nozzle. A man in a blue apron is stacking oranges. How did I ever take such a place for granted? It was an unacknowledged blessing, all these years, to be a short drive from such plenty. I have been fortunate to live so well.

Mala is hurriedly bagging tomatoes, not checking their skins.

"What are you doing, Mala? They will spoil. Your father is taking you to the airport in two hours."

"It doesn't have to spoil."

"There's no time to do anything."

"There's time." She pushes the cart as if to flee from me, haphazardly grabbing produce, no list in her mind.

"What will I do with all this in the house? You see how I am now. I have no strength to cook by myself."

She refuses to slow down or face me. "We can make a month's worth and freeze it. The food will keep for a long time if we freeze it. We can eat it later."

"But your flight—"

"I'll cancel my flight. I'll call in sick." She takes out her phone. "I have sick days. This is what they're for."

I stop the cart with a hand.

"We do not need this." I return the zucchini to the shelf, the onions, the knuckled gingerroot. "Wait until Thanksgiving."

"That's too far away."

I lift the bag of tomatoes. Only six, but they feel heavy. She follows me, the phone returned to her purse.

"I am not going anywhere, Mala."

"Promise."

As if that were in my power. "Of course. I promise."

There. All the food has been returned. I leave the store the way I came to it, nothing in my hand but hers.

Thanksgiving. I am thankful I am here to give thanks.

I used to hate this tradition when I first came here. I shuddered to imagine so much meat being eaten in so many houses all at once. Hundreds of thousands of turkeys. An annual apocalypse for the species. *Gobble gobble* everywhere struck me then as macabre black humor. But you get desensitized over enough years. And now I can see it as a holiday for eating gratefully, and I am thankful I am here. My doctors did not think I would see it.

See it I do, and ravenously. I am quiet in my chair. But I watch as the people I love fill my house. Ronak, Mala, and their families. Sachin's parents have come from India to help him and Mala take care of the children. They allow Mala to spend more time here. His mother is healthy, stout, industrious. She is patient with Shivani's eating, right hand holding the bunched roti until her granddaughter's mouth opens. Vivek has picked up snippets of Gujarati. She will speak nothing else with him. Sachin inherited his height and thinness from his gentlemanly father, who reads biographies on a wafer-thin reader, Sachin's gift. They have been at our house the past week. Sachin's father is very talkative, like his son, and he sits beside me and reports what he is learning about Gandhi, Thomas Jefferson, Mussolini.

Thanksgiving. The house smells like I have been cooking. But I have not entered the kitchen. It is all Mala. She is riding without my hand on the bicycle seat. I breathe in the crackle of cumin and fennel seeds in oil and I think, *That is my hand.*

Mala makes everything, but not without help. Amber, her sleeves rolled up, wears the matching apron Mala gave me. Mixing bowls, cutting boards, both of my blenders, stray clutches of coriander, knobs and nubs of ginger, dark green strips of cucumber skin that smell like the cold, a large stainless steel bowl where dough awaits the kneading—I imagine the preparations colonizing the counter, the kitchen island, the dining table. Sachin's mother offers her able hands, but her handwriting would be different; the girls insist they have to prepare all the food, and by the book, so that I might do it through them.

I am here to see it all. Ronak shows Sachin his new camera, the two men leaning forward, the screen held glowing between their knees. The light on their faces changes subtly as he clicks through the camera's settings. The boys upstairs shout over a match point on the Wii. The playroom has spilled downstairs. Toys cover the floor, but no one minds. Here in the living room, Raj and Shivani decide they want the same Thomas the Tank Engine neither of them cared about for the three past visits. Sachin's father raises it high and lifts a finger at their screaming. In time, they move on to other toys. Sachin's mother sits with me. We each hold a half-peeled banana, coaxing Shivani or Raj over for a bite. She talks about births, graduations, and the marriages of rich men's daughters in Mumbai graced by this or that aging film star; engagements broken off, fallings-out between elderly brothers, houses sold to the hungry new builders of a hungry new India. On the

television I see storms on the coast and gunfire in the desert.
I have the weight of my granddaughter in my lap. She turns
the pages of a book and tells me, at length, what is happening
to the bear, the tiger, the donkey. Hours pass, and the table is
set. Mala, undoing her apron, calls everyone to eat. She goes
upstairs to round up all our boys.

Everyone waits until I come in on Ronak's arm. Amber is
holding my plate. Mala stands beside me. *You fill it*, I whisper
to her. I point, and she fills. Though it is her hand, I am the
one who inaugurates each dish, breaks the carefully garnished
surfaces. This is the first plate. I take everything so I can taste
everything. Not much; I do not have the appetite or tolerance. She rakes the palak paneer to bare the corners of braised
tofu, which we use instead of paneer cubes. Each sweep
unearths more steam. The dahi waits in three stainless steel
dishes, smooth planes, cold and white. We make dahi using
1 percent milk—some might find it not quite heavy enough,
but we like that airy feel. We like the way a bowl of it doesn't
weigh in the stomach. Mala made this dahi from the cultures
I gave her. She spoons a tiny clump of shredded jalapeño, set
aside in its own small glass bowl—Sachin's father is known to
love heat.

At last, after Mala lays a brittle round of papad atop the
rice, rotli, palak paneer, chole, bhartha, after she pours the
dahl in a separate bowl, Ronak guides me to a chair and Abhi
brings a glass of water. The full plate, full bowl, full glass are
set before me. For a time, while everyone else takes their food,
I sit before mine, motionless. When they are all seated, I take
my first bite. Mala urges her family, making sure they take
enough, promising them there is more.

Dinner started very late. No one is holding the children to
their bedtimes tonight. Abhi and Sachin bring out ice cream
from the garage freezer, five boxes faintly ghosted with frost.

Abhi sets up at the half-cleared table between a stack of bowls and a stack of spoons and scrapes, digs, finally stabs in vain. Sachin suggests microwaving them and takes a box of pistachio because that is my favorite. Soon his scoop sinks easily along the edge. Mala takes the bowl and kneels beside my chair, a spoonful held out for me. *Open wide*, she whispers. I open. Ronak hurries to a good angle, kneels, and takes a photograph as I close my mouth. Everyone claps, even the children. I smile. For a moment it feels like my birthday. Mala's eyes were closed in the picture; we restage it with an empty spoon.

When it is time to go to bed, Abhi joins me as usual. He waits. I feel my breathing steady. I feel my breathing slow. I know not to expect much more. This night would be a good night.

I close my eyes. It is still night, but summer. I go upstairs to Abhi in his study. The door leaks the brightness behind it. I push it open the rest of the way. Abhi sits before an open window. The room is hot and full of the cricket-loud midnight. It smells of the outdoors. Four houses down, a patio light is on, but at this hour all the backyards are empty. The light in the room makes it harder to see outside. Abhi's notebooks are on the desk, but he isn't working. His pencil taps idly on his chin when I peek in.

"Is everything all right?"

"I was feeling good. I thought I would come visit."

"You couldn't sleep?"

I point at the window. "People can see you from outside."

He shrugs. "They can see the top of my shiny head."

Abhi holds his arms out. I look through our lit window as he presses his cheek to my fluid-swollen stomach, as though he were a new father feeling for a kick. Seen from out there, we could be a color photograph inside a frame.

"You're feeling better?"

"I am."

"Let's go."

"Where?"

"Follow me."

He leads me downstairs and through the backyard door. Our patio light comes on. Specks, burned out, fleck the glass. Wings have collected like sere leaves around the base of the bulb.

"A walk? At midnight?"

"Better than a walk."

I stop at the top of the deck steps. He stands on the lawn.

"Come on."

"Where are we going? We need shoes."

"Forget shoes."

"Slippers, then. I'll go in and get them."

"Come on," he says impatiently, taking my hand.

I step onto the ticklish grass. Abhi scoops me up—I have a girl's weight, near nothing—and walks me into the dark, across our backyard, and into the neighbor's and across.

"What are you doing?" I whisper.

"Those kids jump all day. I see them having the time of their lives."

The trampoline has black netting around it.

"Shhh!" I whisper. "Abhi! Put me down!"

He slides me through a part in the netting. The trampoline surface is taut and finely crosshatched under my palm. He clambers onto it behind me and stands unsteadily. The surface slopes toward him.

"This is going to break."

He begins to bob in place. "You should see their daughter." He throws his elbows out and puffs his cheeks.

"Abhi!"

"Stand up."

He puts his hands under my arms and draws me to my feet. He bobs higher, his own feet still on the surface, while I go up and down passively, my hands in his.

"Abhi, let's *leave*."

He stops bobbing.

"Is this making you nauseous? You feel okay?"

I realize how much I don't want him to stop. "I am fine," I say. "But what if they see us?"

He starts bobbing again, grinning again. "Jump."

He lets go of my hands. The trampoline is bigger than it seems from the window. There is a lot of room. A few steps away from him, only a vague pulse transmits. I bend my knees and crouch and straighten, starting my own rhythm, half expecting a light to come on.

"Jump!"

His feet leave the trampoline.

"Jump!"

I try. I feel inside me a skyward lurch, but I shy at the last instant.

"Jump!"

I look up at the night sky. I try again. And that is when the moon drops, and I float bodiless above the earth's turning.

ACKNOWLEDGMENTS

Authors aren't granted much insight into their own work, but it seems to me that I write my novels out of fears I cannot overcome in any other way. My first novel sprang, in retrospect, from fear for my sons, the fear of some danger from which I would not be able to protect them. This novel, even though it is written from the perspective of the mother of a family, gives form to my fear of losing a parent.

Thankfully, very little in this story is autobiographical. The main part that is drawn from life, although altered in various ways, concerns my parents' return to India to care for their mothers, who fell gravely ill at the same time. I would like to thank my mother and father first, for everything. Here's to many more years together.

My wife, Ami, and my twins, Shiv and Savya; my sister, Shilpa; my brother-in-law, Devo; my nephew, Shail; my nieces, Keya and Lekha—the love goes without saying, but I'll say it anyway.

Riva Hocherman of Metropolitan Books, who also edited *Partitions*, challenged and improved the manuscript, saving me from myself sometimes. I am in continued debt to my agent, Georges Borchardt, and his assistant, Samantha Shea, who have supported both my fiction and my poetry.

ABOUT THE AUTHOR

AMIT MAJMUDAR is the author of *Partitions*, chosen by *Kirkus Reviews* as one of the best debut novels of 2011 and by *Booklist* as one of the year's ten best works of historical fiction. His poetry has been published in the *New Yorker*, the *Atlantic*, and *Best American Poetry 2012*. A radiologist, he lives in Columbus, Ohio.